THE BROKEN MARRIAGE

ELENA WILKES

Storm
PUBLISHING

Ebook ISBN: 978-1-80508-336-8
Paperback ISBN: 978-1-80508-338-2

Cover design: Emma Graves
Cover images: Arcangel, Shutterstock

Published by Storm Publishing.
For further information, visit:
www.stormpublishing.co

ALSO BY ELENA WILKES

The Son

The Man I Married

Keep My Secrets

For Amy, Ko, and Tess – my writing stars

PROLOGUE

'Rach—? Rachel, are you there? Please! Can you come? I need help, Rachel – I need you to come now.'

'Hannah?'

I hear the instant worry in her voice. And then other voices down the line: hoots of laughter in the background.

'Hannah? Are you still there? Where are you?'

I look around.

The abandoned houses sit in dusty piles of broken bricks. Pits of turned ground yawn in giant bunkers all around me. I'm hunkered down behind a wall, desperately clutching the phone to my ear like a lifeline.

I glance down.

Pools of something sticky mixes with the grey dust. I feel very calm suddenly; calm in a mute, numb kind of way.

'Hannah? Are you still there? I can barely hear you. Are you okay?'

A croon of pigeons echoes down the line. I imagine she's in some garden under the shade of a tree, surrounded by students lounging on blankets. There are bottles and glasses and laughter. Young people having fun. I know I haven't even crossed her mind.

'Something bad has happened. Something really bad. I can't say it over the phone. *Please, Rachel. Please.*'

I hear her take a sip of breath.

The sound of the laughter down the line gets fainter. She's coming, she's moving away. But then there's another, muted, voice. It'll be Alison, nosey bloody Alison. I can't hear what she's saying, but I know she's asking questions.

'Tell Matt I'm borrowing the car, will you?'

Rachel's tone is sharp and dismissive. I like that.

'I'm on that site...' I tell her. 'The one where the houses are being knocked down on the other side of town. You know the one?'

I know she does.

'Are you hurt?' She's breathless all of a sudden. I'm guessing she's running.

I glance down at my thighs, my hands.

'A bit.'

'Okay. Just stay where you are. Don't move. I'll ring the—'

'No!' I bark. 'No ambulances. No police, Rachel. Promise me... Nothing like that. *Promise me.*'

She pauses, then, 'Yes... Okay... Yes... I promise, I promise. Look, I'll get there as quick as I can.'

I end the call imagining her panic. She's doing this all for me. I almost feel bad... but then there's no one else I could've called. Literally. She's the only one.

I stare down at the blank phone in my clenched fist, my eyes fixing on my knuckles; they look like mine, but they're not. Someone else's skin is stretched pure white and there's a rusty-orange crust webbing between the fingers. In the other hand is the bundle of ripped dress. It's the same mustard silk dress I was wearing when—

No.

I squeeze my eyes tight shut, aware that the sunshine has dimmed for an instant.

A slow rumble of thunder gathers overhead as a single splat of rain hits the back of my hand.

It had started to rain that night too. The smell of warm rain on the grass. The lights in the trees, blurring into a myriad of dancing colours. A man's voice whispering in my ear, loud and sticky on hot breath. Laughter whirls in the air somewhere way off. The night sky turning as though on a merry-go-round, circling slowly, with me pinned in the centre like a butterfly, unable to move, staring upward, the tears leaking from the corners of my eyes, clucking into my ears, muting the sound of—

'Hannah?'

Rachel's voice rings out, trawling me back, as my head turns, the sting of gauzy blue sky making me blink.

'*Hannah...?*' There's the crunch of feet as they stumble across the debris.

'I'm here, Rach.' My voice sounding not as it should as I struggle to stand upright, my limbs not responding, my arms and legs quivering like jelly unable to get me up. My phone screen dies into black, and I realise it's been flashing with her calls.

'Jesus, Hannah.'

And suddenly there she is all in a rush, kneeling in front of me, the sunshine behind her casting her halo of blonde hair into shimmering fire. She looks like an angel.

She *is* an angel.

A cry falls from my mouth without my asking it to. The tears come so fast I can't stem them as she's suddenly right up close, scuffing forward in the dirt in front of me, her hands reaching out, her arms encircling—

'Please help me, Rachel,' is all I can manage.

Her eyes are as round as her wobbling mouth as she tries to make sense of what's happened. 'Hannah... Hannah. Oh my word.' She swallows quickly, taking all of me in. 'Look at you. You're hurt. We have to call someone.'

I see her hand fumbling over her phone, and I instantly react.

'*I said* NO.'

It comes out much louder and sharper than I'd intended, and she snaps back.

'No, don't. Don't. Please, Rach. Don't...'

'Who did this to you, Hannah? Please talk to me.'

'I can't. I can't. Please don't make me.' I start to cry.

'Shhh... Shhh, now.' Her hands are soothing, comforting. 'But, Hannah, you can't just... You have to tell someone. You have to.'

I look up at her. I see the pity etched into her face; the need to take care of me. *How I want so much to be taken care of.* I want her to put her arms around me, draw me to her and make it all go away. I want to feel as though someone loves me – that *she* loves me.

'Please, Rach, don't make me. I can't tell anyone. I wouldn't have called you if I thought you'd make me. I would've stayed here on my own, I would've dealt with it on my own...'

'But why, Hannah? Why won't you—' But she breaks off. She thinks I'm not in my right mind, and yet I've never been surer of anything in my life. 'Shh... It's okay, it's okay...' she soothes, relenting. 'We won't do anything you don't want to, okay? I'm here for you. Only you.'

I could weep right here and now.

'No one else knows where you are, do they?' I ask, blinking back at her tearfully. 'You haven't mentioned it to anyone?'

'No, no one,' she reassures. 'I'll make something up about an emergency. They'll believe me. You're totally safe.'

My fingers pluck fretfully at her arm. I want her to remember our old closeness. 'I know you think I should be going to hospital, or seeing a doctor, but I just can't.' I've left a trail of fresh pink on her skin. Blood sisters.

'I'll do whatever you want... Whatever you need me to do.' Her eyes catch the rag-bag bundle in the crook of my arm.

'My dress. I had to take it off,' I explain pointlessly.

'Of course, of course.' She's bewildered. Scared. She doesn't know what to do with me.

'Help me up.' I struggle forward, seeing her hands reach out to support me. 'We need to get rid of this.' I proffer the mess of material and see her flinch.

'Get rid? Why? What do you mean?'

But then her eyes suddenly stop in shock as she sees – she really sees what's bundled in my hands. She glances at the bloodied material in my arms, but then her eyes dart away in horror.

'Don't look at it. Don't look. Don't judge me.'

'I'm not judging you. I would never judge...' She's breathless now, panting, barely able to get her words out. 'Is that... Is that—?'

My swollen eyes search her face. Her mouth is like an 'O'. Her frown quickly crumples as she tries to disguise her reaction – but I see it: the horror of what's plainly in front of her betraying her reaction.

'Oh my God, Hannah,' she whispers softly. 'Oh my God!'

'You have to help me now Rach.'

'Help you? I don't know what you mean?'

But I can't find the words to explain. There aren't any.

'Here. We could put it somewhere here.'

'Put it... Put it? Hannah, I...' There's a warning note in her voice. The terror is ramping up a notch.

I look around me. The rain is starting to come down harder now; it patters into the dust, sending up a warm, almost chemical smell.

'Who—?' she asks. 'When?... I didn't know that you—'

'Please don't ask me anything, Rachel. I can't tell you. You won't talk me out of this. If you don't want to help me, then leave now. I won't be angry. I'll never tell anyone you were involved. You don't have to be here. You can walk away.' A hard constriction in my throat burns at the very thought of her leaving me. *I won't cry, I won't cry.*

She glances up at the sky, blinking into the rain. I think she's going to get up, but she doesn't. Her gaze drops directly to mine, and she presses her lips together.

'You can't stay out here on your own, Hannah. I'm not going anywhere. We'll figure this out together.'

I know what her whole instinct is screaming at her to do. She wants to persuade me, to scoop me up into the passenger seat of Matt's car and drive me to a place where there are proper people: grown adults, not bits of kids like we are. But they're the kinds of people who'll make me talk, who'll push and prod and pry until they have control of me, and I can't have anyone in control of me ever again.

'Over there.' I point to a hole in the ground where a broken concrete pipe has been heaved up. 'We'll bury in there.'

She looks back at me. Her face is white.

'Bury it?'

'No one will know. No one can ever know, Rachel. Will you promise me, Rach? Will you promise me this is just between us?'

'You're not thinking straight, Hannah. You're in shock. You've lost a lot of blood. You need a—'

'I've already *said*... I've already told you. You're not listening, Rachel... You're not hearing me.'

'Alright. Alright. Yes, shhh. I *am* listening. I do hear you... Shh...' Then her eyes spark wide with shock. 'Hang on, Hannah, no... Wait... Stop. Where do you think you're—?'

But I've managed to get up without her, hunched over, walking, crab-like, nearly crying out with each step, my bloodied burden clutched against my chest, as I make for the hole in the ground.

'I said *wait*, Hannah.' She's scrambling after me, glancing around to see if anyone has seen us, but I don't care, I'm focussed and determined, dropping to my knees at the side of the hole and letting the mass of rag slither from my arms into the darkness as though it had never been.

Gone.

There's a chill where the warmth had been.

I glance round at Rachel's face. It's turned from white to grey.

I know I don't feel like she feels; the truth is, I don't feel anything. The only thing I'm aware of, is a slow, creeping paralysis starting in my thighs, spreading into my hips. My hands and arms are numb. I rub my palms together; they stutter and jerk, balling the dried blood into rice grains that fall like confetti. I look down at my shoes. The blood has dried on the leather to a browny-red rust, but beside it, a fresh puddle of red trickles and stretches, beginning to run and seep into the earth,

'Oh my god. Here—' Rachel is proffering a wad of tissues from her pocket. 'Do what you can to stem it. And look, you can have these...' She's suddenly on her feet, hoiking up her dress and pulling down the black leggings she's wearing. 'Put them on. We've got to get you to the car.'

'But we have to—' I glance again at the hole. 'It's easy. Look.' My hands reach to the side and behind me, picking up rocks and stones that I begin to scoop into the opening. I look up into her face. The horror is etched there as she stands, disbelieving, holding the leggings that still contain the shape of her, dumbly watching me.

'Stop. Please stop— We can't. This is all so wrong.'

'The quicker we do this, the quicker we can leave.' I'm breathless with panic now, crawling on all fours looking for rubble, piling it into the blackness.

'I think there are laws—' She breaks off. 'I think there are— I don't know what the... What the rules are...'

'I don't care about the rules.' I can't bring myself to look at her. 'No one has to know anything. There are no rules if no one knows anything.'

I have no idea if she's listening to me, but then suddenly she's down by my side, our hands colliding, shoving anything we can find into the pit that feels as though we might never fill. And then, with a shock, I see we're done: there's no hole, no nothing, just a mound of rubble and dirt, as though nothing else had ever been.

I sit back on my heels, my knees grazed and dirty, the blood on my thighs indistinguishable now in all the churned-up dust.

'Gone,' I say simply.

'God, Hannah.' Rachel licks the grime from her lips. 'God.'

I hold out my hand for the leggings and take them, shakily jerking off my trainers as I try to pull them on, knowing she's watching my every move. I hazard a look. She's cradling her cheeks in her palms; her eyes are huge in her face. The breeze gathers a handful of rain, blowing it past us.

'Wait – let me help.' She sees me struggling to get up and takes me under one arm, looping her other arm around my waist, supporting me.

'The car's just over there. Are you okay to walk? I don't know if the suspension would make it across here.'

I nod in assent, feeling quite strong enough to walk but liking the sensation of her being so close, our shoulders jostling against each other, not quite in step as our feet slip and slide over the wrecked ground.

She pulls the passenger side open for me, guiding me in, gently pulling the seatbelt around. Her breath is warm on my neck as she plugs it in.

'There.'

I smile gratefully, watching her easy movement around the

bonnet, her hair being picked up in damp strands around her face as she drags it under control.

'Where now?' She drops in beside me. 'A doctor? A&E?' She blinks frantically as she thinks. 'You could tell them you were in shock, you don't know what happened. You can't remember. No one will blame you.'

'I'm going away for a while.'

'Away? Away where? You can't. It could be dangerous. You might get sick.'

I say nothing. I'm staring at a torn bag in the footwell. *Potato Chips*, it says. I concentrate hard so that our eyes won't meet and betray me.

'Where will you go?'

I shrug.

'Hannah, listen. You ring me, yes? You ring me all the time. I'll come and get you. I'll come and be with you. I'm always here for you, you know that, don't you?'

I only swallow.

'Tell me you believe me.'

'You'll forget about me,' I whisper. 'Everyone does.'

'Well, not me!' Rachel says heatedly. 'I'll always be here for you, Hannah. *Always*. I want to hear you say you believe me.'

I pause, feeling the weight of her look, and then my head gives an imperceptible nod. 'I believe you, but—'

'But what?'

'I bring trouble – like this.' My hand waves around the car's interior. 'I've dragged you into this awful thing, and now—' I break off.

'Now, what?'

She inhales sharply, gathering her hair in her hands in exasperation, bunching it tight in her fists, pulling at it, hard.

'Right,' she says definitely. 'Right. Okay then. Will you listen to me now, though? Like, just what I'm going to say next. Will you listen? Will you really hear what I'm going to say?'

I nod, quietly. 'Yeah, I'll hear you.'

'Right. Look, I'm right here. I'm always going to be right here, with you for the rest of our lives, yes?'

A soft thrill shivers through me at the sound of her words.

'It doesn't matter what else is going on in my life, or what I'm doing. At some point, it might be in ten minutes, or ten months or ten years. At some point, whenever that moment is, you will call me and when you do, I'll be there. I'll drop everything and everyone.'

'Like you did today.' My eyes flicker up to meet hers.

'Like I did today,' she repeats.

I shift my head to look at her properly now. *You came when I needed you*, I want to say. *You abandoned Alison, and came to me.*

Rachel's lips and cheeks are pink with some kind of natural inner light, a luminescence against my darkness.

'You have to mean it, Rach. You have to really mean it – you can't ever betray me. Can you promise? Can you do that?'

'Of course I can. I'll never betray you,' she says with shining eyes. 'Never, ever, ever.'

ONE

It hasn't been ten minutes, or ten months, or even ten years. It's been seventeen.

I can't believe I'm here, doing this. The thought has been like a drum in my head.

But what will I say?

I've made this situation happen. I've created this.

'In order to move forward, you have to go back, Hannah.'

Theresa's voice is there in my head. Back to where it started. Back to where it all began to go wrong.

I ease myself from behind the wheel of my car, my eyes glued to the retreating back of the jogger heading away from me. *That's Matt, I'm sure of it. Right height, right body shape; it must be. It has to be,* my head says, but the windshield was steamed up and the guy's sweatshirt hood was hiding his face, so I couldn't know for sure.

Her front door stands silently in front of me.

If I'm right, I know she's in there alone.

'Afternoon.' A cheery voice makes me start. A woman is shuffling past with a little dog and a walking stick. 'Brrrr. This wind bites and bit, doesn't it? You want to get yourself inside in front of the fire, love.'

'You're right.' I smile back. 'Mind how you go, though. It looks a bit slippy down there.' I nod to where I see the jogging figure disappearing from view.

'We shan't go far, shall we, Bobby?' She jiggles the lead. 'You take care too, my darling.' And she makes her way carefully down the street.

My smile falters and falls as my shaking fingers reach for the doorbell.

And here I am, about to see the one person who always made it all right. Back to her and back to the me I was then.

The drill of the bell echoes deep into the house. There's silence, but I know she's in there; I can feel it.

Please answer. Please.

Pulling my jacket closer, I gather it tightly under my chin as I glance at the bay window. It's Victorian, ornate stone columns either side, the Ionic scrolls signifying money and class – the people who built it wanting to show how far they'd come, wanting to be something they're not.

The irony isn't lost on me.

The thick door glass reflects only the darkening sky. A couple of snowflakes fall and settle on the windowsill as I glance up. My watch says it's only just gone three o'clock, but it feels more like five. I shiver, trying the bell again, glancing uncertainly back down the road.

Somewhere on the other side of the leadlight door, I hear a voice. Something inside me collapses a little as a shadow twitches and looms.

I shouldn't be here.

I've played this moment over and over in my mind. Every possibility, every reaction.

The voice on the other side grows louder. She's talking to someone.

I could turn around right now. I could turn and walk away before I set something in motion that I have no control over. It's not worth the pain I'll cause—

The door opens.

Rachel's face appears with a phone glued to her ear. She pauses in shock, her mouth moving uncertainly.

'Someone's here, can I ring you back?'

I keep my smile steady.

'Hannah?'

'Hello, Rachel. '

'My god, is it you? Is it really? *My god.*' She laughs, but I hear the hesitation.

Our past floods into the space between us and all the stuff I've rehearsed sticks in my throat, leaving me feeling queasy and shamed. I suddenly think I might cry.

'Wow. What a shock.' Her eyes flicker warily. 'Come in... Come in.'

She stands back from the door gesturing me inside. There she is, golden, tall, shining Rachel, and me back to being eighteen and small and dark, and dumpy. For a second there's a version of me that laughs, makes a sudden excuse, detaches itself from the doorstep like a ghost, mumbling, stepping back, palms held up in apology. *Sorry... gosh. I've stupidly, stupidly left my purse in the car... Won't be a moment...* And then getting back behind the wheel and screeching away.

Instead, I find my feet propelling me over the threshold.

'I didn't quite mean to just turn up like this.' I find I'm pointlessly wiping my feet on the mat over and over. 'I was at a conference in Mexborough... I just happened to be looking on the map at all the bits of this area I never visited when I lived here – too young, I suppose. You know how it is. This always was such a pretty part of the country... I'd always meant to come back and explore it properly...' I know I am gabbling.

I can feel the tension behind Rachel's smile as she stands back to let me in.

'And then I recognised the name of this area, and I thought, *Isn't that where Rachel said she was living?* It was a long shot, I know... I mean, how long ago was it you sent that Christmas card?'

'A Christmas card?' I catch the slight query on her face as the almost criticism of her not keeping in touch hangs in the air between us.

'God, yes. Years and years ago.' I flap it away. 'And then when I realised how close I was, I thought, *Wow! I wonder if she might be in?*' I giggle. I know I sound ridiculous.

Her face relaxes a little. 'Amazing coincidence. Well, anyway, what a fabulous surprise. This is so lovely... Go through. You'll stay for some tea, won't you?'

I am aware her enthusiasm feels a bit forced. *Have I overdone it?* But I shuffle past her anyway, into a hallway with its original tiled floor and high cornicing. A grandfather clock sits next to an ornate mirror on the wall. I catch sight of myself; I'm almost shocked that there isn't the eighteen-year-old me looking back.

'How long has it been?' She deftly scoots past me, leading the way into a kitchen: a large glass-roofed extension. I stand there, awkwardly, as she bustles away from me, going over to the kettle, flicking it on and reaching up to open a cupboard. We're both ill at ease: strangers really, but with too much between us to ever be so. The sound of the kettle breaks the silence.

I am aware that everything in here, every appliance, every shelf and cupboard and picture shouts 'money'. *She's done well*, it screams. And here I am about to be the person who throws the grenade to blow this all to pieces.

'Sit, sit.' She waves a white porcelain mug towards a long wooden breakfast bar. I put my bag down, perching uncomfortably on a stool. It's handcrafted, I can tell. The floor is tiled to make it look like wooden boards. The counter tops and cupboards are clearly bespoke but with a rustic feel. Everything here is trying to be something it isn't.

This room. Her. Me.

I watch her. She hasn't put on any weight. Her thighs look strong and toned in her yoga pants. She's wearing a white linen kurta with a T-shirt underneath. It's designed to look casual but even so, looks effortlessly put-together. I press my lips against my teeth. A strong, clean waft of peppermint fills the air as she brings the mugs over and plonks one down in front of me before restlessly busying herself back at the counter. I get to watch her as she moves: she's exactly the same as she was at eighteen – the yellow gold curls, with that strange shade when it catches the light, almost the colour of olive oil. Her heart-shaped face smiles at me... And those so-perfect wide eyes that I know will get even wider as she talks; the clear translucent skin, doll-like, that you can't help wishing you had too.

'So, how are you? You haven't changed a bit.' She glances over her shoulder but not far round enough to actually see me.

'I'm good.' I smile, touching my hair, knowing she's lying. 'I'm good... yes. Gosh... time marches on, doesn't it? And life...'

'Amazing...' she says, but the expression on her face doesn't match the words. '...That I was at home, I mean. I'm just about to start a new job so I'm using up my leave. Organisational development,' she explains.

I nod as though I know what that means. Now I'm here I can't find the thoughts or words to even know where to begin.

'Where are you living these days?' She turns her attention to finding a spoon in the drawer.

'I'm down south. I bought a flat a year ago. It's only small, but I have a balcony and I overlook the park next door so I get my own bit of greenery.' I smile.

My smile fades. I am about to blow apart everything she holds dear: her marriage, the past, what we did, the enormity of all the things I've faced up to and discovered. All the appalling things I am about to lay in front of her – and all for something she's given no thought to for seventeen years.

The hurt slices quick and easy like a fine blade through my heart.

I've come this far. She needs to know the truth.

A rush of something comes over me – a sudden memory. All those early mornings when she'd leave Matt asleep in their bed and come tapping at my door with a cup of tea, pushing me over into the cold bit to scramble under the duvet, hoisting the pillows up behind her and then both of us sitting, sipping our tea as we chattered on about what we'd do after lectures. Go trawling round the charity shops for bargains, try out a new coffee shop. Rachel Carter, the person people looked up to, had brought me into her orbit. And now here I am, back on the brink of that bubble again. I slide back onto that hook like a fish that's happy to be caught.

I take a breath. For a moment I wonder what is about to fall from my lips. There's an elephant between us.

'It must be, what...?' She pulls out the stool opposite and wrinkles her nose. 'Seventeen years or something?'

I'm aware of the elephant shifting a little.

'Wow, is it? Yes, yes, it must be,' I agree, but all the time knowing it's not.

It was a week ago.

It was in London. Seven Dials. I'd followed her from the Tube station at Leicester Square. I remember the shock of looking up and seeing her on the escalator just in front of me. Five steps was all it had taken to move in right behind her. I almost couldn't believe it. There she was: offered up to me like I'd conjured her up thinking about her so much. *Rachel, Rachel, Rachel...* And there she was. One tiny movement and I'd touched the back of her jacket. My mouth had opened to say her name but then closed again. I couldn't do it then, but I can now. The trammel of my heart ramps up a notch. I take a breath.

'So!' She cups her palms around the mug in front of her. 'So... You said you're at a conference up here? Whereabouts?'

My brain stumbles for a second trying to summon the right information. 'Oh. Yes. In Bradfield. That big hotel not far from the train station.'

She looks vaguely puzzled.

I fumble. 'The Marriott,' I say the first name that comes into my head. 'Or is it the Radisson? I go to so many of these tedious things I get mixed up.' I grin as the clench in my stomach intensifies. 'Endless bureaucracy and presentations about Justice Department waffle. Stuff I'm not very interested in, anyway.' I sigh.

'Oh, are you a civil servant then?'

'Something like.'

'Oh hell, all those late-night hotel bars.' She shakes her head.

Her comment snaps me instantly to her face, but she's only sitting there giving me a cheeky look.

'Nothing worse.' I look away, trying to hide my face in the rim of my cup. 'I don't get involved in any of that. Straight up to my room after dinner to watch rubbish TV, that's more my scene.' I feel my cheeks burning.

I'm a bag of nerves and my brain is numb. I sip my tea. It scours the roof of my mouth.

'And did you say you were in London?'

'Close,' I say vaguely. 'Just outside... Rachel, I—'

Justsayitsayitsayit.

'Right... Rachel... The thing is—'

'I have a vague memory of you wanting to go into the teaching and training side of business management. Have I got that right?' She neatly sidesteps. 'I always thought teaching was far more your bag than business. Justice department, you say? I have a friend who works with offenders in prison – Is that the kind of thing you're doing now?'

'Mmm-mm... Yeah. The reason I'm here, Rachel—'

'Matt will be sorry to have missed you.'

The mention of his name sends a punch to my lungs.

The thing that I need to tell her, that I came here to say, sits hard between my tongue and teeth. I begin to panic, half getting off the stool and casting around for my bag.

'Oh my God, look.'

She's staring up at the glass roof that's darkening second by second. The snow is covering the panes in huge drifts faster and faster, blanketing everything.

'Wow! Look out there too.' She points into the garden where the snow swirls and revolves like thick static on a screen. A weird silence deadens the room.

'It won't take long for the roads to be blocked.'

'I need to go,' I say automatically.

Leaving now would let me off this hook.

This whole idea was madness. I should never have come here. What was I even thinking?

I stoop for my bag.

'Going?' Rachel's eyes follow me upward. 'You can't. It would be really foolish in this. And anyway, go where? It'll be really bad in minutes. Look at it. It's like a blizzard.'

'Before it gets worse then.'

'Hannah, you can't drive. It'd be crazy.'

'I'm sure the main roads will be okay,' I assure her. 'Once I get to them it'll be fine.'

'But we're nowhere near the main road. Firstly, it's Friday and at this time it'll be impossible, and secondly, it'll take ages for the gritters and the ploughs to start clearing. Look at it, Hannah.' She waves at the sight. The windowpane is obliterated with churning snow. 'The fact is, you're staying whether you like it or not.' She laughs.

My heart thumps in alarm.

'Have you got anything with you? I can lend you stuff if you haven't.'

'Sorry?'

'In the car. Any of your things?'

I think of the hurriedly packed case in my car. 'Oh... A couple of bits and pieces maybe, but—'

'No problem. I've got stuff you can have. No worries. We always were the same size.' She grins. 'Perfect. That settles it then. Good excuse for a celebratory bottle as you're staying.' Her head turns at the sound of a clatter in the hallway and I snatch a look at the door. *No, not this. I'm not ready.*

I fumble and drop my bag.

The front door slams. My feet find the floor and I'm already off the stool.

Didn't you want to confront him? The thought comes unbidden into my head.

The door opens.

Matt is standing there.

There's a moment where he and I can only stare at each other.

'What the—' he manages, his hand coming up to steady himself on the door frame. I see his sweatshirt is darkened wet, his trackpants are bloomed with water and white flakes of snow glisten in his hair.

'Look who's here.' Rachel laughs.

Matt blinks rapidly, wiping his palm across his face as though he'd like to wipe the image of me away.

'Wow,' he says with no delight. 'Wow.'

'Goodness. What a welcome.' Rachel gives him a withering look. 'It's Hannah, you goof. She hasn't changed *that* much.'

'Yeah, yeah... Sorry.' He shakes his head, running his fingers through his wet hair. 'I'm soaked.'

'Yes, I thought you'd be back sooner.' Rachel eyes him up and down. 'You're dripping all over the floor.'

The three of us stare down at his feet where a pool of water has gathered on the tiles.

'It got really bad really quickly,' he says distractedly, breathing hard. 'Yes, I'd better...' He backs away, pulling the door closed, muttering. 'Sorry, sorry, just grab a dry shirt,' as his face disappears in the gap.

'I've told Hannah she has to stay!' Rachel hollers, but there's no reply, just the creak of the stair tread.

'God, what's he like?' she tuts. 'That wasn't much of a welcome, was it?' She looks at me, embarrassed. 'Good job you know him.'

The blood fizzes hot in my cheeks.

'It's fine, it's fine. Actually, I won't stay, but thank you for the kind offer. It's really sweet of you.' My breath wheezes a little as I reach for my bag again.

'Hannah.' Rachel's voice has an edge to it. 'You're being ridiculous. Stop all the politeness. This is me you're talking to. You can't leave. You'd have to *dig* your car out. It's not safe on the roads. I cannot, cannot, let you even consider driving.' She makes a snatch for my bag, catching the strap. We stand there, stupidly, wrestling a little with the handbag swinging between us. Rachel giggles. I don't.

'You know I always get what I want.' She raises her eyebrows comically. 'I always win, so there's absolutely no point resisting. Now, stop being silly, and that's the end of it. Sit back down there and I'll find us a biscuit to tide us over until dinner.'

My fingers release the strap and I sit heavily on the stool. I have that sudden sinking feeling of having 'given in'. It's a sensation that I recognise so well. It's what Rachel has always done to me, and is doing to me now. I'm eighteen again, perched here, watching her every move, feeling smaller and less of myself as her personality grows and fills the room. I don't know quite how she does it: it's as though there's only so much of me available and she naturally takes it, like an older sister and it's her obvious right.

She goes over to a cupboard, bringing out a biscuit tin and attempts to wrestle off the lid. I'm glad she's occupied: my hands are trembling, and my chest feels tight. All I can feel behind me is the image of Matt's shoulders silhouetted against that doorway. What was I even thinking, coming here? How did I ever imagine this would play out?

There's a click and Rachel looks round.

'Gosh, that was quick.'

And he's there. Checked shirt. Jeans. Belt. Hair in furrows.

'Yep, two minutes in a hot shower and I'm done.'

His mouth is smiling. But his eyes aren't. They land on me like a cold searchlight.

'Y'know, I saw you sitting there, and I thought, *No, it can't be.*' He gives me a sardonic smile that rips my heart into tiny shreds. He steps towards me so quickly the air is whipped from my lungs. He comes close. Too close as he dips to kiss my cheek. There's an aggression in the action; the feel of his breath and the scent of him as one moment he's looming fast and huge, and the next there's the heat of his hand between my shoulder blades. His face is against mine as he presses, too hard: skin against skin. His hair tickling damp against my temple. He smells of shampoo and shower gel.

'Where have you been hiding yourself all these years?' His tone is genial and welcoming, but I hear the edge. There's Rachel rattling the biscuits from the tin onto a plate. He turns to look at her. The wet hair in the nape of his neck has soaked into his collar. There are seconds as he takes the plate, the muscles in his shoulder blade flexing and tightening. I'd gone to find Matt because he always made me feel safe. Matt was the kind of man who would protect me when I needed protection – a man I could tell anything to. My biggest secrets and everything I'd discovered. *But what had he done?* Duped me. Used my vulner-ability and had come on to me.

I hold on to that anger and hurt and gather it inside me.

Rachel should know. Rachel has a right to know all of it. She should be made aware of the kind of man she is married to. The kind of man who pretends that he's single and tries it on with women who've gone to him for help.

'Really nice to see you again, Hanny.'

He uses the name that no one else ever calls me. It's so deliberate and confident the way he says it. He's so good at lying, my head instantly aches.

The biscuits appear on the table in front of me and he delves to take one, but the plate suddenly shifts away and his grabbing fingers close on nothing.

'They're not there for you.'

Rachel's joking, but there's an edge. Matt pulls away as though slapped.

'Hannah. Here, please.' She proffers the plate, and I can't say no, though I know even a crumb will choke me.

'As I said, what brings you all this way up here, Hanny?'

'She's been on a course,' Rachel answers, stuffing a biscuit into her mouth. 'And how do you know how far she's travelled? She could've been living around the corner all these years for all you know... More tea?'

She reaches over to flick on the kettle again, releasing me from the horror that's unfolding. A horror that I have created.

'A course?' He looks at me wide-eyed. 'What kind?'

My insides crawl with discomfort.

'A conference,' I correct. 'It was a conference.'

'Some teaching thing, wasn't it?' Rachel takes another bite of biscuit, dropping a tea bag into a cup. 'By the way, you heard me saying that Hannah is staying the night, did you? I've told her she can't think of driving anywhere in this.'

Matt watches her stonily as she pours the boiling water from the kettle and then his eyes lock onto mine.

'Wow!' He folds his arms. 'Teaching, eh? You must tell us all about your work over dinner.'

My eyes sting. I know my face is burning.

Rachel glances at him in query. I can't look.

'What school age do you teach?'

'Gosh, what's with all the questions, Matt? Leave the poor woman alone. You haven't seen Hannah for over fifteen years and now it's more like an interrogation.' Rachel laughs, but he's not paying attention.

'Go on,' he continues. 'I'm interested. I'm in that line of work myself. What do you—'

But he stops abruptly as suddenly the light changes, darkening the whole room.

'Wow!' Rachel reaches for the light switch. 'Looks like there's a proper storm coming.' She goes over to draw the blind and the room is plunged into a tinny, muted glow before the worksurfaces flood with the brilliant white of led light.

'That's us for the night then.' She looks around. 'Batten it all down. Could you get the fire going, Matt? It's a good excuse to crack the wine open.' I can see she's trying to lift the mood.

'Sure,' he says, but then pauses. 'How weird is this, though? The three of us all together again: same people, same town, different time. Who would've thought it?' He stares directly at me.

And I find I can't say a word.

TWO

'This is a nice one, let's give this a go, shall we?' Rachel holds up a bottle, turning the label for me to see. 'Shall we go through into the living room?'

Matt is crouching in front of a newly lit fire that hisses in the grate, the orange and red tongues of flame licking the back of the fireplace. A comforting swell of warmth closes in against the chill.

He gets up stiffly. 'I'll just go and get some more logs,' he says gruffly.

I'm aware of the currents of tension in the room as Matt heads for the door. I see a flicker of concern in Rachel's eyes.

'Thanks so much, Matt.' Rachel tries to jolly him. 'Your wine's here, Hannah. Have this chair here, it's comfier.'

She sits, gesturing me to the one opposite, but all I am aware of is Matt's dark bulk disappearing as he lumbers sulkily into the hallway. There's the squeal and slam of the back door and then silence.

A heartbeat. This is awkward.

Rachel's eyes flicker apologetically. 'Don't mind him.' She breaks off and I feel the instant need to swallow. 'I think he's got problems at work right now. Things he won't talk to me about, anyway.' She waves the glass with a tiny shrug. 'It's all been a bit... well, tense, recently. Let's just say that.'

'Right.'

'He works for a conservation organisation. An education programme that goes into schools. He's also been doing work with kids on exclusion orders, therapeutic communities, kids who are struggling to cope in mainstream anything, but what with the cuts—'

'Oh, amazing.' I try to get that pitch of surprise. 'Must be really interesting, but yes, I guess in these uncertain times...' I copy her shrug. A silence threatens again.

'But your new job is pretty secure though?' I ask tentatively.

'Oh, yeah, fine. I'm just about to start as a Team Leader with Children's Services, and with Matt's situation, taking a step up right now is actually perfect timing.' Her expression is enthusiastic, but I hear the doubt in her voice. She goes to say something more, but the sound of the back door opening again shuts her up.

We sit, listening to his huffing and stamping of feet through the kitchen, and the thick rustle of him taking his coat off. His head suddenly appears around the door. He looks straight at me.

'Shall I show you your room?'

I find I can't move.

Rachel takes a sip of wine, putting her glass down and levering herself up. 'Actually, while you're doing that, I'll sort out dinner and then come up and find you some bits and pieces.'

I have no choice. I get up awkwardly trying to avoid Matt's reddened face glaring at me from the doorway. His arm swings the door wide, allowing me through. In those seconds, I'm so close to him that it's almost painful.

'Please, after you.' He gestures to the stairs, but the sarcasm doesn't escape me.

I put a hand on the banister, aware of the proximity of him moving behind me, his nearness intimidating. I want to stop and turn around, confront him with why I'm here in his house, but I can't make a scene right now.

He practically body-corrals me through an open doorway and shuts it behind him, leaning his back against it.

I know what's coming.

It's obvious. This wasn't supposed to be like this.

I was going to tell Rachel, talk to her, tell her exactly what happened, give her my phone number, tell her to talk to me, anytime and anywhere and then get out of there and leave them to it – but now I'm trapped.

For several seconds, all I can hear is him breathing heavily, his fists clenching and unclenching. I am aware of the whiteness of his knuckles, the sheer tension thrumming through him, my heart rate pattering higher and higher.

'I don't even know what to say,' he hisses. 'I can't find the words.'

I stand there dumbly, feeling mutely angry, caught, humiliated.

'You've got *nothing* to say? *Nothing at all?* ' His eyes are hard and marbled with anger.

My head shakes as though on a stalk.

'I don't know how you've got the balls. What the hell are you thinking?'

I can only stare down at the floor. There's a loop of carpet that's unravelling. I can't take my eyes from it.

'I mean seriously, what the hell are you doing here, Hannah, eh?' he spits, the span of his hand jerking angrily to the wall. 'Do you think we're all going to sit downstairs and eat food and drink a few glasses of wine and play like we're old friends catching up after God knows how many years? Is that your plan?'

'This isn't about you, Matt. Really it's not.'

'And you want me to believe that?' He snorts, incredulous.

'Don't get all moral outrage with me, mister. You were the one who wasn't straight with me. You weren't honest. You didn't tell me the truth. That's not fair.' I suddenly think I sound like a child.

'So, you thought you'd turn up here "just to be fair", did you?' His neck jerks back in anger. 'Come on. Even you can't believe that. This is you forcing the issue, plain and simple.'

How the hell did you even know where I live, eh? How did you find that out?'

I look away, my eyes flitting back down to the floor again, remembering his wallet falling out of his pocket when he threw his jacket on the bed and the tip of his driving licence poking up for all the world to see. Five seconds when he went to use the bathroom; that's all it took.

'You're making all this out to be something it wasn't, Hannah.' He turns the palms of his hands, pleading. 'Listen. We got drunk together in a hotel bar. We hadn't seen each other in years. We talked. That was it.'

I stare at him in disbelief. 'Talk? That's what I wanted. We didn't just "talk", Matt. That's just not true. Don't salvage your conscience by minimising what happened and making crap up. Don't do that,' I hiss.

'Look, I was loaded. I can't remember half the bloody rubbish I was gibbering on about. I bet you can't either. I admit, I shouldn't have gone back to your room, but nothing happened, did it?'

'Only because of me,' I mutter stubbornly.

'Still, nothing happened. It was just two old friends catching up. Anyway, you weren't all innocent, so don't give me that.'

I stare at him in mute fury because he's caught me. I can't blurt it all out right now – not the truth, the whole truth.

'So, tell me, Hannah?'

'Tell you what?'

'How you really came to be strolling into that hotel after all these years, because I don't buy your "by coincidence" theory. What's the truth?'

I stare at him.

It wasn't like that. It wasn't how he's making it out to be. It wasn't like that at all.

The Truth with a capital 'T'.

Was I really just looking for Rachel? Is that right? Or is there a tiny part of me trying to kid myself?

'*Go back,*' Theresa, my therapist had said. '*Go back to that time in your life when you were happy. Describe that girl to me. Tell me what she liked, who she loved.*'

See, the thing is... I loved Matt.

But I also loved Rachel.

I was eighteen. The week before uni was about to start. I was moving into a shared house. I remember that shivering thrill as I walked up the road. The scent of the tarmac road rising up in in the heat, and a boy, unloading teetering boxes from the back of a van, attempting to navigate his way up the front path of a house. Then I realised this was *the* actual house, and this was probably *the* actual boy I was sharing with.

''Scuse.'

He scooted round me, and I caught a glimpse of him. Dark and good-looking, all gangly tall and bright-eyed. He winked at me. His eyes were hazel, flecked with green.

'Are you Hannah?' a voice said, and suddenly a girl appeared from the shadows of the hallway. 'I'm Rachel.'

She stood with her hand out and I took it. I was mesmerised by her: that astonishing mass of blonde hair. I remember the washed-out pink Indian embroidered skirt and long lace-up boots. I felt instantly frumpy and small-town in my sad supermarket brand jeans and my top pulled down to hide the size of my bottom.

There was a movement somewhere behind her.

'Oh, and that's Alison,' Rachel explained. 'She makes up the four of us. I'll introduce you later.'

We were forced to let go as Matt bustled past yet again.

'Just in here, Chris,' Matt called out to a guy jumping from the rear of the van before hoisting up a whole stack of boxes. 'Thanks for helping out, mate. I would never have managed all this on my own.'

Chris breathily dumped the boxes in front of us and went off down the path again.

'Hmmm... He's not the only one who's got an awful lot of stuff to carry up those stairs.' Rachel surveys the sight, hands on hips, surveying the mound of black plastic sacks piled up in the hallway. She looked doubtfully at the stairwell and then pouted at Matt.

'Don't you worry. 'Course Chris'll sort all that for you.' Matt pecked his chin in the direction of the van. 'He'd love to show his muscles off to a couple of pretty girls. It'd be a shame to rob him of the opportunity.'

I felt myself colour. I'd never been described as 'pretty' before.

'Great, you're a star.' Rachel turned her sparkling eyes in his direction. 'Oh! Where's your stuff?' Rachel looked at me and then back onto the pavement.

'Umm... I don't really have much.' I'd hoisted the carry-all from my shoulder and dropped it onto the step. 'This is me, really.'

We both looked down at it before Rachel's face broke into a beaming smile.

'Wow! How cool is that? To be so free. I think I'm going to learn a thing or two from you, I can tell.'

Learn from me? A warmth thrummed though me.

'Actually, look, why don't we just leave them to it? We'll only be in the way here. What do you say to grabbing a coffee or something?' She looked at me and then at Matt. 'That's cool, isn't it?'

His face was red-cheeked with exertion as he paused to run his fingers through his hair. 'Err... yeah. Sure!'

'You can put Hannah's bag in my room, and we'll sort everything out later.' She smiled that brilliant smile at him again, and I saw he was instantly lost.

We. My heart had nearly burst.

They.

The two of them, the beautiful people, Rachel and Matt. Taking me under their wing like the three of us had just become a little family. I think I might've been a bit in love from that moment on. I'd never felt like I'd been included by anyone before... Like, genuinely wanted. And now I was.

'But then something happened to you, Hannah, didn't it?' my therapist Theresa had said. *'Something that night at that party that changed everything. That thing you can't remember... So go back just that bit further. You can't go forward until you put yourself mentally back in place – that turning point – where things felt right and then suddenly went wrong for you. Go back to that pivotal moment. Look at the events as they changed and unfolded. Examine them closely. Learn from them.'*

Only I had decided to go one step further. I'd gone back to my flat – my quiet safe space – and with Sophie, my cat, on my lap, I'd opened my laptop, my fingers pausing for a second, making myself think about that night. *That night...* And I don't know what made me type the three words that were in my head, but I did and...

...And.

'Mekborough' and 'Rape' and '2006'.

And suddenly page after page and article after article and I had this feeling like a blanket settling around my shoulders.

I wasn't alone anymore.

There were women, unnamed women, victims that I hadn't known about – eighteen-year-olds, nineteen-year-olds, students, all living in and around the area.

Heart thudding and with a tightening, sick feeling in the back of my throat, I scrabbled for a pad of paper and a pen, and I began to write.

Hours later, I realised the room had gone dark. Sophie squirmed and stretched out on my lap, her claws digging into my knees. The needling shock brought me back instantly to the whirling spin of emotions and memories.

I have to tell someone about what I've found.

Someone who was there, back then, who knew me, and who knew what happened afterwards.

Rachel.

My fingers had typed her name, *Rachel Myers*, but nothing came up... Had she changed her name?... And then tried Matt Glassman. He might've kept in contact with her maybe? And then suddenly up he popped. *Matt Glassman* with a picture of him in running gear... And then a Facebook page that he clearly hadn't used in ages, an Insta account... Trawling through photographs and people who'd commented and liked his posts, cross-checking them with one another for something more recent.

And then by luck, there it was. A workplace charity event, with Matt in running gear, the banners with the name of the organisation in great big letters behind him. It didn't take much. A phone call to a receptionist, who said he was *'at a conference in Bradfield all week'*; a scouring of hotels to work out which were likely to hold conferences; and then a few front desk queries for 'Mr Glassman' and it was easy enough.

I found him in the hotel bar, noisy with crowds of men in suits, guffawing loudly. I was instantly struck by how little he'd changed in the last seventeen years. Same dark hair, long-ish but now with hints of grey, swept back behind his ears; same heavy-lidded, deep-set eyes; same mole on his cheek like a beauty spot. Only some fine lines above his cheekbones when he smiled at a waitress, the lines giving the game away that time really had passed, but nevertheless, I was suddenly unable to breathe.

'Hannah?' he'd said, incredulous.

I'd turned slowly, blinking, slightly puzzled. That contrived shock of one hand on the bar, mouth open as though not quite believing what I was seeing.

'Matt? Matt Glassman? Is it you?' I'd said, laughing.

'Wow! Wow,' he kept saying. 'This is really you, isn't it? I can't quite believe you're standing here.' His hand wavered a little as he pushed his hair back in that familiar way. I wondered how much he'd had to drink.

'Yes, it's me. What an amazing coincidence.'

'What are you doing here?' He'd picked up his drink with an unsteady hand as I told him something vague about a charity event and then asked if he ever heard from Rachel? He didn't look as though he'd heard me properly, bending forward a little, shaking his head in query, and so I tried again, but he'd only nodded as though he hadn't a clue what I'd said and offered me a glass of wine instead from the bottle of red he had in front of him on the bar.

I smiled awkwardly, accepting it, my pounding heart thudding as he pulled out the stool in front of him, gesturing me to sit, leaning in closer, asking had I come far? Where was I living these days?

'I have a flat, you know, the usual, single-person flat complete with a cat I share with my neighbour.' I laughed, skirting around every question, anxiously sipping the wine, being vague and turning everything back to him as he topped up my glass, and then I watched as he topped it up again. Another bottle and time began to slide – along with his defences that were already slurred with drink.

I went to get off the stool, realising with a shock that my head was swimming a little. I staggered and he grabbed my hand to steady me.

'Hanny?'

I looked at him.

'So... So, tell me honestly. I know it's a shock, but how d'you feel about seeing me again?' he'd said, the words stumbling into each other. 'How do you really feel? Be truthful. When we were chatting a minute ago, were you thinking, *We'll have these few drinks, and then we both go our separate ways...* Or—?'

I instantly looked away.

'Or, like... does it bring back... old memories?'

The lights from the bar reflected in his eyes. He blinked as though forgetting where he was for a moment, then he gathered himself.

'Like... like those memories of old times. Of you and me. Y'know... when...' I looked into his eyes to find him looking straight back into mine.

The blunt reminder, just like that, of something that neither of us had even hinted at from the moment it happened. I did something I should never have done: I had betrayed Rachel. Matt had betrayed Rachel. They'd been seeing each other a little bit – and then there was a falling-out between them, at the same time that she and I... and then, well, Matt and I... Well, we...

The lights in the bar suddenly dimmed and came on again, signalling last orders.

'Can we talk, Matt?' I had blurted suddenly. 'I have to talk to someone. It's about the past. You were there and I need to know some things about what happened back then. Can I talk to you?'

'Sure! Absolutely. But like, here? Now? I think they want us gone.'

'My B and B is over the road,' I'd said. 'Like a minute away.'

'What are we waiting for?' he'd said.

He'd grabbed the bottle from the bar and we had headed out. The chill of the night air instantly sobering me, whisking away the intimate warmth of the last couple of hours. He put his arm around me, jokey, friendly, the scented heat of him instantly wafting from the inside of his jacket. We jostled, not quite in step, me leading the way across the street to where a tall house with a coloured fanlight above the door was lit with the word, *Vacancies*. A dead pot plant in the window sparkled with a string of fairy lights.

He had giggled and nudged me as I fished the wooden keyring from my bag and slotted it into the front door. I saw it all then through his eyes, the embossed wallpaper up the creaking stairs, the tatty plywood door that squealed open. I'd left a lamp on earlier, shadowing a room that was completely upholstered in shades of cerise bri-nylon. We went and sat on the bed. It was an awkward moment; Matt pulling out the bottle, pushing it next to the chiffon lamp. Everything felt full of static: the hot nylon, the pink-shirred bedspread, all that uncomfortable slippery heat.

We listened to someone next door urinating loudly in their en suite.

'Do we have glasses, or are we relying on the toothbrush mugs?' Matt slipped his jacket off, swaying a little as he went into the bathroom. I listened to him clattering about in the unfamiliar space, and it was then I saw his wallet and driving licence and a kind of childish curiosity grabbed me, but I had to look away hurriedly as he appeared in the doorway, wrapped plastic cups in hand as he reached for the wine bottle.

'Right!' He handed me one, settling himself on the side of the bed with a knee crooked towards me. 'Go on. You wanted to talk about the past. Us, yeah? Well, me too, me too.' He grinned and bit his lip.

I stared at him. That wasn't what I'd wanted, no. That wasn't what I'd meant.

'Have you gone shy?' He leaned forward a little to take the cup from my fingers, brushing my skin. An unbidden pull of desire shivered through my gut.

'Matt.'

'What?' Sliding the cup back onto the table, he looked back at me, reaching to cup the side of my face in the palm of his hand. It was so long since anyone had been that gentle with me; that caring. I closed my eyes. The pressure of his hand pushed me back onto the bed. I looked at him. Our noses were touching and he was smiling into my face. His eyes perused me, this way and that. He wasn't speaking, and I was suddenly aware of his fingers flicking open the button on the waistband of my jeans and unzipping it.

Did I want this? I wanted to feel wanted. I wanted someone to hold me and take care of me. Someone who really knew the person I used to be – back then when things were all okay.

I squirmed upwards, letting my limbs flex out of the warmth of the material, feeling his pulled-out shirt tails drifting and tickling my stomach as he leant down, kissing under my ear, my neck.

'I want you, Hanny. I want all of you.' His lips trailed over mine, teasing and soft. 'There's nobody, no one, that's ever made me feel so complete.' His fingers flick over the buttons on my blouse, unpeeling each one, laying the material open. Tiny shivers of cold touch me with each one. 'No one ever. If I were to die now—'

'Don't say that.'

'It's true. If I were to die right now, I'd die happy.'

I pulled him closer towards me and let the darkness between us fill all the gaps, our heat, shutting out the room, the sounds outside, letting nothing else in.

'There has never been anybody – I mean nobody, that's ever made me feel the way I do about you.' His breathing tock-tocks in my ear. 'Relax,' he whispers. 'Relax.'

But I can't. There's something, there between us, all the time I'm kissing him, touching him. All the time my head and heart were responding, I had to block out the thing in my body that wasn't going to let me do this, as though a wall of thick glass separated me from him.

'Is this okay?' He slid the blouse from my shoulders.

'Yes, yes it is,' I murmured, wanting him to break through, to free me from this numbness, to take away my edges, to soothe and calm and drift me away to somewhere else.

'*You* got away once, but never again,' he whispered. 'I promise you, as soon as I'm properly free, I'll—'

I was instantly fully awake and totally sober. I pulled back, staring at him.

'I mean, I *am* free, in all the ways it matters, but just not physically… I mean properly. It's not that easy. I can't just walk away.'

'Free? What do you mean "free"? Walk away from what?'

'From… from… well, Rachel…' His hands came out, pleading, but I pushed him away.

'Rachel? *Rachel?*' I screamed at him, grabbing at my clothes and dragging them on. 'What do you mean, Rachel? You're still with Rachel? Why the hell didn't you say when I asked you, you bastard? I asked you about Rachel and you said nothing. Nothing.' Snatching and scrabbling at my things; the burning shame and realisation of his duplicity and my own stupidity sending me running down the stairs with him behind me, as he desperately tried to explain.

• • •

But he's not desperately trying to explain now. All I have are those hard eyes looking at me, asking me to do the explaining.

'I wanted to talk to you,' I say hotly. 'I needed to talk to someone, I told you that. I was feeling vulnerable. You led me to believe you were single.'

'I was wrong, okay? I was totally wrong. You were totally right. We had a drunken kiss and a bit of a fumble. I said things I shouldn't've said... Or... or maybe things I should've said a long time ago. Maybe it's right that you've turned up here like you have.' He rubs his hand across his face. 'Maybe you forcing the issue is a good thing. Maybe you're the one person in the world who could shake me from the appalling situation I've found myself in.'

'Appalling? You mean screwing around behind your wife's back?' I try to sound angry, but a part of me wants to know, because... well, just because.

He stops abruptly, his face changing from anger to something else I can't fathom.

When he speaks, it's a different tone. Hesitant. Hurt almost.

'You don't have a clue, Hanny,' he says quietly. 'You really don't have a clue.' He swallows and shakes his head. 'Actually, maybe I don't blame you for thinking what you're thinking about me right now. Maybe I am the duplicitous, gutless coward you think I am. Maybe you're right...' He purses his lips. 'But maybe when you know the full story, the real story, you'll feel differently.'

'Matt, look, I'm sorry. I'm sorry about...'

I feel his hesitation.

'Why?' He has the decency to go bright red. 'What good will it do?'

'What good will it do? Jesus.' I glare at him. 'Because she's my oldest friend. Because...' I falter. 'Because I feel really bad about what happened between you and me. I would never have gone anywhere near you if you hadn't—' I wave, searching for the words. 'Misrepresented what was going on with her.' I find I'm trembling.

I watch his face working angrily. *He's caught and he knows it.*

'I didn't "misrepresent" anything.' But I hear the uncertainty.

'Didn't you?' I look around me. 'Really?'

'Everything I said. Everything I told you. It's all true.'

'I thought you said you couldn't remember what you'd told me,' I say sulkily. 'I thought it was all a haze. I thought as far as you were concerned, we were just two people having a drink in a bar.'

He looks hard at me for a moment. I see the hurt flinching through his eyes. I don't know whom I'm angrier with: me or him.

He stalks over to the widow, gazing out into the tumbling blindness of white.

I want to hate him. I want to despise him. I want to march down those stairs and call him out for the liar he is, but there's part of me – the part of myself that I hate right now – that knows that I could've asked more questions that night. I could've delved deeper. But the fact is, I didn't. I wanted to be eighteen again; feel like I was eighteen. I let what happened, happen, knowing all the time he was hooking me in that night. Hook, line and bloody sinker.

'We can't do this right now,' he whispers miserably, getting up. 'I have to explain to you. Then you'll understand.' He goes over to the window and leans with his knuckles on the sill.

My eyes are drawn to the curl of hair in the nape of his neck; the moving wing of his shoulder blade under the fabric of his shirt as he leans in, hunching; the sadness etched across his face. I so want to be furious. I so want to maintain my moral indignation and loyalty to Rachel – and I *will*. I will be this person, even though I find him so bloody attractive.

He levers himself up from the sill, suddenly turning with his back to the window and folding his arms. He's there, silhouetted against the boiling whirls of snowy whiteness.

'I want out of my marriage, Hanny.'

It's like a bomb going off in my head. And my heart.

He means it. I can tell he really means it. Something inside me tightens in panic.

'You don't mean that.'

'I do. Oh yes, I do.'

He jerks his head away. 'Can I tell you something?'

I know something big is coming.

I feel a quiet thrill. I stay completely quiet.

He takes a breath, his tongue resting on the tip of his lip. 'So, I'll tell you my truth.' He takes another breath. 'The truth is, I've left her: up here, and in here.' He taps his temple and then his heart. 'I shouldn't stay with someone when I've spent years thinking about being with someone else.'

I can't find any air. I'm aware of my own pulse beating rapidly under my tongue.

'I've been living a lie all these years, Hanny.' He shakes his head as though he can't quite believe his own words. 'I've never really been myself with her. Not properly myself, not truly. And all the time, every night and all through the day, all I could think about was you – so when I saw you standing there at that bar—' He looks at me, incredulous.

I can't drag my eyes away from his face. I'd forgotten just how beautiful he is.

'Rachel has always known that you and I had some kind of connection, she just never knew the depth of it. I think she dismissed the whole vibe, thinking we were just really good mates. In her mind, as we know, no one else can ever actually compete with her, can they?' He widens his eyes. 'Don't look like that. We're both aware that's just how Rachel is. I'm not telling you anything you don't already know.'

I don't know where he's going with this. I want to stop him: I won't betray Rachel, but I don't want to hurt and embarrass him either.

'I mean, in Rachel's world, we're all there to serve a function, aren't we?' His shoulders lift 'That's how things are with all the people in her life. You know how she operates: Rachel makes sure she's at the centre of everything, telling everyone around her how massively important they are to her – but you and I know what's really going on: she's stroking your ego, making you feel like she can't function without your help and support.'

He studies me carefully to gauge my reaction, but I'm not going to openly diss her – sure, she has faults, but don't we all? No matter what else happened, when I needed her, she was there for me when no one else would have been.

'But, deep down, we know it's all one big manoeuvre. We know we're being groomed and managed. But somehow, despite knowing, we just can't help giving her everything she wants.' He pauses and then laughs, sadly. 'But I know you're the one person I don't have to explain that to.'

We. Us. He's thinking there's an 'us'.

'You got away, Hanny. You got out of it. I remember Rachel saying something about you having "problems" and that's why you left, but I always knew the real reason.'

'Problems? What kind of problems?' Now he has my attention.

He wrinkled his forehead. 'Wow! it's a long time ago. I can't think what she said specifically, something about struggling with the coursework – amongst a lot of other things.' His eyes flicker over my shocked ones. 'And that you were giving up and going home for a while. Taking some time out. As I said, I was probably one of the only people who knew what living with Rachel was really like. You'd had enough of being a puppet, and frankly, I don't blame you.'

But I don't let it go. 'Struggling? She said that?'

He shrugs.

'Come on, Matt. Level with me.'

He regards me for a moment. 'Okay, drinking,' he says finally. 'She said you were having problems with drinking too much.'

My shock drops into my jaw. 'And you believed that?'

He squirms, folding his arms tighter across his chest 'Well, after... after that night. The one of that party—'

My stomach turns inside out.

'After that night, when you were so out of it... And afterwards, when you wouldn't come out of your room, and Rachel said you were binge-drinking—'

'I was, but—' I can't find any more words.

'So, it all made sense to me: your need to get away... And that's how I feel right now. Only it's taken me seventeen years to do the same.' He takes a breath, turning back to stare out of the window again, his breath fogging the pane, the intensity of the blizzard dimming the light.

'There were other things too, Matt,' I try to explain. 'That's what I wanted to talk to you about that night at the hotel. Rachel was right, I ran back home, to the very place I thought I'd finally escaped from. But you never really run away from anything, do you? Because you take your sad, sick self with you no matter how far you go.'

'Oh, I get that. Funnily enough, I've been running too – by staying right here.' He gestures to the walls. 'That's a form of running away too. I've been hiding by staying in a relationship I should've left years ago.'

'Matt—' I want to stop him.

'I asked you what the truth was earlier, didn't I? Well, I think either knowingly or unknowingly, something led you to that hotel that night. There's no way you could've known I'd been thinking of you. I said it was magic, didn't I? It was as though I'd manifested you. Does that sound crazy?'

I look at his face now, staring so earnestly at me.

'And now my manifestation has come here to haunt me.' He laughs a little. 'I never dreamed this bit of it.' Matt turns away, taking a deep breath, his finger coming up to imprint itself in the misted pane. 'Now what? Now what do we do with you?' He looks as though he's talking to himself.

'I didn't plan to stay here, Matt,' I say lamely. 'This all just happened. None of it was my intention. I couldn't have known about the snow, but you're right: it's true, I shouldn't have come here. It was a stupid thing to do. I don't know what I was thinking.'

Matt stares sullenly out into the whiteness. 'But I suppose the good thing is, you'll see what I'm talking about.' His finger becomes a spiral, winding slowly down to a full stop. 'You'll confirm that my marriage is a sham. Rachel was seeing someone, Hanny. We've agreed to give things another try, but—' He checks the expression on my shocked face. 'The situation made me realise that I shouldn't have agreed to stay. Seeing you again only hammered that feeling home. And now you're here—'

I'm trying to process the enormity of the situation that I've walked into.

'Now you're here I have a feeling it'll blow this whole charade apart once and for all. It's like a pressure cooker reaching a head of steam. Things have to happen. There'll be no plastering over the cracks. We're stuck in this house, the three of us. There'll be no escaping.'

The terror of what he's suggesting suddenly grips me; this isn't what I came for at all. What does he want from me? What does he expect? A crawl of something uncomfortable snakes its way into the pit of my stomach.

'Matt, I need to say something. When I came here, frankly I

never dreamed… I never thought… I just assumed you were messing about behind Rachel's back.'

'And do you still think that?

Do I?

Matt was always so straight, so decent, such a kind sort of guy, I think I was stunned that he could have behaved like a dick.

I shake my head. 'No. No, I don't. Seriously, Matt, you're an attractive, amazing guy, and if things were different—'

I see his expression change.

'But they're not. Things aren't different. You need to figure this mess out. I won't say anything to Rachel, but you have to promise me you will.' He goes to speak, but I hold up a hand. 'And you need to handle it thoughtfully. Sensitively. This isn't about me, Matt. We both know that. It's about sorting you and her. Let's have no explosions from the pressure cooker. No collateral damage. Wait until I've gone. Have a calm and honest conversation. Tell her how you really feel.'

'How I really feel?' He turns, taking a step towards me, but I put my hand up in case he's thinking of touching me. The tips of my fingers brush his sleeve. A tingle of electricity shivers right up to my neck. My head isn't listening to my heart; I can feel it cleaving wide. I look at him standing there in front of me. It would all be so easy: to start something that neither of us can stop. It would all be so easy – and so wrong.

A sound outside on the landing and we both snap a look at the door. I don't have time to move before it opens, and Rachel stands there with a look on her face that I can't decipher. Matt doesn't speak; we're both frozen. I know I look guilty; I *feel* guilty. Rachel doesn't take her hand from the door edge as she glances from Matt and then back to me.

'What are you two whispering about?'

THREE

'I brought you these in case you needed them.' She steps forward hesitantly. She's clutching a bundle of clothes in her arms. I can only stare at them. There's this mad compulsion to speak, to say something, anything.

'I have to say you two look very serious.' She doesn't meet my eye.

'We were talking about the last time we saw each other,' Matt says quickly. There's no way I can look at him. *Why the hell did he have to say something like that?*

Rachel's spine twitches as she straightens.

'And how long ago was that?'

The air in my lungs flutters pathetically. My eyes glue to the loop on the carpet.

'We were just trying to work that out. It's got to be over fifteen years. Seventeen, maybe?'

I can feel her eyes twitch in my direction. She knows there's something odd here, she just doesn't know what.

Matt, Matt, Matt, what are you saying? What are you doing? my head is screaming.

'Oh heck, it must be seventeen at least.' She pats the pile, seeming to accept the explanation. 'I've put a collection of toiletries together for you – here. There's brand-new underwear too, and a few bits and pieces of casual stuff. Let me know if you need anything else, and we can have a look through my wardrobe.'

'Great, great. Thanks.' I'm desperately agreeing.

'Dinner won't be too long. We'll see you downstairs in a while, yes?'

It's the first time she glances at Matt, who immediately scuttles to the door. Rachel pauses with a hand on the frame as she looks back at me.

'Everything okay?'

Her eyes clear and direct.

'It's fine. Everything is fine.' I even manage a smile as she gives me a little satisfied smile back and then leaves me alone, pulling the door closed behind her.

My god, my god, I'm anything but.

Flopping back flat on the bed, I stare up at the unfamiliar ceiling, trying to stop the rising panic from taking me over completely. The shadows of falling snowflakes strobe around the light fitting, a dizzying pattern, faster and faster.

How could he do that to her, to *me* – like he was sharing some kind of appalling private joke.

You're the one that got away, Hannah.

He can't have meant that, surely? One night, that's all. One stupid night when we were both upset with Rachel over something and nothing.

Not quite. Alison's face comes back to me. *Alison* – who inserted herself between me and Rachel, who was bitchy and nasty to me so many times despite how much I tried to make her like me. If things with her hadn't happened, then strangely neither would Matt and I.

Sighing, I open my eyes. The snowflakes have stopped spinning on the ceiling. The light in the room has changed to a strange blue-white and all I feel is a muted hush filling the house. I'm cocooned here, snug and tight. Swinging my legs from the side of the bed, I get up to go out onto the landing but am immediately aware of raised voices.

I pause at the top of the stairs, unsure whether to go down. The sudden creak of the top step gives me away, and the voices instantly stop and I hear the slam of the front door.

'Your wine's down here waiting for you,' Rachel calls cheerily. 'Matt's just popped out to get some more.'

Slipping quickly down the stairs, I'm suddenly aware of how oppressive the house feels. She meets me in the hallway wiping her hands on a tea towel.

'He didn't need to go out, not on my account. Not in this weather.' I glance through the lounge into the street. The snow has built up in drifts against the bottom panes. It hangs, thick and precarious, from the roof of the bay window.

'Oh, he's only gone up to the shops on the corner. He says he needs the walk.'

There's a moment where our eyes meet. I feel it. I can see she feels it too: the massive weight of things unspoken. *Does she suspect something? Were they arguing about me?*

Turning quickly on her heels, she heads back into the kitchen. There are two glasses sitting on the breakfast bar. I see mine has been topped up.

'Rachel...'

'Hmm?' She keeps her back to me, moving over to the draining board and starting to put stuff away.

'Are you okay?'

'Not really.'

An instant thump of fear drops deep in my gut.

She clatters some forks into a drawer. I don't know how to begin this. Everything I'd rehearsed has flown out of my head. My fury at Matt has been replaced by... What? Christ. A whole raft of confused emotions I can't even begin to unpick.

I'm aware that her shoulders have stiffened. She picks up a Pyrex dish. I can't even begin to think what I want to say. Rachel's hand falters midair; she too seems nervous.

'I'm "okay" in a more or less kind of way,' she says levelly. 'Given the circumstances.' Bending to open a cupboard, she slots the dish inside and then quietly closes the door.

Despite the squall of sick feeling in my stomach, I know I have to do this now.

'I think we need to talk, Rach. Like, about a whole ton of things.'

She looks round at me and I see her face is crumpled with grief. I go to her, grasping her hand. Her fingers hold on to mine as I pull the both of us to sit at the workbench.

'You might as well know: things are pretty awful. You heard us rowing, I suppose?' Her eyes are red and bright with unshed tears.

I instantly feel worse, terrible – more and more like a betrayer than I did before, caught in my own disloyalty with no way out.

She rests her elbows on the bench, burying her face.

'You can talk to me.' I slide the wine glass over to her.

I feel like the poorest version of a friend that anyone would want to have, but right now, I'm all she's got.

'I think Matt wants to leave me,' she says simply.

The squall in my stomach plummets violently.

'I think he's been seeing someone.' Her fingers touch the glass stem. My throat constricts.

'How... how do you know?' The words stick hard and fast.

Her head swings dully. 'I don't really. I know he hasn't been happy for years. Neither of us have. It was a few weeks ago. He went to some overnight event to do with teaching, and when he came back, he was different. I think he was with someone. I asked him, but he just got angry.' Her fingers press into her forehead so hard the tips turn bloodless.

'The facts are we're both just too scared to pull the plug. Anyway...' She lifts her head, shaking her mane of hair back. 'You don't want to get embroiled in all that nonsense, do you? It'll just spoil the evening and I could do with not thinking about it for a while.'

My gut cramps painfully; I suddenly feel sick. *I am the worst person ever.*

'What's the matter?' She's looking at me. 'What did I say now? Oh gosh, have I upset you?'

'No, no, honestly.' I can't even bring myself to look at her. 'It's just all so sad.'

Christ, what have I got myself into?

'And so complicated. I mean, it's not just Matt.'

Her phone on the worktop suddenly flashes. She grabs it up, quickly scanning the message, and then replies, before putting it back face down. When she looks back at me, I can see that other thoughts are filling her head.

'The one that got away.' Her eyes bore into mine.

'What?' My heartbeat thuds under my tongue.

'You can't control who you fall in love with, can you?'

The hammering inside my ribcage won't let me hear the words properly.

'S-Sorry?'

She sighs, rubbing her nose and sniffing. 'Me. It's not just Matt. That's basically it. I met someone else. I fell in love. But it's over now.'

I can only stare blankly.

'Are you shocked?'

'God, no. Not shocked. I...' I shrug. 'I don't know what I am. Things happen I suppose.' I swallow hard. My head is a mess.

'I was stupid.' She bites her top lip. 'He made me feel—' She gives a little laugh. 'Well, young again.' She cups her palms around the glass, swirling the wine and gazing into it for a moment. Her face goes dreamy. 'Silly really. Fantasy stuff. Not real life. Matt is real life, isn't he?' She looks at me with those big eyes. 'Safe, dependable Matt. Solid. The kind of guy you can rely on.'

I nod. Yes, I remember it well. Matt, always being given tasks: deliver this, post that, driving here, there and everywhere. Biddable, dependable Matt, always so wiling and so eager to do anything she wanted – while all the time I knew that one day the sparkling, bright flame of Rachel would tire of the dull, plodding Matt.

'I just need to be more grateful for what I've got.' She looks sad. 'Excitement isn't everything, is it?'

'I suppose not.'

Rachel. Brilliant, effervescent Rachel. But always taking, and Matt always giving —until one person gets tired of the way things are.

'The thing is, weirdly, Matt and I never made a proper real decision to be together, you know? We kind of drifted into it. You remember what I was like in the early days: very political, very passionate about working with the disadvantaged, the vulnerable, the people who had no voice. When we got married it was a kind of, "Well, shall we? We might as well," kind of thing.' She chuckles without fondness at the memory.

'Wow, I didn't realise – but yes, yes, I remember how you were. You were committed and full of fire. I was in awe of you.'

I remember her taking the stage at an event and giving a speech on the council's lack of action on people sleeping rough. I was there, at the back of the room, stunned at the ferocity and fire, almost hypnotised by the dazzling sight of her on that platform. Her sparkling hair, her expressive hands, the way her voice resonated: full of fury at the unfairness and injustice. She spoke and we all listened, like *really* listened. Totally entranced, I would've followed her anywhere. She made me feel like I was not only *doing* good; I *was* good. I *felt* like a good person.

'In awe? Were you?' She smiles. 'How sweet. Matt always

was there with me, a hundred percent, every time – championing me on to bigger and better things. He made me feel as though I could *do* and *be* anything. He was always just *there*.'

Poor Matt, my head says.

'So, what happened?'

'Too many causes, too many wrongs to right. I took on more and more until in the end, I think I burnt out,' she says with a wry smile. 'And without that fire of meetings and speeches and marches and events, what did we have? Just us. Us on our own staring at each other with nothing to say. Matt didn't know what to do. He tried being me. He tried to get involved in the way I had, but he doesn't have the right personality – the right edge.' Her eyes track my face. 'Some people are kings and some people are king-makers. But *you* totally get that don't you, Hannah?'

The words fall from her lips without even a hint of how they might sting. I say nothing.

She sighs again, locked in her own world. 'So, I ended up getting a proper job: social care. I work with Children's Services – did I mention that?' She doesn't wait for me to answer.

'Ironic, as I don't have any.' She shrugs. 'And somehow the opportunity ladder stretched up in front of me, and I took it. Money, money.' She rubs the tips of her fingers together. 'It's amazing how easily those deeply held principles can be bought, particularly as Matt wasn't earning that much.' Her mouth sets in a line.

'But it meant I drifted further and further away from what made me, me.' She picks up the glass and takes a sip. 'I told myself it was called "growing up" and "being mature" when what I really felt was uninspired and flat.' She shrugs. 'And then, through a friend of a friend, I agreed to go to some fundraiser – and this man walked onto the stage.'

She blinks slowly at the memory. 'James Talbot. He began talking... His voice...' She peters off as she recollects. 'And suddenly I was paying attention. He was talking about local businesses offering the underprivileged a way out of their situation. Real, tangible, properly paid work.' Her eyes are alight with the memory. 'He was talking about taking people on who had no fixed address, probably no national insurance number, and no references – unheard of. The whole scheme was fraught with problems, but it was revolutionary.'

I watch her face.

'And that's how I ended up putting money into one of his businesses,' she explains. 'For the first time, I became a follower and not a leader. I followed him.'

And left Matt behind.

'So, what happened?'

She sighs. 'My friend Emily persuaded me it was all madness. The investment, the obsession – *him*. She said I should let it all go. And I finally listened to her. Mainly because she told me stuff about him – like he had a partner and a child he'd never mentioned.'

'Wow.'

'And showed me how stupid I was. As I said, it was all a fantasy, really.'

'You're not stupid, Rachel. Don't say that.'

'I am. She opened my eyes. Made me look at reality and not the romance. All my "championing" and "podcast influencing" had been a romantic ideal.' She gives another wry smile. 'I was going to defend mankind and change the world.'

'So, you came back to Matt?'

She nods wearily and takes another mouthful. 'I asked him if he'd be willing to give it another try.'

'And clearly he was.' I am squirming, knowing what I know.

'He was, he's trying. I'm trying.' She pulls a wry face.

'So, who was that on the phone?'

Her hand automatically comes out to touch it. 'Emily.'

I can't tell if that's the truth or not.

'But you're still in contact with him?'

I see her blanch slightly and know I've guessed right.

'Off and on. I've told him he mustn't...' She gives me a look. 'But he's persistent.'

I almost ask her if she's thought of blocking his number, but I stop myself.

I see the phone suddenly bead with light against the worktop as her hand halts abruptly at the sound of the back door.

'I'll tell you more later.'

The phone screen goes black, and she slips it into her pocket as Matt walks in, stamping the snow from his boots. He has a bottle of wine stashed in each pocket.

'I got white and rosé.' He addresses the comment stonily to no one. His eyes flit over me. 'The walk home chilled them.'

'You really shouldn't have gone to all the trouble,' I offer.

'It was no trouble.' He still can't bring himself to look at me.

'Let me top you up.' Rachel reaches for the already opened bottle. The glug of wine feels warm under my fingers as it slides into the glass. I am aware of Matt's eyes on me the whole time.

'How far did you get with dinner?' he says, gruffly pulling his coat off. Rachel pauses and looks up, mid-pour. 'I'll carry on with it if you like,' he adds. 'Leave you to lay the table and chat? I'm sure you've got loads to catch up on.'

He turns to the hob and Rachel gives me a look. I can see there are things she's desperate to tell me.

She gets up, taking a sip from her glass and giving me a meaningful look before getting up to grab a bunch of cutlery, beckoning me through into the dining room as she begins the lay the table.

I keep catching glimpses of Matt's movements through the gap in the door. He glances over anxiously and then turns away, beginning to make a salad. Rachel fusses with placemats that don't need fussing over and then tries to make banal conversation – am I in a draught there? Would I like water? We all individually hold on tight, pretending that everything is okay.

Matt clatters about, heralding he's about to walk in, appearing with a bubbling pasta dish, silently placing it on the table between us.

There's an uncomfortable moment.

'This looks and smells wonderful. What a treat!' I gush.

Matt picks up my plate and begins to pile it with pasta. Strings of mozzarella hang from his spoon.

'Damn.' His annoyance ramps the tension up a notch.

'Oh, don't worry about the presentation. It looks fabulous.' My laugh sounds forced as he attempts to shake off a lump of melted cheese and then scrapes the handle down the side of the plate. I don't dare look at Rachel. She's not laughing, she only scrapes her chair back to fetch the bowl of salad and then unsteadily reaches again for the wine bottle. I see Matt's eyes flit disapprovingly.

'God, I love pasta,' I mumble appreciatively. The aroma wafting up is amazing. 'I haven't been to Italy for years. I really must go back soon.' I smile at them both, but neither is paying attention.

Matt serves Rachel and then himself, taking the proffered salad bowl before sitting down and picking up his fork.

'Aren't we having a toast?' Rachel's voice is loud and slightly aggressive. She stares at him stonily.

'Well, I'll propose one then: To friends and friendship.' She looks pointedly at me. I shrivel a little inside as we chink glasses. I can't bring myself to even glance at Matt as we do the same. I begin to eat and chatter to cover the moment, going on at length about the recipe and the wine, aware the whole time that I'm talking too much.

Rachel doesn't touch her food, only reaches for her glass and drains it, before twisting off the cap of the new bottle of rosé.

'Should you calm down, do you think?' Matt isn't looking at her, just spearing piece after piece of pasta: *tap, tap, tap*. The hostility is palpable.

'I thought we were celebrating?' she says. I glance at her. She's all wide-eyed with mock puzzlement.

'Yes, *we* are. That means not just you doing the celebrating.' *Oh god.*

'Hannah? Would you like some more wine?' She stares at me. 'There's some red left, I think. Or if you'd prefer white?'

'Oh, umm... No, I'm okay for the minute, thanks.'

'We've got to have more toasts though.' Rachel reaches for the bottle. 'Here. Go on.'

'She said she didn't want any,' Matt says through tightened teeth.

'She's just being polite though, aren't you, Hannah?' Rachel wavers the bottle over the top of my glass. She's going to miss the rim completely.

'Well—'

'See?' She glares a smile at Matt, but it's not pleasant.

'Rachel.' Matt's tone is giving her a warning.

'Matt,' Rachel mimics, googling her eyes at him.

'Hannah said she doesn't want any more wine.'

'When did Hannah know what was best for her, eh?' She giggles. 'I've always been the one who knows what's best for her.'

A sting of embarrassment heats my neck: her words, the atmosphere, the situation.

'I have to say, this is divine.' I shovel up a whole forkful. 'It took no time at all, you'll have to tell me how to make it.'

Matt briefly closes his eyes. Rachel is staring at him.

I can hear myself asking a question, but even I'm not really wanting an answer. All the time, I'm acutely aware that Rachel isn't eating. Her fork is resting at the side of her plate. She has both hands cradling her wine glass, with elbows on the table.

Her shoulders have muscled up around her ears. I can feel the fight in her gathering momentum in the lowered chin and the steely vibe.

'What?' Matt says, still chewing. 'Something the matter?'

She lowers the glass slowly, putting it in front of her and squaring the base carefully with the edge of the placemat. 'Are we really going to rehearse all this in front of Hannah?'

The threat is right there. I have no idea what's going on, but whatever it is, it's unravelling right in front of my eyes. Matt only shrugs. It's a long shrug: the kind that says, quite clearly and candidly that if she wants to go for it, she should go right ahead.

Whatever 'it' is, hangs there in the air between them for several moments, before Matt pushes his chair back with a screech against the wooden floor.

'Are we finished?' He looks pointedly at Rachel and then at her plate.

'If you think so, then yes.'

The meaning is obvious. I'm aware of my eyes flickering nervously from one to the other.

'Hannah?'

I haven't, of course, but dutifully lay my fork down with a nervous smile. 'That was fantastic... Really yummy. Thank you so much...' I trail off as the plate disappears from under my nose and Matt carries the uneaten food back into the kitchen. I reach out to pick up the serving bowls, but Rachel's hand comes out to stop me.

'Leave it,' she says loudly. 'Let him do it.'

'Would anyone like pudding?' Matt calls out. 'I've—'

'No thank you,' Rachel cuts across. 'Hannah and I are fine.' She attempts to catch my eye, but I let it flutter away, concentrating on a bit of sauce that's blobbed on the table. I use my napkin to wipe it up as the moody silence gathers. The only sound is Matt scraping stuff into the bin and loading the dishwasher. The tap gushes and then there's the click and hiss of the kettle. Matt appears in the doorway; he looks like a man uncomfortable in his own skin.

He comes forward and picks up the rest of the serving dishes. 'I'll get rid of this and then I'm going for a walk,' he announces.

'Fine.' Rachel doesn't look at him as he retreats into the kitchen. We listen to the crashing about and then the stomp of his feet in the hall and the slam of the front door.

Rachel slumps at the table, putting her head in her hands. 'God, I'm so sorry, Hannah. I'm so sorry you had to witness all that.' She wraps her arms around herself. 'I'm trying to hold it together. The last thing I want to do is involve you in all this bloody drama.' She presses the heels of her hands into her eyes. 'I'm so embarrassed at dragging you into this. Please forgive me, it's just that I'm under so much pressure right now, I'm not coping at all well. And I shouldn't be using this—' She shoves angrily at the stem of her wineglass. 'God. Let's not rehearse this mess any further... Let's talk about you instead.' Her hands drop to the table and she forces an encouraging smile. 'I've often thought about you, you know.'

'Rachel—'

'No, honestly, it's fine. Tell me. Tell me about your life, after —' She shakes her head a little and presses her lips together. 'After what happened.'

I pause. I remember the look on her face when she dropped me off at the train station: all concern and worry. I don't think I had ever felt what it was like to have someone worry about me.

'You really cared, didn't you, Rach? You were really scared for me?'

''Course I was scared for you,' she splutters. 'I was even more scared when you didn't reply to my messages or answer emails. I remember in desperation I looked up an address online that I thought might be your parents and I sent letters and a couple of Christmas cards on the off chance your parents might forward them to you, but I assumed you'd moved, left, maybe didn't want to answer or something?'

I nod. 'Yeah. Wow! Well, yes, some mail did get passed on, but by then I think you must've moved too...'

But not passed on by my parents, that's a fact. Certainly not those two people I was supposed to call Mum and Dad. The reality was, I was always something to be 'dealt with' until I could 'deal with' myself. I'd gone straight to my parents' house, knowing I'd find it in darkness. The electricity was off. I rang my mother, who of course didn't answer, so I rang her friend Kit, who was too drunk to help me with anything much other than that my mother had 'gone off' to Spain with Juan, her new bloke, and my father was living with his new girlfriend in New Zealand.

Why did my parents even have me? I've often wondered that. Was I an accident they didn't get rid of in time? An expensive annoyance, like a dog you bought on a whim and then really wished you hadn't. The more the marriage fell apart, the more obvious that became. I had parents that looked after but didn't care for me. I lived in a house, but it wasn't a home. Each of them had grown bored with their lives and bored with each other. I was part of some past that neither of them wanted to deal with. There were drunken rows, smashed-up furniture. The fights went from fighting each other over what they wanted, to fighting each other over what they didn't want: me.

Whole weeks spent on my own with nothing but a debit card for company and the threat of Social Services hanging over my head warning me to keep schtum. I pretended both of them were still there: I opened and closed curtains, turning lights on and off in all the bedrooms so that the neighbours wouldn't question. I even taught myself to move the car late at night, so it looked as though I wasn't alone.

'You were okay, though?' Rachel leans forward a little. 'When you got home? There was someone to look after you?'

I waver a smile. 'There were people who looked after me, yes.'

Rachel leans back in her chair looking relieved.

I remember putting the phone down from speaking to my mother's friend and standing there in the moonlit hallway. The shadows, the silence, the nothingness seemed of little consequence at the time. I was barely there either. I dragged myself to my old bedroom that was now filled with half-packed boxes and lay on the bare mattress. I was empty: no thoughts, no feelings. It was as though I was only just there, half in, half out of not really existing at all. I don't know how many days had passed when the police found me, alerted by a neighbour who'd seen movement and thought there were intruders. She was right, I was an intruder. I told the doctors and nurses the same thing at the hospital I was taken to. '*I shouldn't be here,*' I insisted, but they all misunderstood my meaning. All I really wanted was to not be anywhere.

'I've been getting help, Rach.'

'Oh?'

'The fact is, I realised I needed to sort myself out. There was this...' I spread my palms on the table. 'This dawning realisation that I was repeating patterns, getting myself into situations – with men particularly.' I give her an awkward smile. 'You know how it is.'

'Don't I just.' She closes her eyes. 'Anyway, go on.'

'It felt as though after a while everything in my life became toxic. The common denominator was me.' I desperately want Rachel to see how far I've come 'I had a chance to talk to someone, Theresa. She's been fantastic. She told me that I can't move forward until I go back – which I've done. I've come here.' I swallow painfully. 'Rachel.' I stop. 'I need to talk to you.'

Her eyes dart uncertainly.

'I need you to come into the lounge and sit down.'

'What is it?'

'Please. While Matt's out.'

I push my chair back and she follows me uncertainly. I reach for my bag and go and perch on the edge of a chair. Rachel sits opposite.

'I didn't tell you the truth back then,' I gush awkwardly. 'But I want to now. I want to.'

'Now?'

'About why I'm here.'

Her face changes a little. 'Oh?' She looks at me warily. Her expression is very still. I see she doesn't want to guess.

'Me turning up here. It wasn't really by accident. It wasn't on the off chance.'

She still doesn't move.

'I wanted to talk to you about the past... What we did...'

Her face blanches a little.

'We thought...That is, *I* thought I could make it go away. Never speak of it again...'

'Right.' She agrees in a kind of dazed way as her brain attempts to process.

'But things have happened, and I've had to face things I don't want to face.' I swallow, pushing away the hazy images that force their way into my brain. 'I've had to confront feelings I never wanted to feel again, but unless I do, I can't live. Not properly. I'll be running away for the rest of my life.'

'Right. Right.' But she looks unsure.

'I was raped.'

Her head snaps back.

The words hang stark and brutal in the air: almost like I haven't uttered them.

'What?'

I can't repeat it. The words don't belong to me. It feels as though it happened to someone else: a girl I read about but don't know.

'*Raped?*' she says as though testing it out. 'Hannah... Jesus.'

'I know what you must've thought at the time. That it was some boy, some kid, a one-night stand maybe.'

'But why didn't you–'

I know what she's going to ask and I hold up a hand.

'I know. Why didn't I tell you? Why didn't I confide in you? Because I knew what you'd say, Rachel. I knew you'd want me to talk about it – to police, to professionals. You'd want me to re-live what happened. And I couldn't do that. I just couldn't. I wanted to shut it out. I didn't want to think or feel anything. I wanted to pretend that it was some kind of appalling nightmare that I'd woken up from and now everything was alright.'

'But you were alone, Hannah. You were alone. Through all that.'

'I wanted to be alone. I wanted things to be normal. I didn't want the questions and examinations... on and on.' My hands cover my ears. 'I would have had to face the possibility of no one believing me. Staring. Whispering. Judging.'

'Hannah, Hannah, Hannah.' Rachel slips from the edge of her chair to kneel at my feet. There's the warmth of her hands on my arms as she pulls me to her, but I feel myself stiffen at the physical contact. I want to peel myself away.

'I couldn't deal with the pity I knew everyone would feel, Rachel. I couldn't go there and become a "rape victim". Something less than other people, and not me anymore.'

'W-Who... Who? Do you know?' Her voice trembles at the question.

'I have no idea. I was drugged.'

Her mouth falls open in horror. 'Drugged?'

'Yes, yes, yes. That's what I believe. It was Theresa. She's made me go over and over it. She made me think – like, take control. Take action. Not just feel – she told me to *do*. And in *doing*, I began to not only think about what had happened to me, but to other women who might've had the same experience. I know things now – I've pieced things together.'

I unzip my bag. 'Hugo Leach.' She watches me as I draw a file of printed-off papers from my bag. 'Theresa began to question what actually happened that night. Who was I talking to? Was I with anyone? She asked me to try to remember details: sensations, smells, any tiny, tiny thing.'

'*Leach?* Oh my god. Wasn't Leach the guy who attacked girls in their student accommodation?' She's looking at the papers as I draw them out of the folder.

I lay them out so that she can see. 'This is stuff I found on the internet. I know what happened to me isn't exactly the same, but as I started researching, I stared seeing a patten in the offences – look.' I turn a piece of paper round where I've written the names of the victims and the dates. 'Each one two weeks apart, or thereabouts. And here's the date of the party.' I have the 21st July 2006 ringed in red.

'See? Two weeks later he attacks the first girl. The police already know him as a drug dealer, not a sex offender so they discount him. She's drugged. A hood over her head. It was hot. They'd all been outside, drinking. She said she felt ill and went into the house to go to the loo, and he must've been waiting for her. The attack took place in her room. When she woke up, she could hardly remember what happened. Her friends just thought she was a bit pissed and had crashed. Well, you would, wouldn't you? And here, this girl, again at a party, again drugged, and then this on....' I hand the printed-out sheets to her. 'And this one.'

Rachel holds them jumbled, a look of horror on her face.

'I think I might've been the first. He hadn't perfected his process. I was a test case.' I steady myself.

'But *Leach*, Hannah.'

'I know. He was all over the news, but I wouldn't look at any newsfeeds, I closed my eyes and ears and mind. The truth is, even if I'd had a glimmer, I didn't *want* to make the connection.'

Rachel stares down at the bit of paper, not saying a word.

'I couldn't read or listen to any article that even hinted at rape.' I watch the disbelief sink in. 'If I heard Leach's name, I switched off. For years I've checked every TV programme or drama for trigger warnings, just in case, but now...' I swallow. 'I'm confronting every fear I have. I'm staring it in the face.'

'That's good,' Rachel reassures. 'That's good.' She looks up at me. Her eyes are red rimmed with hurt for me. 'I just wish I'd *known*, Hannah.' Her hands lift to her face. 'Where the hell was I when all this was happening to you, for God's sake? Why don't I remember any of this? And afterwards? Surely I would have noticed something was wrong. And Matt? Or Alison? No one even hinted anything had happened. Jeez. We were living in the same house! How did I see nothing was wrong?'

'There was a party at a house with a huge garden. It was all set up outside. You don't remember it, Rach?' My gut burns at the memory.

But she only swings her head slowly. 'There were so many parties, Hannah.'

I feel my chin lifting at the memory of that night, my lungs searching for air.

'No one would've known anything was out of the ordinary. I guess anyone that saw me would've thought I was just wasted and making a show of myself.' I shake my head wearily.

Rachel's face doesn't move. She's frozen in front of me. 'Until now,' she says.

'Until now.' I swallow.

'I just wish I'd known.' She wraps an arm around her gut, reaching for my hand as though she might drown.

'So, the news has prompted all this right now?'

My eyes cloud and then focus. 'What news?'

'You haven't seen it? The local channels have been going mad. Leach. Hugo Leach. He's being released.'

There are moments when the world begins to spin and tilt on an odd axis.

'Leach?' I hear the echo of my own voice in a dawning realisation. I feel sick suddenly.

'You okay, Hannah?'

I realise I'm standing.

'Yeah. Just... Just going to the bathroom. I feel... I'm fine, Won't be a sec.'

My legs manage to carry me to the door and into the hallway. The chill of the space feels like a balm from the sickly heat of the fire. I breathe slowly, trying to calm my stomach and shaking hands that grip the banister for dear life as I haul myself upward.

My head is whirling.

Released?

This is impossible... I reach one hand on the bathroom door when I pause, aware that I'm not alone. There's a faint shift in the shadows.

'Matt,' I whisper. 'Matt, is that you?'

He is silhouetted by the blue snow-light from the window.

'I thought you'd gone out. Are you okay?' I whisper.

I hear him take a breath. 'Not really. I was going to go for a walk but then changed my mind.'

We both stand there in silence for a moment.

'She told you something, hasn't she?' He steps out of the darkness. His voice is soft. 'About what's been going on.'

'We've been talking about the past. I need to talk to you about the past too, Matt.'

He laughs sadly. 'The past is all I cling on to these days, Hanny,' he says, completely misunderstanding.

I don't speak.

'I just want to be happy. I'm cracking on forty and I've

wasted a huge chunk of my life. Would you begrudge me that chance? Would you begrudge yourself? Wouldn't you always wonder if we could have made a go of it?' He shakes his head and looks at me holding out his palm in a question. 'That night. The one when we were eighteen. The one that feels as though it could have been another lifetime... Do you think of it ever?'

It *was* another lifetime.

'Every part of your face is etched into my mind,' he says quietly. 'I don't need to look at you. I can summon you up in an instant. Every day I've kept you with me.'

'Stop, Matt.'

'I can't. That's my punishment. I think I've been waiting for you for years,' he says into the shadows.

Everything inside me shivers.

'We can't do this, Matt. As you say, we were eighteen then. We're not eighteen now.'

But it's like he's not hearing me.

'I often think how I'd like to go back to that summer and change every choice I made from that exact moment on.'

I see it unfolding in front of me like an old film I've watched over and over.

'Let's go back.'

'Matt, you have no idea—'

'Do you remember those times, though? That one time that we—'

'Matt, stop. Please. That isn't what I meant.'

I don't want to think about it.

I can't think about it. Me coming back to the student house in the early hours, not putting the light on – the stretch of moonlight in the kitchen – and then suddenly there he was, unhappy, alone, sitting in the dark because he and Rachel had had a row. I remember mumbling something about needing a glass of water and not being able to get the tap to work and him coming over and then the next thing we were kissing, and he was telling me how much he'd liked me from the moment he saw me, and me saying how much I liked him. And then we were in my room, at the front, and it was sweet and lovely and passionate and nice – and for that time we had let ourselves forget who we were and what we should be doing.

'That was the past, Matt. We shouldn't have done it. My excuse is, we were very young, but it was a truly awful thing to do nonetheless.'

'You're right,' he says softly. 'But it feels like I've paid for it ever since.'

This isn't what I need right now. This isn't what I want.

'We need to stop this, Matt. It's not helping anyone.'

He stops back, his whole demeanour changing.

'Actually, I think I will go for that walk. Clear my head a bit.'

His shape comes towards me. There's a moment when the light catches the side of his face as he passes. He doesn't attempt to touch me, but there's the warm presence of him passing. So close. I breathe him in with the same old feelings that I breathed him in that night, the memory of hi. And yet that *thing* that I know haunts me, is there, again, always, always, aways. Tears threaten, burning the back of my tongue – unstoppable grief for that girl I used to be.

I listen to the quick trip of his feet on the stairs, the creak of the front door opening, and then the soft whump of it closing behind him. I stand for a moment, the thoughts whirling in my head. I'm aware of my heart fluttering beneath my ribcage. That night back then... The night that set off a catalogue of events unfolding like dominoes, the events that have led me full circle, back to here.

Me and Matt.

Rachel and me.

Rachel and Matt.

We got bound up in something, the three of us. Something

that changed all our lives in one way or another. Such a tiny span of time for something so monumental and huge.

A perfect storm, really, that took me to the darkest place possible and then brought me back here and now to face it all over again.

FOUR

I stand in the bathroom leaning against the basin. I haven't put the light on. I stare dully at the face that's reflected in the strange blue-and-grey shadows.

Leach is getting out, my head says. *He'll be walking the streets. He could be sitting next to you in a restaurant or café. He could be the man walking behind you down the road.*

My insides quail and shrivel in on themselves. I try to remember what Theresa told me to do: don't allow the memories of the past to control me. Grab hold of each memory in turn, stare right into it, stare my fear in the face.

I close my eyes.

I deliberately put myself back there, to that night.

There were trees with lights in them. I remember feeling dizzy and lying down in the grass. All I can see is the night sky, the stars... I'm laughing... And then I'm not. There are hands on me, hard hands, rough. I can feel the thickness of the skin on my arm. I can hear people at the party, their voices: so close. I open my mouth, but I can't shout out...

I'm aware of the deep thud of my heart. I want to run away

from this memory, but I don't. I force myself to stay there. To stay with it.

There's shouting and something goes over my face. The lights become gauzy, and then there's this pain. God... a pain shooting right inside me that goes on and on. And air... There's no air. I feel like I'm suffocating, there's a smell choking me... What is it? Oil, maybe. Am I in an outhouse or a shed? I know there's the sound of someone crying. Is it me?... I open my eyes and I'm in a bathroom, hanging over a toilet bowl and being really, really sick. Alison is there... I don't know why she's there – all I know is she's holding my hair back, stroking my back, finding me tissues, and asking if I'm okay... and me saying I am... I am... I'm fine, even though I'm absolutely not.

I open my eyes.

Alison.

We were bound up in something, the three of us, I keep thinking, but there wasn't just three, was there? There were four.

Alison. The fourth person in that house

That girl hiding in the shadows in the hallway.

Rachel inviting me to go for coffee that first day.

She took my hand. I remember the feel of it: small and dry and almost hot, as she led me out back down the path.

'Great. That's us good to go then.'

And then suddenly, there, standing on the pavement was Alison. She must've come around the back and was watching Chris bring the last of Matt's gear from the van.

'Oh, you off?' she queried, frowning. She looked straight at Rachel, ignoring me. I noticed her hair wasn't washed and she had acne tracing a line into the collar of her coat.

The girl's hunted eyes looked back, warily.

'We thought we'd go and explore. Wanna come?'

'If you don't mind?' Her eyes managed a skidding slide over mine.

'Of course we don't mind.' I felt like I was overcompensating a bit. 'It'll be fun.'

'Right.' Rachel wheeled us both round, linking our arms in her own. 'Come on then, girlies.' She laughed. 'Off we go.'

She chatted on about the course in health and social care she was going to start, and how she was looking forward to the psychology modules as she had a real 'thing' about understanding people and their motivations. 'How about you?' Rachel's green eyes were like a radar, drinking me in.

'Business Management. Very dry.' I pulled a face.

'Oh, business is all about people though, isn't it? Everything is about relationships, that's why it's so fascinating.' She carried on talking about relationships as transactions and how that translates really easily to a business model, and all the time I was aware that no one was asking Alison anything, but out of the corner of my eye I can see her feet, trying to keep pace with Rachel even though the strides were too long for her.

'Town centre this way.' Rachel paused at a finger post sign. 'Shall we go and get that coffee first?'

We found a café, busy with students, laptops on tables, bags everywhere. There was a wall of noise. Cramming ourselves into a corner onto cushions at a low table, we all paused to glance up at the board.

'What does everyone want?' Rachel reached for her purse. 'I'll get this.'

'I'm lactose-intolerant,' Alison's eyes scanned up and down the board. 'And gluten. It also has to be salicylate-free. I'm also mindful of where produce is sourced.'

'Cappuccino for me,' I said, eyeing the packed food counter. 'And a slice of cheesecake.' I didn't look at Alison's face. 'Are you sure about paying, Rach? I'll buy the next time we come out.' I'm hoping she clocked the cosy shortening of her name.

'I'll get in the queue while you decide, Alison.' Rachel hopped over the cushions. 'Just give me a shout.'

There was a moment's pause as the two of us sat watching Rachel at the counter.

'I really hate these kinds of places...' Alison slid a look around. 'And I don't know how you could eat poison like that.' She nodded at the food on display and shuddered. 'Have you no idea what it does to your body? That's without the impact your consumerism does to the people's lives who are forced into producing it.' She shook her head. 'Or taking into account the animal suffering.'

I picked up a sachet of white sugar from the pot on the table but then immediately put it down when I saw the look on her face.

'Alison?' Rachel called over. 'So, what are you having?'

'Oh.' She looked flustered. 'Just water, thanks.'

I was pleased to see the look on Rachel's face echoed my own.

'Sure?'

'Sure.'

She came back to the table with a laden tray, depositing, to my amusement, a panini stuffed with chicken and vegetables for herself, the cake and coffee for me, and a sad-looking glass of water which she put down gently on the table.

'I'd be fascinated to hear about a salicylate-free diet.' Rachel jacked her long legs over the cushion and folded herself like a daddy longlegs, all knees and thighs. 'I've never heard of it. Do tell.' She bit into her panini, listening intently and encouraging this great, long diatribe about the poison in plants and how vegetarians are kidding themselves, and how Alison had discovered the dietary light. Quarter of an hour later, and I'd had enough.

'Do you think she's just a bit lonely?' Rachel looked at me as Alison stagged off to the toilet after her third glass of tap water. 'I get the impression that all this food faddiness is less to do with virtue-signalling and more to do with needing to "belong" to something.'

I looked at her in surprise. Her reaction instantly showed me how mean-spirited and unkind I was being judging Alison on face value. in that instant, if I was going to be Rachel's friend, I was going to have to be a better and nicer version of myself.

'Why don't we suggest the three of us spend some time together. It would be nice to get to know her – get her to relax a bit.'

Rachel beamed a warm and encouraging smile. *I'd done the right thing; I'd said the right thing.*

'So, how could we do that?' She chewed her top lip and she pondered. 'Quickly. Come up with something before she gets back.'

'Let's grab some bottles and go and sit by the river,' I said quickly as I watched Alison making her way back towards us. 'It's a nice day. Why not?'

'You're brilliant.' Rachel laughed. 'Of course that's what we should do.'

Alison appeared in front of us, and was about to clamber back to her seat again when I tugged playfully at her sleeve.

'How d'you feel about grabbing some wine or something and spending the afternoon chilling out? I mean, we don't have to go back to the house yet, do we? Matt seems to have it all under control.'

Alison paused and I kept a friendly smile plastered across my face as she weighed me up.

'Okay,' she said uncertainly. 'That might be fun.'

It was much hotter outside on the pavement; a waft of warm dusty air swirled as we kept to the shade of the buildings as we headed for a convenience store. Rachel led the way into the depths of the shop where the brightly lit chiller cabinets sat humming away.

'How about this one?' I levered the door open, reaching for one at the back. 'It says "suitable for vegans". You'd be okay with that, wouldn't you?'

Rachel nodded encouragingly. 'Yeah, we'll all get the same so there's no issue. Is that okay?'

I didn't know if Alison understood what was going on, but it left her without much alternative but to go with the flow as Rachel and I thrust another couple of bottles at her, grabbed some cups, and headed for the checkout.

It felt like something out of a film as the three of us took the street leading down to the river, where a narrow pathway directed us to where the body of water opened up. Bent-over trees dipped their uppermost leaves into the water, creating tiny eddies. We headed for the pools of shade, settling ourselves down, spare bottles propped in between the tree roots as we tore open the cup carton and cracked open the wine. It was deliciously cold. I lay back, propped on one elbow in the dappled sunlight, squinting out across the water, aware of Alison's stiff shoulders beside me as she sat, legs awkwardly to one side, cradling her cup, not speaking.

'Why don't we play a game?' I blurted suddenly. Rachel looked round at me, amused. 'How about we all share five facts about ourselves and our backgrounds?' I grinned.

Alison pulled a dubious face. 'Oh hell, I can't think.'

'Okay.' I nodded. 'Don't worry, it doesn't have to be serious, anything will do.'

'Shall I go first?' Rachel piped up.

'Great.' That gave me time to think.

Rachel shook her spring of blonde curls as she scanned the blue sky. Her skin was flawless. I had no idea how anyone did makeup that made their eyes pop like that.

She picked a couple of daisies and began threading them through each other. 'My mum is a barrister, my dad's a teacher, I've got one older brother, our house is always full of people coming and going, houseguests staying longer than anyone ever expects them to, starving artists, writers, musicians, poets, all of them discussing and arguing about politics and shit.' Her hands sprang apart. 'It's a bit like living in a boho hotel, really.' She laughed. 'But they're lovely. Bonkers, but lovely... So, go on, Alison, what about you?'

Alison automatically twitched as the spotlight moved to her. 'Oh, umm... Okay... Dad's an engineer with a car company. Mum's a secretary. We're not very interesting. I've got two sisters, twins, older. There's a big age difference so... Um... I think I was a mistake.' She snorted a tragic laugh. 'They're both much cleverer than I am.' She broke off and looked at me. 'Which is fine. I don't mind really...' She swallowed and looked at me expectantly.

I carried on nodding as though I was listening, allowing myself time to gather my thoughts. 'My mother runs her own business and is a bit of a high-flyer. I think it's her influence that's made me so independent.' I'm trying to sound like I'm proud of her, but all the while remembering having to sit alone in a classroom, aged five or six, while the teacher tried to contact someone, anyone, who might come and claim me. More often than not, it was a neighbour my mother conned with some cock-and-bull concoction about a family emergency, or motorway accident. Different people every time so no one was putting two and two together.

'So, like you, Rachel, I was pretty comfortable around an endless parade of adults coming and going. It gives you an interesting take on the word at a very early age, doesn't it?'

'And your dad? What does he do?' Alison asks.

'My dad's in business too, but he works away an awful lot.' Which is true.

What I don't tell them is that I was once at a friend's house and her dad was talking to a man I didn't know, and after he'd gone, my friend asked me why I hadn't said hello to my dad – which I would have done, if I'd known who he was.

'Ah. Hence the business management degree,' Rachel interjected. 'It's clearly in the blood. They must be very proud of you?'

And I said, yes, they were. Very proud, and maybe we should all drink to being strong, capable, independent women who were going to do amazing things with their lives.

'I'll definitely toast to that,' Rachel said, reaching for the bottle.

'Me too,' Alison added, holding out her glass.

And we all lifted our cups and cheersed in the sunshine, congratulating ourselves on the people we were going to become, grinning at each other, me all happy on the outside but dying a little on the inside at the fraud I was.

'Here.' Rachel knelt up, holding a loop of daisy chain in her hand. 'Let me crown you with blessings for the future.' She placed the circlet of flowers on my head, my scalp tingling with her touch.

'And for you I've made a brooch.' She held out a tiny plait of daisy heads, one threaded through another. She went to tuck it in the top pocket of Alison's shirt, but it broke and scattered, the petals tumbling into Alison's lap,

'Oh no. Oh dear.' Rachel sighed.

But a tiny, tiny childish part of me was happy that somehow Rachel's gift to me was still intact. I felt suddenly delirious, the crown of flowers in my hair tingling my forehead as we played yet more games, throwing sticks into the sparkling river and having 'stick races'. Drinking our wine as the shadows lengthened, and finally we lay napping as the heat went from the sun into the ground, sending it shimmering around us, and I thought I had never been more perfectly happy.

'Should we be getting back, d'you think?'

The sound of Alison's voice made my eyes spring open. I

turned my head. She was sitting up, pouring the last drips of wine into her cup and finishing it off, smacking her lips. She looked so funny. And then I remembered she'd had nothing to eat – she'd only had water. I looked over to see Rachel shielding her eyes with her forearm.

'Yeah, let's go and see what Matty-Boy is up to.' She got up, dusting herself down as I gathered up the empty bottles and cups and looked around for somewhere to dispose of them.

Alison was struggling to get to her feet.

'Here.' Rachel held out her hand, hauling Alison up as I found a wastebin and then glanced back. Alison was swaying alarmingly.

'She okay?' I called over.

'Hmm, not sure. Can we find her some water maybe?'

I glanced around. There was a mobile coffee cart just along the towpath.

'Hang on,' I shouted, hurrying over and grabbing a couple of bottles of water from the surprised vendor without waiting for the change. But when I looked back, I couldn't see either of them. Scanning up and down the river, I saw there were boats moored and a row of public toilets just behind. Maybe they were there?

I ran over to find Rachel standing outside, looking worried.

'I didn't know where you'd gone,' I panted. 'Is she okay?'

Rachel wrinkled her nose. 'She's in there throwing up. Such a shame, isn't it? What an end to a lovely afternoon. I thought we were really getting somewhere with her, didn't you? Poor kid. Sounds like she's got a shit time at home. No wonder she's a bit uptight. You were doing a great job though, Hannah, so well done you.'

I felt myself going pink with pleasure at the outpouring of praise.

'I was just... well, y'know, doing what you do.' I squirmed.

'Well, it was very nice to see. She's not that easy to get along with, is she?' Rachel leaned in conspiratorially. 'She's a wee bit prickly,' she whispered.

We heard the flush of a lavatory and then water running. Rachel googled her eyes for us to stop talking as Alison appeared, pale and a bit wobbly still.

I offered her a bottle of water, which she took gratefully, and then the three of us started walking back the way we had come. The path narrowed a little in places and we were forced to walk in single file, Rachel and Alison in front and me tagging behind. I could hear Rachel asking her questions about diets and food and sounding like she was genuinely interested in the answers. A couple of dog walkers came past us, forcing me to hang back. I had to stand still while Rachel and Alison carried on walking, unaware that the gap between us was growing longer. Rachel had her head bowed, nodding earnestly at something that Alison was saying. I couldn't call out to them – I would've just felt silly – so I walked as fast as I could to catch up, hoping they'd notice I was missing, but they never did. I knew I'd been instantly forgotten. All that earlier warmth and friendship petering away with my ragged breath, as the sparkling sunlight on the water faded to a dull brittle, and all those lovely feelings fading along with it.

FIVE

I tell Rachel I'm sorry but I have to get some sleep.

She fusses over me, but I can tell she too needs time to process what I've told her.

I lie, fully clothed on the unfamiliar bed, listening to Rachel moving about downstairs. The grandfather clock ticks in the hallway. The sound is a comforting as a heartbeat. There's the creak of her tread on the stair and the click of the bathroom handle.

'Just talk to me, please... Say something. Don't hang up.' I hear Rachel's panicked whisper from the landing. My head jerks to catch the sound.

'Please don't do this.' I hear her beg as the bathroom door lock shunts. Sitting up, I tiptoe to the door and ease it open, listening, but now there's only the tick and roar of the boiler as Rachel runs a bath.

So, I'm guessing she's still seeing James then.

A rush of sadness comes over me.

Rachel, typical Rachel, hedging her bets.

With a sigh I go back and lie on the bed. And I'm also guessing Matt has no idea.

Rachel's drama, Rachel's relationships, Rachel's needs, *Rachel, Rachel, Rachel.*

Matt's right: we're all there, like willing satellites circling her orbit, waiting for crumbs of attention, and being so grateful when her attention comes our way.

I know why Matt has taken her back: she's a compulsion, she's our addiction. She's at the centre of everything good...

And everything bad.

That night when it happened.

She was there, wasn't she? But was she?

All I have is a broken film reel – snatches of celluloid, frames missing, disjointed images that make no real sense.

The heat of the memory comes flooding back yet again. Weird images. A garden. Something bad had happened, I know that. Why do I keep thinking it <u>was</u> something to do with Rachel? There were snatches of remembered conversation. Had I been drugged at that point? Did I think I'd just drunk too much?

There was music thudding through the trees, laughter hooting up from huddles of bodies; people sitting and lying on the grass, the sounds weaving up into the branches. I remember feeling desperate, forcing myself to be happy. I wanted to block out everything... experience this single moment, absorb it, bathe in it. The sensation: of the slick slide of silk fabric over my bare skin, the heat of the evening seeping up through the grass between my toes. *Where were my shoes?*

I'd felt powerful in my own skin. I remember dancing – alone, not caring. The dress made me feel I could dance – spinning round, the silk ballooning, the draft around the tops of my legs. Someone dancing with me, their hands touching mine, clutching my waist for an instant and then releasing me, laughing.

A sob choked in my throat as I stumbled through the darkness, away from the lights and the music and the laughter. I collided with something, winding me for a moment.

'Hey... hey... You okay?' There was a male voice in the shadows as I broke out into a clearing. I realised I'd only circled the trees and was back in the wheeling lights from the open doors of the house. The music boomed into my ribcage.

Boom, boom, boom

I wanted a drink. I wanted a drink really badly as I stumbled towards the open doors, heaving myself inside and into the thronging bodies.

The voice behind followed. 'You sure you're okay? If you're looking for something to drink, take this one. You look like you need it. I can always get another.' A guy, no more than a boy really, thrust a drink into my hand, fighting his way through the crush towards the drinks table. He disappeared into the melee, and I suddenly felt alone, so alone standing there clutching a sticky warm cup.

I felt like I couldn't trust anyone. What had made me feel so hurt?

Downing the cup of sickly wine in one go, I spied a half-full bottle on a windowsill. Grabbing it, I slewed another few slugs into the edge of the cup. Someone jostled my elbow, sending a splash of liquid over my hand.

'You should be dancing, not drinking,' someone shouted over the din.

I turned to find the boy jigging about behind me. He grinned, taking the cup from my dripping fingers, depositing it onto the windowsill before taking my hand. We danced, the music thudding up through my heart; twirling, letting the spin of the lights take me away, not caring that I felt giddy, wanting the music to transport me somewhere else, and not caring where. My dress stuck to my legs, my hair clung in hot tendrils in the nape of my neck, the sweat trickling down my temple to my chin. The boy lifted a finger to wipe it off, laughing, and then he's gone... Someone gives me a drink and I gulp it down, not caring, only wanting oblivion, not caring what shape or form it took – I just *wished and wished and wished* to not be feeling what I was feeling.

'*Be careful what you wish for, Hannah,*' a voice whispers close to my ear.

My eyes drop open with a start, not knowing where I am for a second. The clock in the hallway chimes midnight.

Somewhere in the lingering shiver of the last bell-strike, the voice still resonating in the darkness. That was the last thing I remember that night: the boy, the heat, the thud of the music inside me. I try to regulate my breathing, concentrating on counting as the air inflates my lungs.

In for five, hold for three, out for seven... in for five... slow, slow...

I can feel the memory of what happened next, somewhere in the periphery of my mind. It's like a thing just in the corner of my eye that I can't quite see, that I'm always aware of but can't quite grasp. *He* is that something.

Him.

The shuddering becomes so violent I can feel the bed shake beneath me. I glance over at the rectangle of the black doorway. My dressing gown is hanging on the back: it looks like a figure with a bowed head. My heart trammels wildly. *Stop this. Put those thoughts out of your head. You're safe. You're at Rachel's. He's not here. You're safe.* The heating system gurgles somewhere and the radiator makes a tiny tapping sound. My eyelashes scratch against the sheet, and I have to push it back in case it disguises some other sound. There's the sound outside on the landing and my eyes flit to the door. I think I hear the sound of the bathroom handle. There's another creak and I wait. The sound of someone cleaning their teeth and water running. *Matt.*

Their bedroom door opens and closes and the house is suddenly silent. And the sound in my ears thuds slower.

Click.

I am instantly back on full alert.

My head lifts from the pillow, heart thundering.

Click.

I sit up, not daring to breathe.

Click.

My eyes snap to the window. Something has hit the glass.

Sliding from under the duvet, my feet find the cold carpet and I shiver. *It could be Matt though,* my head says. *What you heard before must've been Rachel. It's just Matt and he's locked himself out, he's forgotten his key.*

My hand reaches for the curtain and the sudden gap lets in a shaft of white moonlight, brilliant against the snowy garden.

Something moves.

My eyes catch it before my brain registers.

There, in the snow are footprints. Crisp and black. I track them carefully from the far side, across the lawn: definite, purposeful, leading right up to the house. I move closer to the glass, pressing my forehead against the cold pane to see.

A shadow lengthening through the open doorway and disappearing inside.

I leap back, my breath coming out in little pants of quick air. My ears strain. A movement downstairs: faint, but definitely there.

Crack.

A sound behind me and I wheel round. Somewhere, out there on the stairs, there's the quiet shift of someone coming up the steps. The tiny increments of sound are very careful not to be heard; they tread, slowly and deliberately. I count: close... closer... They've reached the top step... they're passing my door now. Each step slow and methodical, heel to toe, pausing in between each considered effort.

Heart hammering. *It's Matt. It's only Matt.*

My mouth opens to say his name.

There's a pause.

Whoever it is on the other side of the door has stopped. They are standing motionless: me listening to them and them listening to me. And then a shift.

My eyes scan the wall, boring through the plaster and paint, acutely aware of their presence. The shift becomes steadier: a definite movement now, a rolling transfer of weight to toe.

I could scream.

My eyes flit quickly to the wall space behind the door. If I tucked myself behind the dressing gown, I could press myself in its folds and bury myself in the shadows. If someone came in here, I could buy myself some time.

Almost not daring to breathe, I feel for the end of the bed. Easing my weight forward onto the heels of my hands, I slide myself towards the hiding place, trying not to make a sound. *Listening, listening* all the while, until the safe patch of shadow engulfs me. I stand there, shivering, furious that even that might give me away, holding my breath, aware that the movement on the other side of the door has stopped. I swallow. If I listen carefully, really, really carefully, I think I can hear their breathing.

Then the dressing gown moves.

My eyes snatch up. In the darkness I can see it swaying a little, right and left, almost imperceptible. And then the doorhandle twists. Tiny movements inching from right to left, an infinitesimal squeal. My heart rate ratchets up: any moment now, any moment and I will see the frame and the door part company – the black strip growing wider as whoever is out there pushes the gap into a widening yawn.

I'm paralysed.

The black door becomes a dark hole. There's a gust of cold air and I see the figure; its shoulders filling the frame. It leans in, whispering to me.

My open mouth tries to scream but can't.

'Hannah.'

The sound won't come out.

'Are you okay?'

Matt.

My knees won't hold me. I find myself clinging to the side of the bed.

'Matt... Matt...' I struggle, not able to get my words out. 'There was someone... I saw someone...'

'Saw someone? Where?' He comes into the room, quickly glancing round.

'Out there.' I point shakily to the window. 'Throwing stones to get my attention. I thought it was you. I saw footprints... There are footprints outside.' I'm breathless with panic.

In two strides Matt is across the room, yanking the curtain back. The room is suddenly flooded with moonlight. He fiddles with the sash, and suddenly there's a massive blast of cold air as he leans right out. 'Where? Where did you see them?'

'The door, Matt. I saw the back door was open. I think someone's in the house.'

He instantly jerks back, bare feet pounding across the floor as he runs down the stairs. I can hear doors crashing open and light from downstairs pools into the snowy garden.

Pulling the comforter from the foot of the bed, I wrap it around me, trying to stem the violent chattering that's racking my body. I peer tentatively around his shoulder. It's started to snow again. Matt appears, breathless behind me.

'There's no sign of anyone down there. The back door is locked. Did you say you saw footprints?'

My eyes strain into the gauzy whiteness, trying to make out the imprint of what once was there.

'And someone was out there? Whereabouts?' Matt leans out further. He's only dressed in T-shirt and sweatpants. I can feel the cold skin of his arm against my cheek. 'I can't see any sign, but I'm going down to check.' He pulls the sash closed and locks it.

'I saw… There was someone,' I manage.

'You came into our room. I thought something was wrong.' He swiftly draws the curtains.

But I'm shaking my head. 'Your room? I didn't come to your room.'

He stops, his hands bunching the fabric. 'You came into our room, Hannah. I thought you were feeling unwell or something—'

'I haven't been anywhere. I was here, awake.'

'But you…' He pauses. I can tell he wants to say more. 'Maybe you only thought you were awake.'

'I was, Matt. Honestly was.'

'Maybe you were sleepwalking or something?'

I blink blindly.

'You were standing in the bedroom. Just standing there.' He shrugs. 'I spoke to you, but you didn't reply. I was scared of waking Rach.'

My eyes bat slowly. A numbing kind of headache begins to pulse in my temple.

'What's going on?' Rachel appears in the doorway, sleepily rubbing her face.

'Bad dreams I think.' Matt looks at me. 'But I'm just going down to check again to make doubly sure.'

'My god, Hannah, are you okay?' Rachel scans my face, touching my arm gently. She lowers her voice. 'I'm not surprised you're having bad dreams after tonight's conversation.' We stand for a moment listening to Matt moving about downstairs. 'What's he checking?' She looks at me. I can't stop shaking.

'I thought I saw someone outside, but I didn't; I couldn't have, there was no one there.'

Her face drops. 'What? Out… outside here?' She looks at me, horrified.

'There were no footprints in the snow. I must've been dreaming, Rach, like Matt said. It's fine, we're okay…'

Rachel's face is a mask of fear.

'What is it?' Matt appears on the landing looking from me to her. Rachel and I can only stare at each other. 'What were you two whispering about?'

'I was being stupid. Ridiculous.' I'm aware Rachel's face is burning.

'Being ridiculous about what? Just tell me what you were whispering about? It's clearly something.' Matt's face is a mixture of frightened anger and frustration.

I take a breath, but Rachel's eyes fix on mine for a second.

'There's something... something we haven't told you.' She catches my eye.

'Oh?' I can't read his expression.

'The real reason Hannah's here.'

Matt looks from me to her.

'She's been in a relationship... A bad relationship that she needs to get away from. She's terrified he might be following her. You're scared, aren't you, Hannah?'

My cheeks burn fiercer. I can only stare at her.

'Following her here?' Matt snaps a glance at me.

'So, I've said she should stay with us as long as she wants. He's abusive... I've told her she can't go back. I've said she can stay until she sorts things out.'

Matt's eyes manage to get as far as my shoulder, but he can't look at me.

'You can see why anyone would get freaked out and imagine things.' Rachel waves a hand in explanation. She can't look at me either. 'It's enough to make anyone terrified.'

The heat in my face spreads down my neck, and I find my fingers fluttering to my throat to cover it.

'Wow! I had no idea.' I can see the hurt etched into his mouth. 'Not a clue. Well, that explains things then.' A tic of anger works in his jawline.

My heart flutters in panic.

'She's been having a hard time, haven't you, Hannah?' Rachel stares pointedly at me.

'You should have told me.' Matt's voice is stony. 'I would have understood.'

'I'm sorry for making a fuss,' I mumble lamely. 'I must've heard you come in and...' I trail off, mortified.

'Well, let's see if we can get some sleep now, shall we?' Rachel turns back to her bedroom.

'Actually, I'm too wired right now,' Matt says bluntly. His eyes won't meet mine. 'I'm going to go down and make a hot drink, maybe watch TV for a bit.'

'Oh, okay.' Rachel glances nervously my way. 'How are you feeling now, Hannah?'

'I'm fine. Fine. It was nothing, just a bad dream.' I feel her eyes assessing me for a moment and then she nods, satisfied.

'Come and sit with me for a while.' She pulls her gown tighter and her eyes flit to her bedroom door. Her eyes are wide with meaning. 'I don't think any of us will be sleeping for a while. Come and sit in bed and keep me company. It'll be like the old days, won't it?' She grins. I can't bring myself to smile back.

'I'll keep the volume down, make sure I don't disturb you.' Matt looks pointedly at me. 'I'll leave you to sleep in tomorrow. I won't come knocking on your door with cups of tea. Sounds like you could do with a bit of peace.' His eyes trail away, leaving me standing there, mute with embarrassment, unable to say a word as he heads off down the stairs.

Rachel leads the way into their room. I stand dumbly in the doorway, aware of the canopy of shadows on the pinky-grey walls, the rumpled duvet, the pillow where Matt's head has lain.

She clambers onto her side of the bed, pulling the duvet up and patting Matt's side encouragingly.

I don't think I can move closer.

'I'm sorry about saying all that, okay?' She shakes her head. 'But he heard what we said, didn't he?' she whispers. 'I had to say something, *anything*. It was just the first thing that came into my head. The fact is, you can't tell Matt the truth, Hannah. If you tell him the truth, then he'll know I was involved in what happened... in what we did on that building site. I've kept my promise to you. I've never breathed a word.'

She's saying it like it's all to do with me.

'I shouldn't have come here, Rachel. I've started something that I don't know how to deal with.'

'Yes you do, Hannah.' She reaches for my hand. 'You said you had to face your fear. Hold fast. You knew it wasn't going to be easy, but like you said, it's something you have to do.'

'Matt said I was standing in your room... Was I?'

Rachel hugs her knees closer to her chest. 'Hannah. You'd had a terrific shock over Leach. You're in a strange house. If you were having nightmares, I'd say that was a pretty normal reaction, wouldn't you?'

'I have no recollection of sleepwalking, yet Matt says I was.' I shake my head, puzzled. 'Matt said the doors were all locked tight and there weren't any footprints.'

I see the footprints in my mind's eye, clear and black against the white. *But it snowed again*, my head says. *Are you completely sure?*

I look up at her. The memory of the footprints and the shadow in the open doorway burns into my mind.

'I feel overwhelmed. I'm scared I'm becoming paranoid.' My mind trawls back. *Did I manifest the whole thing?*

Rachel slumps back a little on the pillows and snuggles back. 'Stay here a while, Hannah. Matt'll be ages watching TV. Don't sleep in there on your own. Lie down here and I'll turn the light out and we can talk in the dark like we used to when we were kids.'

Rachel pulls the duvet over my legs. 'I can't imagine how

they hell you've processed all this on your own. I mean, piecing it all together – working your way through the horror that happened to you. And alone... All alone.' Her hand creeps across the duvet towards me, the fingers begging me to take them. I swallow; I can't not. Her skin is hot to the touch. She strokes the back of my knuckle with her thumb. All those old feelings of how connected we were come flooding back.

'Why didn't you get in contact with me, Hannah? Why didn't you let me share what you were going through? Why did you keep the... the...' She can't bring herself to use the word 'rape'. '...assault quiet? You know I would have supported you through anything, you *know* that.'

Needy.

That word comes out of nowhere. It's a punishing description. *Pitiful. Me. I'm just something pitiful.*

I shake the unbidden words out of my head.

'I couldn't.'

She stares at me. 'But why, Hannah?'

The shadows in the room make her eyes look like huge dark holes.

'You would never have seen me the same way,' I say. 'I would've always been a victim in your eyes.'

'Is that how you felt?' Her voice is a horrified whisper.

'The morning after... after 'it' happened, I woke up in my own bed. Everything looked the same. I could almost believe it had all been a nightmare. Even when I saw the blood.'

I hear her take a little gasp of air.

'Even when I saw all the blood down my legs and on the sheets, I tried to pretend that I'd maybe cut myself on some glass. All I had to do was get myself into the shower and the bedding into the washing machine, and the whole lot would be washed away.'

'Hannah—' I hear the break in her voice.

I lie down facing away from her on the edge of the bed.

'It felt the easiest thing to do. It was a simple way out. Everything was just the same as it was: my bedroom looked the same, the house looked the same, the sky looked the same, people went to lectures and sat in the Student Union bar and laughed and joked. Nothing was any different.'

The light goes off.

'But it was,' she whispers in the darkness. 'It was.'

'Yes, it was,' I say softly. 'But I wasn't even prepared to face how different things were. I don't know how long I would've let it go on for. Every day I closed my eyes to it all and before I knew it, weeks had passed. I knew somewhere in the back of my mind I hadn't had a period, but I kept thinking that maybe I'd just forgotten...' I put my hand up to my cheeks. 'I was in shock, traumatised, I wasn't thinking straight – I was trying not to think at all.'

'Yes, yes, of course.'

'God, Rach, how I'd love to stop thinking now.' I screw my eyes up tight in the blackness, watching the blue and red zigzag lights burst and disappear. 'Can we talk about nice things? Like, non-scary things? Can we?'

I hear her take a slick of breath in the darkness. 'Do you remember us doing this in those first few weeks when we used to come back from the pub?'

There's a smile in her voice, I can tell. She desperately wants to distract me.

'Yeah. It was nice.' I so want to be distracted.

'Remember that lock-in we got because the landlord fancied us?'

'No. No, don't think I do.'

'Yeah you do, Hannah.' Rachel giggles. 'Him. The one with the false teeth.'

Despite myself, I join in at the memory. 'What happened in end?'

'You don't remember?' She laughs.

'No.'

'We said we were both going to the loo, and we legged it out of the toilet window.'

'Oh god, yes... Yes, now I do. Wow! How did I forget that.'

There's the sound of Rachel chuckling and it makes me smile. I have this instant recollection of us walking back to the house together in the early hours. I see that summer dawn, still spangled with night-time stars, the dusty pavements, the weight of my sandals in the hook of my fingers, the feel of the warm concrete beneath the soles of my bare feet, that gauzy sky-blue day just waiting to be born, and the waft of bread from a local bakery. We were laughing. She'd reached out to grab my hand and I felt that sudden press of warm skin, feeling more like I belonged and was wanted by someone than I ever had in my life before.

My eyes bat open. All I can hear is Rachel's soft breathing behind me. I lift my head a little, realising I must've fallen asleep. I feel calmer now, more centred: back to myself. The truth is, here, in this house, are two people who care about me. Their own lives are uncertain and in tatters, but both Matt and Rachel want the best for me, I do know that.

Easing myself from the side of the bed, I pull the covers closer around Rachel and lean over to plant a kiss on the side of her exposed cheek.

'Night night,' I whisper, before creeping out onto the landing and pulling the door closed behind me.

I stand for a moment on the landing, my fingers letting the catch click into its housing, listening to the rustle of the duvet as she turns over. There's the soft shift of Matt downstairs moving about, and I wonder if he's heard me.

I glance down the stairwell and watch as his shadow looms and lengthens along the hallway.

'Hanny?' he hisses.

I glance back once at Rachel's door, before tiptoeing my

way down. His face gives nothing away as I follow him, only holding a finger to his lips as he goes into the lounge.

The only light in the room is the glow from the dying fire. We look at each other. His hands come up in surrender. I know the questions are coming: he takes a breath, his shoulders raising in exasperation, but then his arms drop with a slap against his thighs.

'I don't even know where to start.' He sighs. 'I need a drink.'

He wheels round, going to the cupboard, and brings out a half-full bottle of whisky, holding it up in enquiry.

'Yes, please.'

Without saying a word, he goes off into the kitchen. I sit, staring into the glowing embers of the fire. A piece of grey ash falls away into the grate leaving a deep pulse of red. Matt reappears carrying two glasses. Setting them down, he roughly twists at the bottle neck and glugs a couple of fingers into each.

'Here.' He hands it to me, slumping into the chair opposite and taking a long slug.

He sighs: a tired and weary sigh as though he's had enough. My stomach somersaults.

'So.' He bites his cheek.

'Matt—'

'No, please don't say anything. You don't have to say anything.'

'Listen. What Rachel said—'

But he shakes my words away with a swing of his head. 'Forget it. Jeez, what a night.'

He slurs his words a little after his hours in the pub.

'I'm sorry, I just don't know why she said all that.'

'What have you got to be sorry for? You haven't done anything.' He looks up at me, his elbows resting on his knees, his hands cupping the glass. 'It's not you who needs to apologise – it's me putting pressure on you, it's *her* and her lies.' He jabs an angry finger at the ceiling. 'I suspect you've had the pleasure of listening to her phone going off constantly, have you?'

My brain stumbles and drags, not knowing how to answer. He takes another gulp of whisky before looking off into the distance.

'She switches it to silent thinking I won't notice, but of course I do. She sneaks off to the bathroom.' He looks back at me. 'She runs a bath thinking the sound of the water covers her whispered conversations – to *him*.'

I stare dumbly, not knowing what the hell to say.

'Yeah, yeah.' He chuckles bitterly. 'She has no idea I've sussed her. And she's mentioned this partner in crime of hers, too: this Emily woman? Has she told you it's her who is constantly ringing, or has she told you the truth?' He's angry, but then his face changes and he holds up a hand. ' No, don't answer that. I don't want to put you in the middle of this appalling situation. All you need to know is she covers for her all the time: backs up her lies.' He's lost in thought for a moment and then his head snaps up. 'Y'know what?'

I can only stare back.

'I'd prefer it if she was just totally and utterly straight with me. I don't know what game she's trying to play or why the hell I'm putting up with it. Why doesn't she come right out with it. Tell me the whole dirty truth, instead of all this charade.' The whisky sloshes dangerously in his glass. 'I don't know who I'm more disgusted with: her or me.'

I'm aware he's winding himself up. His feet scuff the carpet as he shifts.

'What a bloody mess.' He stares gloomily into the middle distance. The fire pops and the wood beds down.

'Actually, you know what, Hanny? I bet it was *him*.'

'What?'

'I bet it was him,' he says resignedly. 'I bet that's who you saw outside sneaking around.'

I can only stare, dumbfounded.

He rakes a hand through his hair; the gesture is so familiar.

'I've known there's been weird stuff happening for ages: there's been a car sitting outside for hours, the phone calls, shadowy figures, all the whispering I hear when she says I'm imagining it. Christ, she must think I'm stupid. She kept telling me I was going mad, that I was paranoid and jealous.' His head whirls round to stare at me. 'But now. Wow, this is a new one. Jesus, fancy coming up with that cock-and-bull story about you being harassed by some bloke. Wowzer. She's really trawling the depths now. I have to give it to her, though. That was a fantastic performance. It was amazing she could think on her feet like that.'

A log in the fire grate fizzes, cracking in half and sending a scattering of red sparks up the chimney breast. I stare into the glow, hardly daring to swallow.

'I can't carry on, Hanny.' Matt's voice is dull in the quiet room. 'I can't live like this. It's killing me.'

'No,' I whisper. 'You're right, you can't.' I don't know what I should be saying to him.

'Do you want to know something?' he says quietly.

'What?'

'This is history repeating itself.'

I look questioningly.

'That night when we were kids at uni, that night when we—'

'Matt. Don't go there. Please.'

'Did you know why I was sitting in the kitchen in the dark? Did she ever tell you what had happened that afternoon?'

'No.' I'm aware of my own heart beating.

'Then I'll tell you. It was to do with Alison,' he says simply.

'Alison?'

'Do you remember that weird girl who shared the house?'

'Alison, yes. What happened to her?'

'Not a clue. I didn't ask and I didn't care.' He looks at me quizzically before sitting down heavily, reaching for the bottle again and viciously twisting the cap. 'Once she was off the scene, suddenly Rachel and I had a completely different relationship, but my God, that girl was poison. Were you aware she hated me?'

'*Hated* you?'

'Yeah, she was always trying to cause trouble, meddling. Creating arguments. She told people that I kept staring at her. It was all to get Rachel to not trust me. God, we had some rows back then.'

I watch him steadily.

'She basically knew Rachel was getting tired of hanging out with her, so she'd deliberately create drama, knowing that Rachel could never pass up the opportunity to run off and save someone.' He stares deep into his glass. 'As you're aware, Rachel loves being needed. All the time you're that broken bird, she's there, fussing over you, giving you all the attention. Once something new comes along, something more challenging, then she's off and you're left in the dust.' He looks up; his eyes bore into mine. 'But then, you're very familiar with that scenario, aren't you?'

His words dig up old feelings, but I swallow them down.

'Well, Alison had all that down to a fine art. It's like there was always a competition for attention going on. You must have felt that too, surely?'

I don't answer.

'Well, like some desperate sucker, I joined in the competition. I couldn't walk away. I was desperate not to lose Rachel. It made me want to fight even more for her. Which, of course, brought out the worst in me.' Matt's head swings slowly from side to side. 'I think I would have let her get away with anything. Even though I knew she was messing around with other lads, I chose to turn a blind eye because I couldn't bring myself to confront her.'

'Rachel went off with someone else back then?' I'm astonished.

He catches my eye. 'Yeah, I'm amazed you didn't know. There was at least one. But that *particular* time, that *particular* night, it was a bloke called Jake. That was his name.' His jaw tics. 'Did you know she was seeing him?'

'No,' I say, although my memory instantly scans back.

'It was all a manoeuvre: a plan to get me out of the way so that her and Alison could...' The whisky sloshes over the side. Matt glances and licks his fingers. 'Play their little games.' I don't move, keeping my face expressionless but remembering things as they all come flooding back. Matt runs his tongue over the side of his thumb where the whisky has spilt. I have to look away.

'My intuition told me there was something going on. I told her I'd be out all day, but that was a test. I came back early and found the house was empty. I sat at that kitchen table for hours, just waiting.' His head snaps up to look at me. 'I've always felt like that, Hannah. I've always felt like I've sat waiting for crumbs from her.' He thumbs towards the door. 'Sitting for years, head blank, body numb, never knowing how to confront her, or even *if* to confront her. Truth is, I never really had the balls, knowing at every turn, she'd have the likes of Alison to back up any crap explanation she came up with.' He pauses. 'Only that night, that one *particular* night, was different to any other night. Because you walked in.'

I can't speak.

'You walked in. You were always so different; you were straightforward, decent—'

'Boring.'

'No, no, never that.'

'I was though – I was never someone that people noticed.'

'I noticed you.'

I blush furiously.

'I was a fool not to walk out of that house with you that night. We could have walked away and had another life, but instead—'

'Matt. You need to stop this.'

'I know, I know – I'm making this impossible, aren't I?'

'You and Rachel have agreed to try and make your marriage work and this won't—'

But he only snorts with derision. 'Oh, come off it, Hannah. You know what's going on here just as much as I do. Just like back then, I've kidded myself that it's all to do with someone else's influence. But it's not, is it? It's Rachel. It's the way she is and has always been.'

But something grips me as I hear all this. Something making me want to draw back.

'I just can't do this, Matt. I'm sorry. I want to be the person to listen and to help, but I can't. I should never have come here.' I bring my hands up to my face. 'You don't understand – how could you? You couldn't have any idea.'

He looks back at me, shocked.

'Things happened back then, when we were kids. Things you had no idea about. Things that involve me and Rachel.'

'What are you talking about, Hanny? What things?'

'I will tell you, I will explain, but just not right now.'

'Hanny...' He makes a sign he's about to question me further, but I jerk back to stop him.

'No, Matt. Like I said, not right now. I can't. A whole host of things happened – like dominoes, each one had a knock-on effect on the other. What happened with you and me and Rachel and even Alison – I see it now... the sequence of events leading me to the point that changed my life. I'm sorry about what you're going through, I really, really am. When we met up at the hotel, I was in the process of trying to piece it all together and I needed help. I never dreamed you were with Rachel... And you're right, you're so right, part of me was looking for revenge by turning up. Looking back, I see how selfish that was of me. But now things have happened; I've found things out. Things I can't talk about right this minute.'

I look into his face: his mouth has dropped open with puzzlement and alarm.

'What I do know is, the things that happened between us back then, Matt, set something in motion. I mean, not directly, but everything that took place led me to make the choices I did; the choices that changed my life from that moment on.'

'Hannah. You're saying that there was something bad? Something that involved us all? What, Hannah? Please talk to me.'

'No, please, Matt, leave it. I will explain soon, I promise. It's late. Go to bed now.'

'You can't just leave this conversation like this, Hanny.' He looks at me appalled.

'It's okay, honestly,' I say to him. 'It was the past. I'm dealing with it. You don't have to worry about me.'

He goes to speak again, but I silence him with a hand on his arm.

'Now go to bed. Get some sleep. The truth is, it will all still be here in the morning.' I manage a grim smile and he reciprocates, getting up unsteadily and making his way to the door.

'Night night,' he whispers.

'Night night.' I smile.

But my smile drops as the door closes behind him and I shiver.

The fire's dying ashes glow red and orange behind the grey. *But you're not okay*, the voice in my head says. *You're as far from okay as it's possible to be.* And *dealing with it?* I lift my hand into the light of the fire and absorb its tremor with a clench of the fist.

I, just like Matt, was desperate back then. Desperate to belong, desperate to be liked, desperate to keep in that little family that I'd somehow become part of. Maybe in the same way as Matt, my desperation made me vulnerable, made me open to hurt. My hurt weeping like a tiny drop of blood in the water, letting the circling sharks smell the pain, drawing them in, making me defenceless to the kind of people who liked to hurt people like me.

SIX

That summer.

'Have you got a minute, Hannah?' Rachel called from her room.

Got a minute? I so wanted to spend time with her, all she had to do was click her fingers.

I came out of my room and looked up to find her hanging over the top banister on the stairs, head upside down, hair like spun gold in the sunlight.

'Come on up. I want to show you something.'

I'd stood in the doorway of her bedroom, not knowing if it was okay to go in, in awe of the casual, chic way she'd decorated it with junk-shop flair: a heavy gilt-edged mirror leaning against the wall, a huge black lacquered Chinese box, her jumpers spilling out of it, the bed piled high with silk and velvet cushions. *The colours.* The madness of all the colours and textures that somehow worked.

'This music gig thing tonight,' she'd said, flopping down on the bed, 'you are coming, aren't you?'

I must've looked surprised.

'You *have* to, Hannah. You *havetohaveto.*'

The thrill of the invitation. My nearly laughing out loud with pleasure at the thought.

'Because...' She sighed and raised her hands theatrically. 'Because Matt's gone off out with his mates, and I'll said I'll go to this gig. It's a charity-raising thing, but I won't know anyone who'll be there.'

'I can't believe that.'

'Seriously. Honestly. Truth is...' Her hands flopping onto the mattress. 'I'm scared to walk in there on my own.'

'You?' I looked at her, astonished. 'Rachel, you know everyone and everyone wants to know you.'

'Yeah, but then I'm left on my own. I always feel awkward at these things without a wing woman.'

I couldn't get my head around it.

'So, what I'm saying is, would you be her? Would you be my wing woman?' She grinned.

'Me?'

'Yeah.' She looked away shyly. 'Oh, go on. It'll be a laugh. I'll owe you one. A huge one.'

'Me? Are you sure?' *Had she actually chosen me?*

'Purrleese...' she implored.

'I haven't really got anything I can wear.' I glanced round at the jumbled piles of clothes on the floor.

'Take anything – anything.' She scrambled off the bed onto all fours, diving into a pile in front of her and dragging out a dress. 'This. Now, this would be *perfect*. Look at the colour on you.' She grabbed my arm, hauling herself up and twisting me round to look in the mirror. 'See?'

I saw me: dowdy, frumpy me, with some crumpled rag bunched at my shoulder.

'Put it on.'

'What?' I looked at her laughing reflection.

'Now. Put it on. Let me show you how good you can look.'

She started pulling at my cardigan, peeling it from my arms.

All I could think was how appalling my underwear was, my rolls of puppy fat, how she'd see and be embarrassed and wish she hadn't asked me, and I would never, ever be asked to anything ever again. But she'd already dragged the cardigan off and was pulling up my baggy T-shirt.

'Come on. Come on,' she urged. 'We need something to go with this. Hang on.' She turned away to rummage in the pile behind her, thankfully allowing me a little dignity as I slipped off my jeans and tried to fathom how to put the dress on. I'd just about got it over my head when I felt her yanking it down. It slid down my back and hugged my waist.

'There,' she said proudly. 'Look.'

I glanced at my reflection. I suddenly had a figure.

I tugged at the hem. 'It's very short.'

'With these underneath!' She shoved a pair of shorts into my hands. 'And these.' She found one embellished kitten-heeled shoe, and then untangled another. 'You're about my size. Oh, yes... Earrings.' She went over to a box on her bedside table. 'These would look fab.' She held up a pair of sparkly chandelier earrings. 'And then we'll do your hair like this...' She grabbed a handful, twisting it up into a messy pile on top of my head and pulled down some strands to frame my face.

'Perfect,' she breathed. 'Transformed. And look – look.' She snatched up a red dress from the pile. 'I'm wearing this. They'll think we're sisters.'

A thing inside me, a dormant thing that I had never felt before, quivered and squeezed with a rush of joy. A warm cascade of light and bright happiness thrummed joyfully. I saw what she was meaning: there I was, reflected in the glass just like she said, but the truth was I couldn't take my eyes from her laughing face bobbing at my shoulder. There she was, her flashing eyes oozing the absolute unwavering confidence that I looked just how she said I did and that was all that mattered.

It was sheer *bliss*.

Sisters, she'd said. *Like the thought had even crossed her mind.*

And so she helped me get ready, washing my hair for me, doing my makeup.

I stood there in my bathrobe in the kitchen, ironing my dress and hers, not quite believing this was happening.

The doorbell rang. There was the thudding scamper of Rachel's bare heels along the hallway, the sound of the front door opening, and then the rise and fall of raised voices. They sounded panicked. Rachel appeared in the kitchen doorway.

'I've got to go. There's an emergency.' She sounded breathless.

'What?'

'Is my dress ready? I'll go straight to the gig and I'll meet you outside, okay? You know where Headrow House is, yeah?'

I looked at the iron and the shorts that were still crumpled on the hanger.

'Maybe I should I come with you? Like, now?'

'You can't,' she said, holding out her hand for the dress. 'There's a girl at the refuge who wants to talk to me urgently. I have to go.' And with that, she'd snatched the dress from the ironing board, chucked off her dressing gown and pulled the neckline over her head. Ramming her feet into her shoes, I saw a flash of red skirt, and she was gone.

But we hadn't said what time we were meeting?

Slowly, I finished ironing, putting the iron and board away, checking the clock over and over. I felt a bit mean and not very compassionate; I should be thinking about this poor girl, not about my own spoiled evening. I stood, biting my lip, considering messaging Rachel to see where she was, then thought that might put pressure on her.

I could just go there, couldn't I? Sit at the bar, have a drink. The thought of being alone in the corner of a club being stared at, terrified me. *I'll walk there slowly*, I decided. *Take my time.*

I'll give it half an hour and then ring her; half an hour would be long enough, wouldn't it?

I looked around and realised that Rachel had forgotten to bring down the shoes I was borrowing.

Making my way up the stairs carrying my hanger of clothes, I went into her room, took off my dressing gown, and put on the dress and the shorts. Sliding my feet into the heels, I stood for a moment, gazing at myself in the mirror. The room was quiet and I held my breath, gazing at the length of my legs, the way my waist cinched in. My skin radiated gold. My hair shone with strands of auburn in the dark waves. The dying sun filtered through the grimed window. An orange flash lit the edge of the frame.

Rachel had done this for me; I looked how I always should have looked. This is the me I should have always been, and thanks to Rachel, I'd discovered her.

I took a deep breath, looking out at the early evening sky as the light faded. It would get cooler out there and I didn't have a decent coat to go with all this. Looking around at the cast-off clothes heaped on the floor, I spied a sleeve of denim and pulled it out. The casual jacket was perfect.

Tripping down the stairs, I pulled it on, grabbing my handbag and stepping out into the cool evening. *I felt free and my own person.* The thought came to me as I swung happily down the street. I felt free, and new, and... *loved.* And I knew right then that I never wanted to feel any other way ever again.

Even as I turned into the Headrow, I heard the noisy chatter from groups people out on the street. Slowing my pace, I fished out my phone, checking it for the umpteenth time. I'd sent Rachel three messages already but saw she hadn't picked them up.

'Oi oi.'

A boisterous bellow echoed across the street. There were

two lads, feet scuffing, hands stuffed into the pockets of their jeans, crossing the road towards me.

'We know where you're off to.'

I quickened my pace to where the sea of people outside the club spilled across the pavement. I realised if I slowed down and waited for Rachel here, I'd be a sitting target.

They fell into step behind me, leaving me praying that Rachel would already be there, waiting for me.

The covered walkway to the entrance meant the gig-goers were herded into straggling groups, blocking the path. The lads moved in closer behind. My eyes scanned and scanned again over the faces of the girls. I lifted a hand, pretending to wave at someone. A girl I didn't know looked up in query.

'Looks like she's got a mate.' The first lad guffawed. 'That's one each.'

Panicked, I didn't know what to do. I couldn't see Rachel. I couldn't stay here, outside though. I'd have to go in.

There was a chap on the door. 'Ticket,' he said.

'I need to see if my friend's here.' I waved my phone pointlessly towards the bar. 'She has the tickets.'

'Try ringing her,' he said gruffly. 'But you can't come in, love. Not without a ticket.'

I thought about arguing the point, but I could see he wasn't going to budge. Sighing, I scrolled for her number. It went straight to voicemail. I decided to try pleading.

'Look... All I want to do is see if she's there.' I waved again at the bar, and then suddenly saw her. 'Oh, there she is.' I pointed and waved. 'Rach... Rachel.' Rachel half turned but clearly hadn't spotted me. I looked back to the guy. 'You can see she's the blonde girl over there at the bar. Honestly, two minutes and I'll get the tickets and be straight back. Promise.' I looked at him imploringly.

'Go on then.' He pecked his chin. 'Two minutes or I'll be after you.'

I darted gratefully over. 'Rachel.' I put a hand on her shoulder. 'Where have—?'

But the girl turned round in shock. It wasn't Rachel.

'Oh god, sorry,' I flustered. 'I thought you were someone else.'

She looked wordlessly away, rolling her eyes to her friend sitting opposite. I swallowed nervously. I half-recognised the other girl. Yes, bright-red lipstick, hair tied in a bandeau. I'd noticed her in lectures.

'You haven't seen her, have you?'

Lipstick girl gave me a withering stare.

'*Sorr*-ry?' she said slowly.

'Rachel Myers. Do you know her?'

'Yeah, I know her.' She looked away again.

I tried again in my meekest voice. 'I wondered if you'd seen her at all?'

Please don't do this. Please.

'Yes.'

'In here?'

'Yes.' She smirked.

'Oh, for god's sake.' The other girl snapped round. '*Yes*, we know Rachel. *Yes*, she was here, and no, she's not here anymore. Does that answer all your questions?'

''Scuse me, love?' I turned to see the man on the door beckoning to me. 'Have you got a ticket or not?'

'*Not*,' the two girls said in unison, and then burst out laughing.

Face burning and eyes stinging, I managed to stumble away.

'Freaking freak,' I heard one of them say as I floundered past the bemused-looking guy and found myself back on the street. The tears brimmed and fell. My mascara felt thick and sticky on my cheeks as I smeared it away. I didn't care who saw me and who cat-called me now. I couldn't believe how horrible people could be. Why treat someone like that? And where the hell was

Rachel? I scrubbed angrily at my face knowing it was ruining my makeup but not caring.

Where was she? How come she left? Why hadn't she rung or answered any of my texts?

It was Friday night and the students were starting to party. Everyone was out and having a good time. Everyone apart from me. Young people, dressed up, drinking, happy, spilled out onto the pavement from all the bars. I knew no one. I didn't have any friends, only Rachel. Those girls called me a freak. *Maybe they're right. Maybe I am.*

The sound of my heels slowed on the pavement as a shriek of laughter ricocheted through the evening air. I turned my head, half-recognising the sound. *Alison.* Her laughing mouth caught sight of me and froze, grinning.

'Hiya. Goin' somewhere nice?'

She was drunk. Sad, uptight, intense Alison was *drunk.*

'Have you seen Rachel?' I asked wearily.

'Yeah, she's here – over there.' She waved her glass and there was Rachel, her hands gesticulating wildly, her hair springing in manic coils as she excitedly told a story to a group of boys I'd never seen before.

I walked over. She was sitting on one of the wooden tables, her feet on the bench. The boys looked enraptured, laughing at her jokes, egging her on. Their eyes grazed over me, making her look round.

'Hannah.' She looked vaguely surprised, but not in the slightest embarrassed. 'How brilliant to see you. I didn't know you came here.'

I didn't reply.

'Do you want a drink? Here, let me get you a drink.' She reached for her bag.

'I thought we were meeting at the Headrow?'

'I bumped into Alison,' she said distractedly, pulling out a twenty-pound note. 'While you're at the bar I'll have a vodka tonic. Anyone else?' She looked around expectantly.

'You said you wanted me to go in with you because you wouldn't know anyone. You said Alison was driving you mad.' I heard the whine in my voice.

'Did I?' She lifted her head, puzzled. 'Oh, you know me. Very forgiving. I don't bear grudges for long.' She wrinkled her nose as she gestured across to her friends. 'I think Jake will have another pint. You should have enough there.'

'And what happened with the emergency?' I took the money she was offering.

'Oh, Alison was with the girl when I got there.' She nodded matter-of-factly. 'Alison's really, really good at counselling the women you know. I think it's her forte. She's totally come out of her shell. Getting involved at the Sanctum Shelter has been really good for her. I did say all she needed was a bit of looking-after, didn't I?'

'Alison volunteers at the refuge with you?'

'Yeah, but you knew that. I told you.'

No. You didn't. You didn't tell me anything of the sort.

'Oh. You're getting the drinks, I see.' Alison appeared at my elbow. Her kohl-rimmed eyes drifted drunkenly from the twenty-pound note to my face. Her garish red mouth split into a grin. 'I'll have—'

But Rachel interrupted her, tutting. 'You've probably had quite enough, girlie. Hey, come here a minute.' She caught hold of Alison by the collar of her jacket, drawing her closer and used her thumb to wipe away a smudge of eyeliner from her cheek. The action was both nurturing and intimate. Something inside me went suddenly cold.

'There.' Rachel smiled. The feeling inside me gripped hard as stone. I pulled my jacket closer across my chest, holding on to that burning tearful sensation in my throat that was threatening to blurt out in front of all these people.

'Hang on, isn't that Rachel's?' Alison's moony made-up face peered closer, her fingers coming forward like pincers to pluck at my sleeve. I yanked it away. 'Yeah, that's Rachel's jacket,' she said frowning, her eyes scanning downwards. 'And her shoes. You've nicked her shoes.'

'I haven't *nicked* them, as you put it,' I answered hotly, glancing at Rachel for confirmation.

'No, she hasn't,' Rachel piped up. 'She's just borrowed them without permission.'

My head snapped round. 'I haven't. I wouldn't.'

'It's no big deal. There's no drama.' Rachel shrugged waving dismissively. 'Don't worry about it. I don't *mind*, honestly. It's cool.'

Alison was standing there, swaying a little, with a stupid look plastered across her face.

'We'll all have to watch you.' She winked at me, lazily licking her lips. 'Keep our gear under lock 'n key – or you'll have your sticky little fingers in there,' she sniggered. 'Any- Anyways... Where are these drinks you're getting? As you've nicked her clothes, 'spect you owe Rach a round or two, doncha?' She plucked the note from my fingers and stuffed it back into Rachel's breast pocket, pressing it firmly twice.

I saw Jake's eyes following her hand.

'Chop-chop.' Alison gestured me away. 'Mine's a vodka tonic, same as Rach.'

'Vodka? Is that on the approved list of drinks then? Is vodka vegan then?' I kept my tone lighthearted, but I knew I wasn't being nice.

'Totally pure, isn't it?' She smiled clumsily back. 'Just like me... *Not*.' She laughed, turning away and saying something to Jake, who laughed back. They'd shut me down. Between them all, they'd completely frozen me out.

I tried to catch Rachel's eye; I wanted her to see how hurt I was, how embarrassed, how I hadn't deserved any of that. I took a couple of steps back. I was stunned, reeling with humiliation. I'd done nothing, *nothing* but be a good friend to Rachel. She said she'd needed me, and I'd been there for her, only to be stood up and treated like this.

I turned away as if to go to the bar, stumbling, my feet catching on the entrance step. She'd lent me these clothes – I would never have taken them, *never* ever. I thought we were friends, proper friends. *Like sisters*, that's what she'd said, wasn't it?

A sob caught in my throat, the lights in the bar blurred into a myriad of colours. I made a half-strangled sound, a hiccough of pain, and the chap behind the bar looked at me to take my order. I couldn't stand to be there a moment longer. I ran – ran out towards the toilets, my chest heaving, gulping for air as I sobbed and sobbed, heartbroken and angry and completely confused.

The rear door to the pub yard was ajar and I pushed straight through it, out where the barrels and crates were stacked, yanking blindly at the bolts on the back gate, not caring where I was going as I practically fell out into the street. I tried running, but the stupid shoes ricked my ankles, so I wrenched them off, throwing them as far as I could.

I don't know how long I kept on running. I didn't care how the sharp stones cut and sliced into the soft skin, I didn't care that my toes were bruised and grazed, all I wanted was to be as far away as possible.

The road opened out. It was familiar. It was a road not too far from home.

Home.

The idea of that house filled me with a sad dread: the thought of going back in there, seeing it just as I'd left it, all that excited anticipation of the evening ahead, and then walking back in... to nothing but emptiness. The thought of lying in bed, listening to Rachel and Alison coming home all giggling and girlish, squawking and shouting as they recounted the night's events. No. It was too, too much: I just couldn't do it.

Collapsing tearfully onto a low wall, I leaned back into the hedge bordering a row of terraced houses and rested my head in its twiggy depths. All I wanted was to close my eyes; close my eyes and go to sleep and pray that when I open them again, tonight would never have happened.

Some warbled strains of a woman singing drifted by me, fading away into the night air. I opened one eye as the sound came again. An old-fashioned pub, its blackened facade lit only by muted lights though the frosted windows, shone dimly in the gloom. I listened as every so often the door batted open, and the warbling wafted stronger. Levering myself up, I made my way across the street and gingerly pushed open the door.

It was like some cave from another world. A man in a corner was playing an organ for the woman singing. She was squeezed into a red dress and clutched a microphone close to her thickly shining lips, singing a song I'd never heard. The dress instantly made me think of Rachel. I nearly walked straight out.

'You alright, love?' An old woman with a perm was sitting by the door. Her pink lipliner went way beyond the confines of her own thin lips.

'I'm fine, thanks,' I mumbled. 'I think I might be in the wrong place.'

'Well, I think you're just in the right place.' The pinkness stretched into a smile. 'Why don't you come an' have a drink, darlin'. Just stop for one. We don't bite.' She patted the seat beside her. 'You look a bit upset, love. Come and tell Aunty Pam all about it.' She peered closely at me and I felt the burn and smart of more tears.

'Pretty thing like you. T'isn't right at all. You come and sit with me. I'll make it all better.'

She held her arms out, and suddenly I found myself crumpling onto the bench seat beside her, a hiccoughing sob choking my throat as she grabbed my hand in her gnarled fingers and gestured over to the girl behind the bar.

'She'll 'ave a brandy, and I'll 'ave a top-up please, Cheryl.'

I wasn't sure if I even liked brandy, but withing seconds a glass of shining amber appeared on the table in front of me.

'Drink that up, luvvie, and tell me what's been going on. Tell a stranger your troubles. You'll be amazed how good you'll feel after. Trust me. I've done it many a time.'

I sipped gratefully, mumbling my thanks, and gradually told her all about Rachel and the dress and what Alison had said and done, and how I'd felt like I had a proper friend for the first time in my life, and now I had no one.

I drank, and she stroked my hand and listened, and I drank some more, and all the time a woman was singing about love, and heartache, and I knew precisely and painfully, precisely what she meant.

SEVEN

The clock in the hallway ticks its beat. My eyes scan the lounge ceiling as I hear Matt's bedroom door click shut. The house goes quiet. My head isn't.

I have so much going round in there I can barely cope with one image and sensation before the next comes tumbling in: the past and the present all jumbling and blurring one into the other, Rachel... Alison... Matt... Theresa... Leach...

Leach is getting out, my head says, and my stomach somersaults in a bundle of sickening tension. *And here you are, back in the place where it happened, back with the people who were around you back then. You made choices back then that led you to that terrible place. Are you doing the same now?*

My breath drags deep into my lungs. I can't breathe suddenly. Getting up, I open the lounge curtain a little, feeling the relief of the chilled pane. The world is completely white, hushed with the kind of silence that only snow brings. There's no movement out there. My face is reflected back in the windowpane, a distortion of it: my mouth slurred into a dark gash, the lines of my cheeks hollowed out in two half-moons as my heart thuds away inside my chest.

No... I need to breathe... like, properly breathe. Pulling the comforter around me, I go into the kitchen heading for the back door. Turning the key in the lock as quietly as I can, I feel the door give a little as I ease the handle and a fine whistle of cold air prickles my skin. The ice of it instantly chills in my lungs making my head sing, but at the same time, gratefully, cleansing me.

The moonlight has turned the world blue. I peer out into the quiet, pure blanket. There's nothing here: no shadows, no creeping figure, no footprints. Nothing. Just me with echoes of the past in my head and the horror of Leach somewhere in the edge of my sightline.

It had to happen one day, my head tells me. *You couldn't escape forever, could you? He'll be on licence. He'll be monitored. You'll know he's out there in the world, but he never has to come near you ever again.*

Easing my neck and shoulders, I breathe out, watching the plume of anxiety disappear into the night air. Putting my hand on the door edge, I'm aware of how thick and solid it is. A good old-fashioned door, heavy and strong. A thing that's held back the worst of things for probably a hundred and fifty years. Nothing and no one could get through this. *You're* safe *here*, it tells me. *You have nothing to worry about.*

Going to close it, I move to step back, when something makes me look down.

There, on the step, is a snowman.

It can't be. I stoop to see a little closer. It's a bank of snow, oddly formed, but no, it's a snowman, standing about a foot high: its little, black, beady eyes skewed at an odd angle; its mouth a wonky 'O' of grit; the nose, a broken peg. But it has arms made of twigs that have been bent into shape and criss-crossed in a hug. There's something clutched between the sticks. Moving back a little, I allow the moonlight to cast its gleam across the step. There's a heart: bright red against the luminescent white, caught lopsidedly amongst the stems. A wooden heart.

You're Mine, it says.

My head jerks up and my knees almost crumple. I glance across the expanse of lawn, heart pounding. Something out there shivers in the darkness. There's a creak of snow and in that instant, I'm leaping back, shutting the door quickly and reaching up for the top bolt. The key turns shakily in my trembling fingers, as I try and test the lock over and over to make sure it's held fast. I pause, my heart yammering, as some quiet antennae of wrongness prickles into the nape of my neck. My eyes shift slowly round. I stare, wide-eyed, around the shadowy kitchen. A pall of creeping dread inches carefully up my spine. But there's only me and the sound of my ragged breathing – nothing else.

It's him, my head says.

It can't be, I answer. *How can it be?*

It is, and he knows where you are.

No, that's ridiculous, you're being stupid. He's behind bars. It's like Matt said, it's something to do with Rachel. He told you, didn't he? He'd seen someone hanging around?

It's Rachel's bloke. He could easily have left something like that. That'll be it, won't it?

Of course it is. I breathe out.

However, I still don't go back to bed.

I sit at the kitchen table, a knife in front of me, as I wait for the dawn to creep across the floor. My mind feels as though its axis has been jolted off course and is slowly spinning, spiralling away into some dark hole. This feeling... this feeling... I can't get a grip. The clock in the hallway ticks louder. I keep very still in the darkness.

The house is quiet. There's no one here, but I'm not taking the chance and going upstairs.

This kind of darkness, this too quiet kind of darkness, frightens me.

I've felt it before.

When I wasn't well.

But I am well now. I've come this far, haven't I? That's how I'm able to deal with things when bad stuff happens. I know how to take control and stop my mind from spiralling. I know that the darkness frightens me. We're all like children; we're all afraid of the dark.

But it's the kind that's in my mind that's the scariest.

I can never go back to the darkness I felt those first few days in that hospital.

'*I shouldn't be here,*' I told them...

Out of the shadows come the calm, pale faces of kind doctors in their hospital whites; the ones that pretend to understand, but never can, with their notepads, and scratching pens and their probes and their questions, their hushy coffee-breath and their round, earnest eyes. *Men,* trying to push their way inside in all the ways they can think of.

Tell us something, Hannah. Open up. Give us some bit of you. Their patient staring eyes boring into me.

But I wouldn't give them anything.

I thought about it, though: the things I knew they wanted. Me behind that bathroom door at my parent's house. That fine, satisfying sensation of a tiny slither of a blade between my thumb and forefinger. The cold tiles of the floor. No mother, no father, no Rachel, no no one. The dust of that waste ground and the dried blood still clinging under my nails. No one to find me sitting there slumped behind the door – the whiteness of my inner thigh, so smooth, but silvered here and there with tiny lines of old cuts between the fine blue veins.

My eyes were drawn to the press of the blade edge as it

depressed the skin, tightening it more and more, my breath held with the tension... Just a bit harder, just a bit... And then it gave in a gush of blood and the relief, the absolute relief... Then suddenly that neighbour's appalled face in the doorway. The shock. The disbelief. The horror.

'*Hannah*,' she whispered.

My head snaps back in alarm. It takes a second for me to register where I am.

Rachel's kitchen.

'Hannah,' a voice says.

I snatch round. The room is still dark. The whitened rectangles of light from the glass roof cast the shadows into grey canopies. There's a faint shuffle of sound from the hallway as my fingers grip the table edge. I wait. Nothing.

Was the voice in my head?

And then I hear it: the crack of a stair tread... But then, silence.

Easing the knife into my hand, I inch towards the door, peering out into the hallway. It's empty. Taking a careful step, I glance through the banister towards the dark landing.

Something flickers up there – an odd kind of light, moving and swaying. I look back into the kitchen. The door is still firmly bolted, the windows are locked. I peer back again at the strange lights that dance, lengthening and weaving – and put my hand firmly on the newel post.

'I know someone's there,' I whisper forcefully into the quiet. 'Show yourself.'

Legs trembling, my every footstep fights me as, eyes fixed on the lights, I make my way up the stairs, hesitating fearfully as I reach the top step. The bathroom door is open, the swirl of lights spilling out across the landing as, knife pointed, I venture another step forward.

It's a moment before I see what's right in front of me.

Rose petals. A line of them strewn prettily on the floor, red and pink furls in the fluttering light of the candles laid around the edges of the bath. The water laps a little at the sides as though only recently drawn. The tap plinks softly into the quiet. A scent of something, maybe sandalwood, drifts in coils of steam, condensing on the walls.

My head spins as I stagger back against the door, my eyes casting this way and that.

The landing is quiet; Rachel and Matt's door is firmly shut.

'Hannah,' a voice says close to my ear, and I whirl round, heart thudding, knife swishing through the darkness as a shadow moves past me in a breath of air. I hear feet tripping quickly down the stairs as I rush out, seeing a hooded blackness disappearing around the last stair edge, and then the front door is flung open. I race down after it, my feet skidding on the tiles as I come to a halt on the threshold, my breath billowing into the cold night air. I step out onto the path, my eyes searching frantically for shape of a running figure, but the snow lies there, heavy and undisturbed. I check the street desperately up and down, but there's no one there: no movement, no sound echoing back.

There was someone there; I know there was.

Heart hammering, I go back inside, easing the front door closed with a soft click.

'You okay, Hannah?' Rachel's voice jolts me round.

'God, Rachel.'

'What's going on?' she whispers, coming halfway down the stairs.

'Rachel... Rachel... Oh my god.'

'Shhh. What? What is it? Do you want me to wake Matt?' She looks behind and then past me.

'No, no. Don't. There was—'

'What? What did you see?' Her face looks ghostly pale in the moonlight.

'There was someone... It's in the bathroom...' I stammer.

'In the bathroom?'

I grab her hand and drag her up the stairs. 'Come. Come and look.' I lead her along the landing. 'This is madness, I know it is. But seriously, Rachel—'

I'm aware of her eyes trawling the side of my face as we reach the bathroom door and we both stare into the space. There are no rose petals. There are no candles. All there is, is a bathroom in shadows, calm, quiet, and still.

She pulls on the light switch and the room flood with white light. 'What, Hannah? What did you want to show me?'

I don't know how to answer her.

I stare into the empty bathtub. 'There was—' I start.

'There was, what?' I feel the heat of her glance as it travels down from the side of my face to the sight of the knife clutched in my hand. My palm feels bruised with tension.

'Hannah...? What's that for?'

We both gape down at it as though we have no clue what we're looking at.

This isn't happening. Did I dream all this?

'Come on, Hannah, let me help you.' The warmth of Rachel's fingers slides across mine as she prises the knife handle from my grip. 'We've been through this: you're having the worst time right now. The absolute worst.'

I'm aware of her other hand on my forearm as she gently plucks the knife away, guiding me with more insistence than I'm comfortable with, back to my room. She closes the door behind me, pulling the rumpled covers back and leading me to the bed. She tucks me in, bending to plant a kiss on my forehead. She's tender and so gentle, I could actually weep.

'Now, night night,' she says gently. 'Get some sleep. Please.

You're perfectly safe here, Hannah. Nothing bad is going to happen. Honestly. Trust me.'

She strokes the side of my face with the back of her fingers and pulls the covers tighter under my chin.

Is this possible? Things happening that make no sense: shadowy figures, whispering, hallucinations... *What's going on with me?*

'Do you want me to stay with you?'

'No. Please don't. I'm fine.' I don't think I can bear the expression on her face.

'Really, truly, Rach.'

She pauses for a second, assessing.

'If you're sure?'

'I am.' I nod. 'Perfectly.'

'Okay, then.'

She tiptoes out of the door, pulling it closed behind her, blowing me a kiss goodnight as the room fades to black. I lie there for minutes not sure how I should be feeling, listening to the creak as she crosses the landing, and the house settles down. A tremble of something bad, and dark and frightening skims again and again in the recesses of my mind. *Am I losing my grip? I wasn't well once. Understandable, but—*

The scratchy cleanness of the duvet cover against my cheek reminds me suddenly of the hospital bed all those years ago. I remember the hours becoming days and days became weeks. I remember the bedsit unit the hospital moved me to; the kind and bubbly social worker who called in every few days telling me how far I'd come, as the weeks rolled into months...

You're doing so well, they said.

But I'm not sure now what 'well' means. Could I become 'un-well' again?

'It's all about *control*, Hannah,' Theresa had said gently. 'You're scared of being out of control again, but you were a child back then. No proper support, no resources, no tools to deal with the enormity of what you were being forced to face. It's different now. *You're* a different person. You've given yourself a voice, you have a strong sense of self. You're not buffeted by the whims and abuse of others anymore. Look how you handled your last relationship. You created clear boundaries, Hannah. You confronted him. You walked away. You did that for you.'

The darkness in the room stays thick and comforting. I hear nothing but peaceful silence as I turn on my side, dragging the scratchy cover under my chin, and begin to concentrate on the air filling and leaving my lungs.

Theresa was right. I'm not the kid I was. I can choose to take control. I can choose to confront. I can choose to walk away... And then I suddenly become aware of something tickling the skin of my palm and my eyes spring open. Fumbling for the bedside light, the sudden glow pools on my palm. It takes a moment to register what I'm looking at before it slowly dawns with the rise of my beating heart.

It's a pink petal.

EIGHT

'Oh, morning.'

Rachel looks up, attempting a bright smile as I walk into the kitchen. I attempt to mirror her brightness.

'Get to sleep okay eventually?' She pulls a concerned face. 'What a night. Would you like tea?'

'Yeah...' I rub my face to hide my real feelings. 'Tea would be great.'

I want to ask her about the snowman, but can't. Somehow, deep inside, I'm frightened to find that I imagined that too, and right now, I really don't want confirmation.

Rachel turns to the kettle, and I pretend to look out into the garden, my shaking hands touching the kitchen counter for something to hold on to. I don't know what's happening to me. I couldn't find the petal this morning. I searched and searched the floor, the bed, everywhere, leaving me feeling weird and unsettled.

Rachel gives me a look over her shoulder. 'Can I say, you don't seem very fine. You don't have to pretend with me, you know.'

'No, I'm okay. Really I am.' I grip the edge of the work

surface harder to give me the strength to convince her. 'I actually didn't get much sleep, to be honest.'

'No, well...'

'Because I've been thinking.'

'Uh-huh.' She hands me the cup of tea.

'Um... perfect. Thank you.' I take the cup. 'I lay awake, all these thoughts spinning around in my head. What I found out yesterday, Rachel... about Leach. I mean, is it a coincidence that I wanted answers to what happened to me and I come right back here? Is that pure chance? I feel like consciously or unconsciously, Rachel, I've been drawn here. It's like it's a test. I've been terrified all my adult life. I've lived in the shadow of what I believe he did to me. That fear has ruled me. Caged me. Stopped me from living.'

'Hannah, I can't say I get it, because I don't. I can't imagine it. But all I can tell you is—'

I hold up a hand. 'And I came to the decision that I'm not going to let that fear rule me any longer.'

'That's so good.' She's trying to be encouraging. 'That's really, really good to hear.'

'Because I'm going to confront him.'

Her smile drops and a crack of floorboards overhead sends us shooting a glance to the ceiling.

'What do you mean, confront him?'

'He's here, isn't he? That's what you said? He's going to be released from the prison right here?'

Her eyes widen in horror. 'You can't be serious, Hannah. You can't honestly be serious?'

'I've never been more so.'

'What are you talking about? How? This isn't possible.'

'I've decided I'm going to the prison.'

'*What?*' Her disbelief turns to open-mouthed fear.

'It's HMP Crowden Lea here, isn't it?' I reach for my phone and scroll for the article. 'It's going to be soon, it says so here.' I find I'm no longer calm: my breath is high up in my throat.

'Hannah. You can't walk into a prison, for God's sake,' she hisses.

'Yes, I know. I've been online this morning. I've booked a visit.'

'You've done what?'

My voice is shaking. 'I have to know. I have to find out if it was him.'

All I can hear is the sound of her breathing – or my own; I can't tell.

'You're actually going to see him?' She's appalled. 'When?'

The blank numbness; the ordinariness of the action: going onto the prison website, typing in the name as though it was the most normal thing in the world to do.

'There's visiting at the prison this morning.'

'This morning.' She stares at me. 'You just turn up?'

I shrug. 'I've put my name on their list to see him. If he chooses not to see me, then there's nothing I can do.'

Rachel's eyes are full of worry as they blink slowly over and over.

She swallows. 'Are you sure you're feeling strong enough? To deal with him, I mean.'

'Confronting him is not just about what happened to me, it's about the possibility of it happening to some other woman once he's out. He didn't pay for what he did to me, Rachel, and if I can prove it, or... or if I can put pressure on him make him confess, he'll do more time – and more time inside means the longer women are safe.'

'But... but how can you possibly—?' She breaks off, staring at me, swallowing again and again. I know what she's thinking: if I drag all this up, there's a possibility there's a price for her as well. I know why she's scared: about the newspapers, the police, her job, her reputation. I see it all – *flash, flash, flash* – across her face in seconds. Her throat gulps. I'm fully aware of what I'm suggesting. I know I'm opening up the thing that we swore. *We swore...*

Sudden images come back to me like a flick-book cartoon: *a building site, that broken wall. That hole.*

'People need to know what he did, Rachel. He'll do it again.'

Her eyes haven't moved.

Our web of silence.

'But what about what *we* did, Hannah?' her voice shakes.

'We were practically *children* when it happened, Rach. *Children.* We panicked. We didn't know what we were doing. They won't see us as culpable.'

'You don't know that,' she says quietly. 'It'll be in the news. People will think things.' She takes a sudden breath. 'Jesus, *Matt* will know what we did.' She shakes her head quickly, trying to compute. 'Christ, Hannah, this is so...'

The enormity of what I'm asking comes over me.

'Rachel, god, I'm so sorry...' The full force of what I'm asking of her hits me in one great swell. I hold my hands out to her. 'What was I thinking? There are massive implications for you too. I've been totally self-absorbed and hell-bent on this personal mission. Look... You're right, you're absolutely right to challenge me. I mean, I'm the one who's stirred all this up. I'm the one who's so gung-ho talking about taking a sledgehammer to your life and I haven't even consulted you. What an indescribably selfish thing of me to do. You're right, you're exactly right. How the hell would I prove it anyway?' I lift both hands in surrender. 'I don't know what I'm even saying.'

Her mouth moves awkwardly and she reaches forward to grab my raised hand, holding on very tight.

'Hannah. My god, listen to me. You've got nothing to be sorry for. You're not the one who should be sorry for anything. The truth is, I've lived my life selfishly, oblivious to what was happening to you. Of *course* you have to confront him. Of *course* the person who stole your life has to pay for what they did. None of this is about me, Hannah. None of it.'

The floor overhead creaks violently. I know we don't have long.

I feel myself beginning to backtrack and wobble. 'But if I tell someone – the police, the prison – they're going to ask questions, Rach. They'll want more than me recounting some hazy story about a night I can barely remember.' I turn my hands over in hers. 'Who's going to be interested in that?'

'They might, you don't know,' she encourages, but we both know the reality: once I make the accusation, then all hell breaks loose, for me and for her.

'They'll want some kind of evidence for sure.'

'But we don't have any, do we?'

I love the way she says *we*.

'Well...'

'Do we?'

'That's why...' I falter. 'That's why I've been thinking about what we did and how I can use it.'

Rachel's face blanches a little. 'How do you mean?'

'That site... What happened... What we left behind...'

The whiteness of her face pales a little further.

'But surely, whatever was there, on that site... I mean... so much time has passed.'

'But he doesn't know that, does he? He has no idea.'

Her grip tightens and she searches my face. 'And are you absolutely sure you want to put yourself through this, Hannah? I mean, haven't you been through enough already?'

'That's the problem, Rach. Nothing I've done so far has been enough. I've done all the therapy, all the regression sessions and the visualisations, all the letter-writing and then burning it. I've done the whole lot.'

I feel very still and very calm.

I look into her face. Lovely, well-meaning Rachel, who has

never faced up to anything. Who ferociously reads all the books and passionately talks all the talk and says all the woke things in her safe little bubble. How could she know anything of the raw scourging wound I have inside me?

'I know it was him, Rachel. I don't care what he, or anyone else, says. It was *him* that night, Rachel. He's the one who attacked me. I know it, and he knows it.' I feel my teeth clench together. 'He can only guess what I have on him. He's going to have to take a very big risk if he wants to call my bluff.'

Rachel nods, but I can see she's scared and not convinced.

'I know what I want, Rachel, and I'll use anything I can to get it.'

She knows she has no choice. She's in this with me.

'And what is it you actually want, Hannah? I mean what's the core compulsion that's driving you?'

'I don't want him back on the street so he can line up his next victim.' My jaw juts vehemently. 'I want my evidence to get him a life sentence this time to make sure he never, ever does this to anyone else.' I pause. 'But for me, there's one thing I absolutely have to have.'

'And what's that?'

'I want to hear him say the words, "I raped you."'

NINE

'We thought we might take a trip into town.' Rachel doesn't look at Matt as he walks into the kitchen. She slots some bread into the toaster. 'Toast okay, Hannah?'

I look at her, surprised.

I'm acutely aware of Matt trying to catch my eye, but I don't let him.

'Yeah. We want to revisit all the old haunts that are still open.' She reaches for some plates. 'They'll have cleared a lot of the snow by now. We might even go for some lunch. What do you think, Hannah? Do something. Like the old days.'

His look drifts over me again as Rachel's phone buzzes and lights up on the countertop and she swipes it up.

'Just Emily,' she breathes. 'I'll ring her back.' She looks up at Matt's bemused face. I can see he's deliberately not going to challenger her. 'Umm... I was wondering if you'd mind clearing the car for us?'

'Sure, no worries. Let me do that now so by the time you've finished, it'll be all ready to go.' He's being too affable, too polite as he wanders off to find his boots and Rachel leans in, lowering her voice.

'You don't really think I'd let you do this by yourself, do you? I'm driving you, right?' She's conspiratorial but stern. 'Seriously, you need to let me take charge of some things, Hannah. Let me be there for you.'

Matt appears carrying his boots, pausing by the back door to wrestle them on. Grabbing a scarf, he opens the back door in a blast of arctic air as I look nervously past him to the step to spot the snowman, but all I can see are mounds of snow.

Rachel's phone flashes again. 'Oh, sorry, let me just get this.'

She disappears out of the kitchen and Matt mutters something under his breath I don't catch.

'Did you see that thing outside?' I say quickly.

'See what thing?'

'There was a... a snowman.' It sounds weird even saying the words.

He frowns, puzzled. 'I went out first thing to clear the worst away. I didn't see any snowman.' But I'm already marching to the door and pulling it wider to show him.

And there's only the swept track of brushed snow, bits of leaves and twigs dotting the sparkling pathway.

'Could have been the neighbour's kids.' Matt reaches for a padded jacket and some gloves. 'Their football does sometimes come over the wall. Maybe they came in to retrieve it and left us a present.'

'Who are we talking about?' Rachel comes back in. I see her face is flushed. I wonder if Matt notices it.

'The kids next door,' he explains, delving into his coat pockets and bringing out a handful of rubbish. 'We get their chocolate wrappers and all sorts blowing into the yard.' He opens the cupboard under the sink and shunts open the waste bin.

My breath stops in my throat at the sight of what he drops amidst the twigs and bits of foil.

The red heart.

You're Mine.

I'm aware Rachel is speaking, but I'm not registering what she's saying.

I blink, realising there's a plate of toast and preserves in front of me. I look round, but Matt has disappeared.

'There's no point looking like that.'

I snap up to find her studying me.

'I'm coming with you whether you like it or not.'

I gather myself, shaking my head, feeling a little sick suddenly. 'I'm not really hungry. Sorry.'

She flips the trash can open and I get another flash of red as the toast slides on top of it. It closes it with a clang.

'I don't blame you, I'm not either. The sooner we get this thing over and done with, the better.' She gives a ragged sigh. 'Let's just get out of here and face what we have to face.'

The confusing, crazy, fear-filled enormity of what I am about to do washes over me in a tidal wave. Rachel sees my expression and instantly puts her arms around me. There's the sudden heat of her, the tickle of her hair against my cheek; a surge of closeness.

'We're going to do this thing together, Hannah. We're like sisters, aren't we? Didn't I always say that?

'You did,' I say steadily. 'Sisters. That's what you always said.'

'So go and get your things together. I can't sit here a minute longer.'

I make my way up the stairs. The bathroom door sits slightly ajar, innocuous and ordinary. Could I have imagined it? Is that possible? I don't know what to think – about anything.

Rachel's words swirl and beat around my brain. *We're like sisters, aren't we?*

Are we?

'*Didn't I always say that?*'

She did.

Sisters.

There are flashes through my mind of the warmth and closeness we once shared. I remember how I craved to hold on to that feeling. The loss of Rachel to Alison that night, her humiliation of me, felt like the worst thing in the world. Worse than knowing that my parents didn't love me, worse than them abandoning me, worse than anything I'd ever felt before in my whole life. It was as though she'd suddenly woken up to feelings I'd never felt before.

And so when I came home and found Matt sad and alone in the house...

We were two lonely kids who'd suffered the loss of the same person, coming together to comfort each other in our shared sadness.

Rachel was like a drug to us; she gave us a high we'd never had before. I remember feeling that I wasn't alive without that intensity. The sensation thrilled me, delighted me, but ultimately terrified me.

We drive in silence towards the prison. There's a constant shiver of nausea in my gut that I'm just about managing to keep under control. I breathe, counting out, slowly. Any moment, and I know the panic will overwhelm me.

I stare resolutely out of the window as the gritted roads unfold into white banks churned and criss-crossed with car tracks, as we pass the end of the street where we used to live, heading towards the town centre, and then out the other side where the run-down housing was.

A chain-link fence takes over where there houses end, and builder's billboards advertise the company name. With a lurch,

I realise we're passing the derelict waste ground, still undeveloped all these years on. Rachel sees my glance, and speeds up a little, yet somehow, I'm slowing down, the whole world moving as though it's in slow motion as if we're all caught in a bell jar, my past and present colliding, sending my stomach somersaulting.

Rachel glances over again. 'Yeah, I know,' she says grimly. 'I live with the reminders of the past every day, but for you, coming back here... It must be so hard. I just can't imagine how you process it all.'

'This... this thing I'm doing, Rach. Going to the prison. This is part of my recovery. Thank you for being here, Rachel. This means a lot.'

'I told you. I'm here for you. Sisters, yeah? You're not on your own.'

We pause at the traffic lights and I look over to a street name that instantly jolts me back.

Argyle Street.

The shock of it, and with Rachel's words still ringing in my ears, the shame of it too.

Argyle Street. Sanctum House. The refuge where Alison and Rachel volunteered.

'Oh, Alison's really, really good at counselling. I think it's her forte.' Rachel's words come back to me.

Rachel, Alison, the drinking, the cosiness and intimacy – all laid out to make me feel everything that I wasn't.

Which is why I did what I did to try and separate them.

If I hadn't done that, then I wouldn't have been alone at that party.

And if I hadn't been alone at that party...

I set it all in motion.

I did it.

It was all me.

• • •

I'd pressed the buzzer on the door of Sanctum House. The eye of a camera blinked down blankly at me. I noted the patched-up panels, criss-crossed sheets of studded metal, and wondered what on earth went on here?

There was a sudden shunt of numerous bolts before the door opened a few inches on a thick chain as an eye and the side of a cheek appeared.

'Can I help you?'

'I'm looking for Alison. I think she mentioned she's volunteering today?'

A freckled nose turned away to speak to someone behind. 'One moment.' The door closed in the gap, and I glanced back into the street as a whip of wind sent a scutter of newspaper past my feet. A squeal of metal and the door opened again.

'Can I take your name?'

'It's Hannah Waters. She knows me. We share a house actually. I said I was interested in the work she was doing here and she said to drop by.'

The eye swivelled away.

'Hannah Waters,' the voice repeated, and then the door swung open. I stepped inside.

I found myself in the hallway of an old Victorian house. The 'eye' belonged to a small, dark-haired woman, pale skinned, with a wide, generous mouth.

'I'll see if I can find her for you. I'm Marnie, by the way. Come on through.'

She showed me into a large area, clearly two rooms that had been knocked into one. There was a green, L-shaped sofa down one wall, and three slouchy beige armchairs with stained seats. In one corner was a square playmat, heaped with children's toys. A young girl, brown hair scraped into a ponytail, came through from a back room carrying a cup of tea. She stopped when she saw me.

'Uh. Hello.' Her huge eyes regarded me, slightly warily.

'I'm Hannah,' I said reassuringly. 'I'm a friend of Alison's.'

'Right.'

She appeared to relax a little, gesturing for me to follow her into a kitchenette where a couple of mis-matched units and a sink served as a kitchen. The sink was piled with baby bottles soaking in a washing-up bowl.

'I'm Sadie,' she said, picking up the kettle and going to the tap. 'You coming to volunteer here too then?'

'Might do,' I said brightly. 'Looks nice.'

The bush-baby eyes turned doubtfully to take in the whole room. 'You think so? Not much of a life though, is it? Waiting for your ex to bring a sledgehammer to the door.'

'A sledgehammer?' My god. You must've been terrified.'

'Like he did two nights ago. I thought we were all going to die.'

Her tone was so matter-of-fact I was too stunned to speak.

'But the police have arrested him now, right? He can't get to you again?'

'Police?' She shook her head with a little laugh. 'Took them an hour and a half to get here. We're all trash as far as they're concerned; we're all stupid enough to put ourselves in a situation, it's up to us to get out of it.'

A kind of fizzing rage rippled through me. 'But you're out of it now. You can start a new life.'

But she only shrugged. 'Out of it? Nah. He knows I'll go back.'

She saw the look on my face.

'He's in here, see?' She tapped her temple. 'He knows he's got me. He plays me like a fiddle. He'll smash doors down and then act all sweet and I'll believe him. I always do.' She sighed. 'I know you think I'm stupid, but he's like a drug: he's bad for me. Just like a drug that I can't leave alone. I know one day it'll probably kill me, but I'm like an addict, see? I just happen to be addicted to him.' She smiled, but it didn't reach her eyes.

'There you are.' I turned to find Marnie hanging round the door frame. 'Alison's outside in the garden. It's a real little suntrap out there.'

'Really nice to meet you.' I wavered a smile at Sadie. 'Hope to see you again sometime.'

Her big eyes watched me as Marnie led the way along a passageway and out through an open back door. I squinted into the bright sunshine. Alison was sitting on a canopied swing seat in the shade, rocking gently to and fro. She brought up a hand to shade her eyes.

'Hey,' she said, surprised. 'What are you doing here?'

'Curiosity – and I happened to be passing,' I said casually.

'I'll leave you to it.' Marnie raised a hand. The two of us watched her as she walked back down the path.

'So, how are you?' I kept smiling as though we were old friends.

'You want to sit down?' She scooched over in the seat. It put us too close, but my smile stayed rigidly plastered.

'Umm... Thing is, Alison...' I found I couldn't meet her eye. 'I wanted to talk to you about the other night.'

There was a lull where we both took a moment. The garden we were sitting in was overgrown with all kinds of grasses and tall weeds, filled with the comforting rumble and buzz of so many bees poking about from one flower to another.

'I suppose I felt a bit...' I couldn't find the words. 'I don't know what it was. A mixture of things. A bit ganged up on, if I'm honest.'

'By me?' She looked shocked.

'Excluded. I don't know if you're aware, but Rachel was supposed to meet me earlier, but didn't show up.'

'Really?'

Was she lying? I felt a prickle of irritation.

'Rachel had asked me... actually she begged me to go with her to this charity thing, and then didn't show up. No call, no text, nothing. Then I find her with you in that bar. I was so awkward and so embarrassing.' I sigh. 'I suppose I feel... well, "dropped" is the word. Someone more interesting turns up and I'm forgotten.'

Alison frowned. 'Maybe you misunderstood the arrangements?'

'I don't think so.'

'Or misinterpreted what happened? Read something into the situation that wasn't intended? That's really easy to do when you're feeling a bit—'

I knew she wanted to say 'insecure'.

'Let down.'

I bit my lip. All this hostility wrapped up in empathy. My irritation morphed into something stronger. But I held my feelings tight to my chest.

I sighed loudly and looked away. 'Y'know what? Maybe you're right.'

Alison looked slightly surprised.

'I mean, you've both got a lot on your plate right now organising this trip. I'm not surprised there's a load of miscommunication.'

'Trip?'

I watched the puzzlement drop into her jaw.

'To Spain... Madrid, isn't it?'

Her puzzlement turned into a tiny shake of the head. 'Spain? No, we're not going to Spain. No one has talked about going anywhere.'

'Oh, I thought you were... Sorry, my bad. I must've got confused. No, ignore me. It was noisy in that bar and Jake had drunk quite a bit when I got there, so I probably misheard and got the wrong end of the stick.'

'Jake?'

Now that has piqued her interest, but I only shrug.

'Yeah, I heard him say the group of them are going.' I pulled a confused face. 'I just assumed that meant you and Rachel too—'

'But Rachel hasn't said anything.'

I looked away, blinking. 'Umm... I thought he said she had organised it, but obviously you'd know better than me.'

I knew I'd hit home; it was written all over her face. I could tell she didn't know which way to play it: *should she lower her guard and pump me for more information?*

She chewed her cheek. 'But she would've said something.'

I felt the wall between us crumble a little.

'Of course she would. You know what Rachel's like: brain like a sieve. She probably thinks she's told you already.'

Alison didn't look convinced. I took my opportunity.

'But yes, you're right, you're definitely right in what you said before.' I mirrored the way she licked her lips and pushed back her hair. 'Rachel wouldn't intentionally exclude anyone, least of all you.'

There was a sudden shout from the house. A woman screamed something I couldn't decipher, and then a load of high-pitched yelling filled the air. A number of voices, all tumbling over each other, shrill and panicking, rang out from the windows. I felt Alison jolt from the seat beside me and she ran down the path towards the back door of the house.

Marnie appeared, her face white and shaking, but Alison pushed past her.

'What's happened? What's going on?'

'Sadie's husband... Her husband—'

There was a sudden tremendous crash from inside the house that juddered the ground beneath my feet. A whole cacophony of screaming went up a notch.

'He's got an axe. He's trying to smash the windows,' someone yelled.

My hand instantly fumbled for my phone. I couldn't find the numbers; I couldn't find the words to ask for the Emergency Services; I couldn't hear the woman on the other end of the line, the noise around me was thundering so loudly. My hands shook and I dropped the phone as Marnie grabbed my arm. 'We need to get everyone upstairs. The rooms are safe. Come on.'

I felt myself being dragged back inside the house where there was pandemonium. There were women everywhere, shouting and crying, babies and small children wailing, as Marnie bundled me up the stairs.

'Alison... Where's Alison?'

But before I could get an answer, I was being hauled along a landing to where a bedroom door sat open. I was pushed roughly inside and then the door slammed shut. Marnie stood with her back against it, breathing heavily, her hand holding on to the last of the three bolts she'd shunted across. There was a tiny shift behind me and I wheeled round. There was Alison crouched on the end of the single bed, clutching a towel to her head. The white fabric was slowly turning red under her fingers.

'Oh my god. What happened? Did he attack you?' I crouched by her side, tentatively touching her arm. She was very pale.

'No, no, nothing like that... I panicked and slipped on the stairs and banged my head. I'm sure it's much worse than it actually is.' She wavered an unconvincing smile and then swallowed thickly. I thought for a moment she might be about to pass out.

The sound of police sirens blared out and I realised the banging and screaming had stopped.

'They'll send an ambulance too,' Marnie reassured us. 'You'll need to get that looked at.'

'It's nothing. It's honestly nothing,' Alison protested.

'You don't know that,' I insisted. 'Here, let's get you so you can lay back a bit.' I shifted a pillow up behind her shoulders.

'Just relax. You're doing great.' I patted her arm. 'We'll soon get you sorted.'

There was the tinny chatter of police radios and the thumping of feet coming up the stairs.

'There we are,' Marnie breathed. 'Won't be long now. You'll be able to go with her?' She looked at me.

'Oh absolutely.' I nodded. 'There's no way I'd let her go through something like this on her own.' I smiled, but Alison's eyes sprang open in alarm.

'Oh. You will let Rachel know what's happened, won't you? You will tell her?'

'Of course I will.' I glanced over my shoulder to see Marnie had unlocked the door and two paramedics bustled in. 'Don't you fret or worry about anything, Alison. I'm in charge here now. It's all going to get sorted.'

Clambering into the ambulance, I squeezed in beside her, watching as she tried Rachel's number but hearing it go straight to voicemail. I took the phone from her hand.

'Look, no signal.' I held it up, waving it. 'Why don't you let me try to get hold of her? You just need to relax. I'll get through to her and leave a message and tell her what's happened. I promise.'

I paced back and forth in the Emergency Department, glancing again and again at my phone screen, my thumb fluttering over Rachel's number but not quite making the connection.

A nurse came rustling though some rubber stripped doors and glanced around the waiting room.

'Anyone here waiting for Alison Birch?'

'Me.' I touched her arm. 'I am.'

'She was asking for you. Do you want to go through?' She held open the rubber strip and I ducked inside.

I was in a cubicled area, endless staff buzzing about. There were trollies and banks of computer screens. I just didn't know where to look.

'Hannah,' a voice said behind me. 'I'm here.'

I whirled round. Alison was propped up on a bed, alone, the wad of bloodied towel lying in her lap.

She shrugged. 'I've got to wait now and see someone. God knows how long that will be. Have you got hold of Rachel yet?'

'I've been trying.' The discomfort of the untruth squeezed in my gut.

'You don't have to hang around, you know, Hannah. I'm honestly fine.'

My phone vibrated in my pocket and my fingers immediately clutched to silence it. I pulled it out and pretended to read the message. 'Oh, it's Rachel.'

'Great.' Alison's face lit up. 'Is she here then?'

'Oh, umm...' I chewed my lip. 'She says she's going to check how Sadie is doing.'

There were faltering seconds.

'Let me just text her and tell her where you are.'

My thumbs tap quickly across the keys. *Have you got a minute?* I ask, and press 'Send'. The phone beeped again almost immediately, and I held the screen out. 'She says: *Busy right now, I'll msg l8r.*'

'Busy?' There was a look of hurt shock on Alison's face. 'Did she even ask how I was?

'You know how dramatic Rachel's life is.' I rolled my eyes and tried to make light of it. 'There'll be some emergency somewhere. I'm sure she'll be here really soon.'

'Well, you're here,' Alison muttered angrily. 'You've shown how much you care. Much more than other people I could mention.'

I didn't reply. Her face was pink with hurt.

'So, thank you for being such a good friend, Hannah. It's at times like this you really get to see who your true friends really are.'

'We're here.' Rachel's voice jolts me back and I stare round at her.

'You're so incredibly gutsy, Hannah.'

I look up to see the long grey wall coming into view. We pull up to a barrier and wait for a few moments before it swings high.

'You're driven by this real moral core of steel, aren't you?'

Her words send my stomach and head spiralling: at what I did back then, and what I am about to do now.

'God, I'm not, Rach, I'm not. I'm nothing like that at all.' Shame, terror, appalling dread, and a grind of sickness, tumble through me over and over.

'You need to see yourself as I see you.' Rachel squeezes my knee encouragingly. 'I think you're the strongest woman I've ever met.'

I manage a trembling smile back. 'I'm not, Rach, honestly. I'm not what you think I am at all.'

TEN

The intensity of my fear ratchets up another notch as I walk resolutely towards the main gates. In twenty minutes from now, I will be sitting opposite the horror of the man I have tried so hard not to face.

Even the thought of him terrorizes me.

He took a part of me back then. He took my joy and my carefree youth. He took that special bit of me between being a girl and being a woman. He took it and defiled it, and now I'm resurrecting him like some dark demon from my nightmares, bringing the darkness into the daylight.

I take my place in the queue of visitors. There's a woman in front of me carrying a little girl nestled into the crook of her neck. The child stares balefully at me over her shoulder and then tiny finger appears from under the collar of her jacket and she points.

'Baby,' she says.

The women looks round and we smile at each other. She has a nice face: very young and very kind-looking.

'Where's baby?' the child tries again, and I feel my face drop.

'Gosh, I'm sorry.' The woman grimaces apologetically. 'She's obsessed with babies at the moment, she thinks everyone should have one.'

I manage to waver a smile back, but something clenches in the pit of my stomach as the queue begins to move forward in earnest. My feet feel as though I'm wading through treacle. Every fibre of me is resisting what I am about to do. The prison gates loom up in front of me. It will only be minutes before I step over the threshold from this world into that one. I take my last look around. The imposing grey walls with their curls of razor-wire stretch out on either side as far as the eye can see. The slitted windows of the cell blocks stare back blankly. There's someone's horror behind each of them.

And my horror is in there, waiting for me.

We step into a holding area. A female prison officer unlocks a gate at the far end, and gestures us over.

'Apologies for the delay, guys. We've had a disturbance on one of the cell blocks, but it's all in hand now, so if you're ready?' She unlocks a wooden door.

The cold wind whips around the side of the gatehouse building, rattling the chain link fence that borders the walkway into the main prison.

'Brrrr. Wow! It's enough to freeze your butt off, eh?' She looks round at me. 'I should've put my padded jacket on.' I can tell she's trying to be friendly. I'm guessing she senses my anxiety. 'Is this the first time you've been in here?'

'Yeah.' I falter a smile back.

'Husband? Fiancé? Boyfriend?'

The notion makes me feel ill.

'I'm here to see Hugo Leach, but I don't know if he'll see me.'

'Oh... Right.' I see the look on her face. She fiddles with the radio on her belt as a kind of embarrassed distraction as we crunch along the gritted path. Plumes of our breath Intermingle in the cold air.

'I suspect he will.' She doesn't look at me.

'It's not because I want to... It's... well, it's complicated. I have to speak to him.'

'Oh, reporter, eh?' She zips her jacket closer under her chin. 'Mmm...' She looks at me sympathetically. 'These editors have a lot to answer for. Soon as the news broke about his release, a whole load of female journos got sent in. They use them like bait. It's disgusting having to talk to a man like that.'

'I'm not a journalist. I'm...' My brain scrambles. 'I'm doing work for one of his victims.'

'Wow.' She looks at me. 'Good stuff.' She shakes her head. 'Tschhh... He's such a disgusting piece of garbage.'

She jangles a key, ramming it into a lock and turning it. 'I shouldn't be saying this to a visitor really.' She rolls her eyes. 'But they talk about "rehabilitation" and "challenging offending behaviour", but it's all codswallop as far as I'm concerned. It's actually one of the reasons I'm jacking this job in, in a couple of months, and doing something worthwhile with my life. You have to wonder what these "professionals" actually know about dangerous men. The psychologists, the behaviour specialists, all banging on about how they can change these animals.' She shrugs. 'When what they're really doing is lining up the next victim for these predators.'

She swings the gate wide. 'Anyway... Here you go.' She holds it open for the group to troop through. 'Most of you know the way. Follow those signs if you're not sure.' She points to where the path disappears into the underbelly of a walkway. I peer into the shadows as the walls of the concrete tunnel grow darker, where even daylight can't penetrate. Tumbling litter and bits of paper whirl and catch. The intermittent gaps in the breezeblock wall are barred, revealing dug-over flowerbeds of white-flecked turned earth. They look like rows of snowy graves.

The entrance to the *Visits* room is pegged open. An officer sits behind a desk in the doorway, holding his hand out for my ID and paperwork. He doesn't raise his eyes, but I know he's clocked the name of who I'm seeing.

My eyes instinctively stray over his shoulder into the Visits Hall. The sick feeling in my throat rises up to almost choke me as terrifying flashes of a face – a face I'd looked at so many times on the internet – dart in front of my eyes. I'd made myself stare and stare at the photos, trawling my memory, hoping it would jog some inkling of the man of that night, but it didn't.

He's sitting where he can watch the door.

I can tell he's been watching for me the whole time. The blue latex-gloved hand of the officer gives me back my I.D. and I find my feet are making me walk over to the last place I ever want to go.

I can't quite believe I'm doing this.

There's a sudden disconnect. He looks nothing like his photographs online. It's as though he's picked out by a search-light in the cavernous warehouse of the visiting space. He's sitting at a small table, hunched forward slightly, his fingers loosely linked in front of him as though about to conduct an interview. Only the orange bib gives it away. He's slim, oddly younger-looking than his pictures, dark-haired as he turns away from me, blankly somewhere off into the distance. Despite myself, I can't take my eyes off him the whole time. There are seconds before he looks up at me, blinking, and then his face breaks into a smile.

Close-up and in the flesh, he looks different than I thought: all fresh-faced and slightly tanned, as though he's spent the last seventeen years in some kind of therapeutic sunshine retreat rather than a dirty, dim-lit prison wing.

'You must be Hannah.'

Good-looking. My brain registers what's right in front of me, but my whole body shakes with instinctive revulsion. *This man raped you,* my gut is screaming. *He violated you.*

'Can I get you some tea?' His head cocks in enquiry as his eyes flicker past my shoulder. I take a quick glance round.

'My friend just there will ask his visitor to go to the tea bar for us.'

Us. My stomach shrinks at the use of the word.

'Troy.'

A lad in his twenties saunters over.

'Get your visitor to grab us two cups of tea, would you?' Leach motions over to the far side of the room where there are two ladies in aprons serving tea and cakes from behind a roller-shuttered hatch. Without questioning, the boy speaks to his visitor, who obediently goes and stands in the queue.

The ordinariness and yet the complete oddness of the action has every warning bell in my head going off.

'Please, have a seat.' Leach gestures with a slim, manicured hand to the chair opposite. 'It would have been nice to do this in more' – he glances at the room – 'salubrious circumstances, you know? A nice café somewhere. You know they're considering my release, don't you?'

'Yes.' My voice sounds thin and reedy.

'And when I do, we could go for a decent coffee,' he offers genially. 'I've had a couple of practice days already – you know how it works with long-term offenders. The idea is to acclimatise me to life on the outside.' He inclines his head in mock-seriousness. 'With an escorting officer of course. But it's so I can get the *feel* for life out there.'

The way he emphasises word sends a prickle of unease down my spine. I try to steady myself.

'Such a surprise to get a last-minute visitor.' He clasps his hands on the table. 'So, how can I help you, Hannah?'

His voice is low and soft as he sits there, half smiling,

eyebrows raised expectantly, his blue eyes crinkling at little at the corners.

I almost couldn't speak.

'I read about you.'

'Ah yes. There's quite a bit to read.' The grin broadens.

'You were convicted of attacking women.'

'I'm pleased to see you didn't use the word guilty there.' He licks his pale lips. 'And, Hannah, can I say, I'm so, so glad you used the past tense.'

He keeps using my name as though he knows me.

'I *was*,' he says pointedly. 'I *was* that person. I used to be that man, but now I feel as though I'm someone else entirely.' He purses his lips as he considers. 'I was a terrible, terrible human being, Hannah. I barely recognise that person who acted purely out of a desire for power, and control, and fear.' He pauses. 'Actually, do you want to hear all this? I don't want to bore you.'

My head says yes without my asking it to.

'Would you like to know my motivation? Is that what you're here to talk about?' he queries, quite seriously. 'It's what I'm normally asked by journalists and authors and the like.' He smiles, totally comfortable, as though he's had this conversation many, many time before.

I give an imperceptible nod.

'Oh. Okay. Right... Here we go then.' He settles back in the seat. 'Yes, Hannah, I was *afraid* of women.' He frowns a little, but it seems rehearsed. '*Was* afraid,' he emphasises. 'However, I've come so far now in the rehabilitative process, thank God. That that's no longer the case.'

A hand comes to his chest. 'It's thanks to all the support I've accessed while in here. I'm no longer the same person I was back then. I've *learned*, you see. I've learned a lot about myself. I'm far more—' He pauses as though searching for the right expression. '*Insightful*. Self-aware. And far, far more aware of others. Of women, especially. Yes, especially women. How intimidated they can feel. How threatened... ' He smiles broadly. His teeth, I notice, slope inward slightly. I blink.

Something inside me...

'So, who do you write for? Or are you one of my female fans, maybe?'

The question doesn't register properly. It's the way he talks about women: lingering on the words, the hum of his savouring them. The lips coming together and then the teeth, that slight click...

A figure appears carrying a tea tray. Troy, the prisoner, bends to unload a tray with two cups of tea and a plate piled high with small packets of biscuits.

'Thanks, Troy, mate. Appreciate it.'

The use of the word 'mate' feels incongruous.

Troy wanders off as Leach nudges the plate towards me. 'Untouched by human hand, see? Quite safe.' His eyes drift from the plate to my shoulder and across my chest. 'We were talking about whether you were a fan or a writer.'

But my head can only scramble in an attempt to answer.

'Oh, don't look so shocked that I'm guessing you're a fan.' He laughs. 'You'd be amazed how many letters of appreciation the men in here get. You'd think that women would be afraid of rapists, wouldn't you? On the contrary, they're fascinated by them. Intrigued. Drawn to them, I'd say.' He picks up his cup and blows across the surface. The smell of the tea and the thought of his breath curling across the table makes my stomach roil.

'I came here to ask—' I force myself to stare directly at him. 'I came here to ask if you know me? Have you seen me before?' I don't drop my eyes, searching for a sign.

His lips pause mid-pout on the edge of his cup before it descends slowly into the saucer without him taking a sip. His mouth puckers into a comic frown as he ponders.

'What an odd question. Umm... Nope. I don't *think* so. Can't say for absolute certain, though.' He waves the cup distractedly. 'But you know how it is. People. Faces. *Women*. So many come and go.'

'I was...' I falter. 'I was at—'

He suddenly lifts a finger. 'Oh. Oh... hold on.'

My stomach and heart collide.

'No... No...' The finger drops, and he purses his lips again. 'No. Sorry. I think you just look very much like someone else I met once. They used to live in this area, so that can't be you, can it? I must be getting muddled.'

He pulls a sad face that suddenly brightens as he leans surreptitiously across the table, the tips of his fingers touching the cup edge again.

'Are you disappointed?'

'What?'

'That I have no knowledge of you?' He smiles with those teeth aligning together. 'Would you like it if I had?'

I can't breathe. I can't move.

'I've studied you women, you know.' He steeples his fingers sitting back. 'All those tedious psychologists have it pinned that us rapists are obsessed with power. That rape *isn't about sex, it's about having complete control over the victim*.' He makes rabbit ears in the air, his voice drops into a comical mimic. 'Pah.' He snorts. 'They have no idea. Shall I tell you what we're all obsessed with? What all men are addicted to?'

I can't take my eyes from his face.

'*Fear.*' He leans forward, half closing his eyes. The lids flicker as he savours the thought before dropping open to stare at me. 'Look around this room now, Hannah... Go on, look.'

My chin twitches round; my eyes are forced to follow.

'See this lot?' He gestured round 'The prisoners, the officers, the male visitors? Do you see them? Well, even without looking I know that every man in here has seen you. They know what you're wearing, how loose or tight your clothes are. Even one of them has run his eyes over your hair, your breasts, your hips. Every one of them is wondering what's between your legs.'

The corner of his mouth tilts with amusement. 'Every. Single. Man.' His eyes stare like dead things before slowly closing. 'But I'm the lucky one. I'm the one sitting here savouring the memory.'

My spine suddenly yanks back, pinning me in the seat.

Leach's eyes grow wider. 'That's shocked you, has it?'

'You... you said mem-memory,' I stutter.

His neck cricks back and he frowns. 'No I didn't.'

'Yes you did. You said—'

'*Moment*. I said *moment*, Hannah.' He flashes a smile. 'Gosh. We have got you all jittery, haven't we?' The grin widens. 'This is what we enjoy, this is what we get off on...' He licks his lips. '... your squirming discomfort. We all have the power to make you afraid. Every man knows instinctively how to do it.'

His neck cranes left and right in one great sweep and then leans forward towards me. 'Every man in the world knows all he has to do is walk over to you without dropping his gaze. He just has to come right up close, too close, invade your space, and your heart rate will be through the roof.' The tip of his tongue rests on his top lip.

'That fear is like a pheromone to all us men. In fact' – he glances quickly down into his lap and then slowly back up, his eyes fixed and glazed – 'I'm getting a hard-on just thinking about it.'

The skin on my arms and neck, my whole body, ripples with loathing. I would love to reach out across that table and feel my nails sinking into the flesh of his cheek – to feel the sudden give and rip; to make that self-satisfied smirk turn instantly to shock and pain.

I stand abruptly, sending my cup of tea spilling across the

table. The visitors on either side look round and I see a couple of officers begin to come over. I hold up a hand to signal that everything is okay.

'I'll get a cloth.' I'm up and away from the horror of that monster, heading towards the tea bar. A woman behind the counter looks at me expectantly.

'You okay my love?'

'Yes. Thank you. I just need—' I begin, and then my eye sees it. She's still standing patiently waiting for me to speak, but I can't tear my eyes away from an over-filled box on the counter.

Red wooden hearts.

My hand automatically reaches out to pick one up. They have copperplate writing on them.

You're Mine and I'm Yours.

'Two pounds for that please. Anything else?'

'A cloth,' I say. 'I've spilled my tea.'

She hands me a roll of Kleenex.

I can barely think straight as I hand over the money, slipping the heart into my pocket as I make my way back to the table and begin mopping up the liquid, aware of Leach watching me intently.

'Do you ever have weird dreams, Hannah?'

I can't bring myself to look at him as I feverishly tear off wads of paper, scooping the spill, watching the Kleenex bloom from white to brown.

'I ask all my visitors the same question. You'd be amazed at some of the answers.' He chuckles. I pile up the soggy mess on the table. He's controlling every moment I'm here and I hate myself for it. I hate the way I've just given in. I hate the way I feel powerless and weak and that I'm allowing him to carry on doing it.

He tips his head on one side. 'I have some very strange ones, I must say.' His voice trails as he muses. 'I don't know if they're dreams per se, or fantasies really. What was it last night...? Oh yes. A beautiful woman bathing naked by candlelight.' He sniggered. 'You wouldn't imagine me as the romantic type, would you?'

My hand pauses around the fist of tissues, and I think my knees might give way.

'Masses of rose petals and hearts. Maybe I'm going soft in my old age.' His eyes flicker from side to side as he leans forward on splayed elbows into my sightline.

I stare down at my knuckles as I clutch for the chair back. My eyes are drawn to the table in front of me that is etched with obscenities, with an even bigger obscenity sitting there, laughing at me.

'I know it was you.'

My voice comes out stronger than I feel.

'What are we talking about here?' His head tilts again.

'I know it was you. All those years ago.'

The tilt of his head inclines a little more. 'You've lost me, Hannah.' He raises his eyebrows in mock query.

'No I haven't. Would you like me to go and speak to someone in the prison?' I sweep a hand across at the prison officers over at the desk. 'Or maybe call in at the police station and tell them? Would you like me to add that to what I already have on you?' I can feel the quiver in my voice, but a steely resolve grips my gut.

'I'm not quite sure what you believe or what you *think* you believe.' Leach lowers his eyes to the tabletop and he begins to trace a line of graffiti with one finger, tracing each obscene word with a dirty nail. 'But whatever it is, you might end up a little embarrassed. My dear, I'm already serving a prison sentence for the crimes I have committed. For the ones I've confessed to. I've owned up to them you see. *All* of them.'

I keep my eyes locked on him as he tick-tock's his head in amusement.

'So what you actually have on me, Hannah, is precisely nothing.'

'You're sick.' I hear the tremble in my voice.

He inclines his head gracefully. 'You say the most flattering things.'

'But I'm onto you.' I can feel my heart drumming; I won't let him intimidate me now.

He lowers his cup, and slowly leans forward. 'And I, Hannah,' he whispers, 'am onto you.'

The air leaves my lungs. I'm struck mute.

He leans back expansively and takes a breath. 'So, where were we?' His eyes narrow. 'Ah yes, the facts are, you're saying you've "got something", yes? Which means you're going to try to negotiate with me. Have I got that right? And now you're just about to use it as leverage, which means I have something you want? How am I doing so far?'

The tip of his grey tongue runs across his bottom lip. I try not to watch it.

This is it. This is what you've wanted all these years.

I am aware that the front of my jacket is shaking. I can feel the flutter of it against my skin. His eyes flit to my throat and the corners of his mouth lift a little.

'So,' he continues. 'I give you what? Some kind of confession? Is that it? I tell you all about what happened at that party?' His index finger halts in its tracing.

A punch of fear thumps through my gut. 'You know… You're admitting you know?'

But he ignores the question.

'So, I'm asking myself why would I do that?' He's toying with me. 'Because of some vague unsubstantiated threat? Is that what you're hoping?' His eyes crinkle.

There's a tremor running the length of my spine that won't stop; my legs are trembling. This man is a creature. He has defined and shaped my whole life. I belong to him whether I want to or not.

Fear.

He's crippled me with it.

My own fear.

But the fear is all yours, a voice says.

The voice is right.

The fear belongs to me; I feel it, I own it, I'm sitting here shivering and shaking with it. It's *mine* – to do with as I please.

I don't blink back. I stare into his eyes: into the tiny black circles of darkness. I hold myself very, very steady.

'You first then.' His amused dead eyes map my face. 'You show me yours and then I'll show you mine.'

'I want you to admit that you raped me.' I feel no emotion. 'That night. Seventeen years ago. At a student party. You know the one. You were there,' I bluff.

But he hears the slight quiver of uncertainty in the last sentence. His tongue darts out again like a lizard.

'I was at a student party, Hannah?' He frowns, all concerned, as he leans forward. 'I would've been a bit old for all that even seventeen years ago.'

He has an expression on his face that I've seen so many times: all those super-professional counsellors and therapists, all hushy-breathed and earnest-eyed. It's all there – the copying every mannerism, every vocal tic.

'The police said you were a drug dealer so they overlooked you initially. It gave you access to young, vulnerable women. I think I was your practice run. I've studied your other victims. I think I was your first.'

He nods solicitously like some overzealous social worker.

'And what makes you think you were the first?' He's all mock query. 'Just so I can understand your train of thought here.'

'Because what happened to me is so similar to what

happened to them but doesn't completely follow the same pattern. I was drugged so there are things I can't remember – and I *want* to remember. I *need* to remember.' I swallow my fear down. I'm breathing heavily.

'Right. I see. I understand what you're asking.' He glances away to see if anyone's listening. 'What can you possibly have that would incriminate me after all this time?'

'Because I have something of yours. Something you didn't know I'd taken from you.' I make my voice go dead.

There's a slight tic, but he doesn't stop smirking.

'And what might that be, sweetheart?'

I reach down for my bag and open it. Delving inside I draw out a folded piece of paper and push it with one finger, across the table to him.

His thin hand appears above the table edge. 'Nuh-uh.' I shake my head slowly. 'Wait a minute. There's something else you should see.'

I dip again, bringing out a cutting from a local newspaper.

'What's all this supposed to be?' His eyes narrow.

'This,' I said slowly, 'is a photograph of a building site that's about to be developed right here in Mexborough.'

'A mini housing estate of affordable homes has been granted planning permission by Bradfield City Council. Permission for twelve entry-level homes has been granted under the "Right-to-Regenerate" scheme to Miller-Framlin Developers,'

I read.

His expression drops into a dismissive twitch. 'Fascinating, Hannah. And a worthy project I'm sure, but I'm not sure what private redevelopment plans are to do with me?' His smile is effortlessly patronising.

I take my finger off the piece of paper, swivelling it round. 'Think of it as a kind of puzzle. The clues are: These people are going to develop it. They're going to dig. In digging, they could very well find things, especially if someone tells them precisely where to look.'

His eyes flicker warily as he attempts to work it out. Then they lift to face me in a sneer.

'Like what?'

I don't speak.

His face doesn't falter, but his Adam's apple does.

'Dig?' He collects himself. 'Dig for what? Even if you do have something, and this is all probably a lie, whatever it is, you'll never be able to find it again. You know that.'

'Won't I?'

'And whatever it is, it will have rotted or rusted. They'll get nothing from it.'

'Is that right?'

I can see his brain whirring behind his eyes.

'You're lying,' he says, but he's not so confident now. I hear it in his voice. He's worried.

A thrill goes though me. 'So, you're just going to have to take a chance, are you? When you're this close to being released?' I hold up my thumb and forefinger. They don't shake.

He blinks as it dawns.

'But you're prepared to tell me where... whatever this thing is is buried?'

'If I get the truth about what happened to me. And I'll know if you're lying. I want the details.'

His eyes are dead holes in his skull. I see his jaw moving as though savouring something on his tongue; his cheeks suck and fall.

'Okay.'

I instantly think I might throw up.

'I'll make you a deal, Hannah.'

My throat closes involuntarily.

'You describe everything you can remember from that

night.' His eyes widen a little. 'Every tremor, every panic, every little frisson of alarm... I want to know what it felt like, what it smelled like, how every nerve ending shimmered and sparked. And in return, I'll give you the minute details so you'll know it was me.'

It feels as though there's a trapped bird caught my ribcage; its wings beat and beat, desperate to get out.

'It'll be a journey, Hannah. You and me. A re-connection. We can find your missing past. I'll help you.'

The caged bird beats and beats its wings. I want to scream.

'I will fill in all the gaps. I will give you your memory back. That little something of yours that I have, in exchange for that little something of mine.' He shows his shark teeth again.

I think I might heave. Something sour rises up on my tongue. I want to let it come up and out, sliding over my teeth like poison. Get it out of me: gag it up, dry retch it, until there's nothing left but a gasping purge of all the darkness inside of me.

But I don't.

I get up as slowly as I am able. I won't let him inside my head, but I'm scared my face will give me away as I silently lean forward and leave a tiny, folded piece of paper on the table in front of him.

'Had enough?' The officer walking towards me enquires, jangling her keys and turning to the door to unlock it.

'More than enough,' I mutter through tightened teeth. 'I need a bath, a shower, disinfectant. I need to burn my clothes. I feel like I'll never be clean again.'

The officer lets me out of the gate and I walk steadily back down the walkway to the main gate, keeping my shoulders stiff and my head held high despite the churning that's happening in my guts.

All I can see in front of me is that look on Leach's face as his disgusting hand slithered across the table, greedy to know what was on the paper. The way his tongue bobbed from between his lips as he scrabbled it up. In those seconds I watched his nails pick apart the paper folds as I turned to go. He read what I'd written there, his face pausing for a second in shock, and then setting into something hard, something dead behind the eyes as I began to walk away.

'You stupid bitch.' His voice shivered between my shoulder blades and into my hair line, but I kept on going.

'I know where you are, Hannah. Remember that.'

His voice hissed through the air, whistling past me, aimed at me, and me alone. I felt something flick against my hand and I glanced down. There was the piece of paper tumbling at my feet as I lifted my heel to step onto it. My heel lifted and the four little words I wrote were exposed; four little words that had all the power to topple his filthy world.

I have your DNA.

But I've just made a pact with the Devil.

ELEVEN

The huge prison gate shunts closed behind me. The snowy car park is still: nothing moves. I can't remember where Rachel was parked and a run of anxiety shifts through me. I need to get out of this place, and quickly. I feel for my phone, glancing from left to right, desperate to see a friendly face. She answers straightaway.

'You okay?'

'Where did you park? I can't find you.'

'I can see you. I'll get out and wave; hang on...'

I look up and spot her, only a few cars away, slotted in behind a truck. She disappears below the roof line as I hurry over, my eyes registering that something is different somehow, yet my brain can't quite fathom what it is. I go to reach for the passenger door and then stop.

There's a stranger sitting there. She looks round in greeting, gesturing towards the back seat.

'Hello,' she says brightly, offering a hand between the seats as I slide inside. 'I'm Emily.'

I dumbly take it.

'Emily, Hannah – Hannah, Emily Travers.' Rachel's palm

sweeps from one of us to the other. 'I think I might've mentioned that Emily works at the prison, didn't I?'

'No, you didn't. Hello, Emily.' I'm trying to act normally.

'But I had no idea we'd bump into her. It's the perfect opportunity for you two to meet,' Rachel continues while Emily is smiling and nodding, nodding and smiling.

I'm aware of Rachel scanning my face. 'Everything okay Hannah?'

'Fine.' I automatically give the right response.

'How did it go?'

'I think I got what I needed.'

'Right. Good.' Rachel's eyes flit briefly to Emily. 'Em and I spoke briefly on the phone. I told her a bit about your situation.'

I can't believe Rachel would do such a thing. She doesn't pick up on the look on my face.

'It was such a coincidence that she should be walking across the car park,' Rachel starts, hesitantly. There's a pregnant pause. 'And I suddenly wondered if it might be useful for her to wait for you to come out? You two could talk.' Rachel is measuring her words.

'Emily knows all about prisoners being released on licence. I was thinking she could advise you how to handle it.' She looks meaningfully at me.

I'm aware of the ache in my cheeks as I try to hold it all together.

'So, you've been to see Hugo?' Emily says, not missing a beat.

The use of his name stuns me.

'Maybe I should explain, Hannah.' She smiles. 'I do a lot of work with a whole range of police departments.' Her smile has a dead quality to it. 'I advise them on cases. On supporting victims of crime – particularly violent crime.'

I'm a case. I'm a victim.

'And part of that process is working with violent offenders who are due for release.'

She looks at Rachel who hasn't taken her eyes from me.

Emily keeps an inane grin plastered across her face. She has that no makeup scrubbed look and her fair hair is piled up in a messy bun, with tendrils of it hanging in curls around her dangly boho earrings. I am trying so hard not to judge her, not to see her like all those others who don't ever really understand but think they do.

'I don't know much about your situation, but I know how terrifying it must be for you to think of these people wandering about free on the streets again.'

No you don't. You only think you do.

'But we have to find a way of dealing with it so that you're able to live your life without fear.'

'This is what Emily does, you see,' Rachel puts in enthusiastically.

I feel myself go very still.

'Emily runs Victim Awareness courses to help offenders understand the impact of their crimes. So she understands, Hannah. She gets it.' Rachel skews around in her seat. 'She sees both sides.'

Both sides?

'We have to manage the behaviour of offenders when they leave prison. We have to support them, but at the same time, we have to support the victims too.' Emily's earrings bob and sway with earnest zeal.

'I guess it must be really hard for you right now, Hannah.' Emily's fingers grip the back of the seat as she tips her head to one side. 'Just let me say, if I'm able to help you in any way at all, whatever you'd like to share with me, just know I'm here for you.'

'Thank you,' I hear my voice saying. 'That's very kind.'

'Should we go for coffee, do you think?' Rachel looks from

me to her. 'It might be really nice if the three of us could spend some time together?' I see Emily is in agreement. 'Maybe find somewhere for lunch at the same time? Get to know each other properly? Does that sound good?'

I don't know what else I can say.

'Love to.' Emily and Rachel share a look as I sit silently in the back in my seat. We make our way out of the car park. I watch their faces in profile as they chat and exchange glances, sharing amiable snippets of conversation I can't hear. I am aware of Rachel occasionally snatching looks at me in the rear-view mirror.

Everything has an air of unreality. I have just faced the worst thing in the world and suddenly it feels like it's forgotten. Is this how it always was with Rachel, but I've never acknowledged it before? Is Matt right – is she totally on your side until something new and more interesting comes along?

The emotions come at me thick and fast: anger, hurt, sadness, terror at what I have to face – and me sitting in the centre as they swirl around me. Where has Rachel gone when I need her the most? I'm thinking Matt was right.

'So, where do we fancy going?' Rachel looks across at Emily, and then briefly at me in the mirror.

'What about that Italian café place – you know the one we really like?' Emily suggests.

'Oh yes. Yes, let's go there.'

It's as though this isn't happening. *What is she thinking?*

I say nothing as Rachel indicates to turn into a side road and I watch the streets, familiar, yet unfamiliar, unfolding in front of me. I see myself, my eighteen-year-old self, crossing this road, going into the little grocery shop – one that's no longer there. The bakery has gone too, the shoe repair shop, the antique dealer, all these markers of my past have disappeared. Maybe confronting Leach is just some crusading fantasy. Maybe the easiest option all round is that I should just disappear too?

'I'm going to pop into the shop next door.' Emily peers out of the window. 'If you two don't want to join me, you can wait for me in the café. I won't be long.'

'That vintage shop?' I watch Rachel's eyes widen in the mirror. 'Wow! We'd love to go with you, wouldn't we, Hannah? Gosh, I haven't been in there for years.'

'Great. It'll be fun,' enthuses Emily.

'Rachel.' I am aware my voice sounds flat amongst all the chatter.

'What?' She parks up, glancing round at me. I realise this is the place that Rachel and I used to come to at weekends. This was 'our' place; this is where we spent hours poking about, giggling and being silly. The memories come at me thick and fast.

'You remember this place then? You remember what fun we used to have here?' Rachel grins round at me.

Emily is already halfway out, heading to get a ticket from the machine as Rachel swings open her door.

'Rachel,' I say again, and she pauses, aware of my tone. She reaches over the seat and grabs my hand.

'Trust me on this one,' she says quietly. 'The moment I saw Emily in the car park, I realised that she would be a brilliant ally for you. She's a great person to talk to and she knows Leach. Confide in her a bit, Hannah. Seriously. I know she'll be an amazing person to have on your side. I can see how defensive and tense you are, but you two need to get to know each other; just go with the flow and open up to her a bit.'

I feel my insides melt a little with gratitude. *Maybe I'd overreacted. I'd read her all wrong.*

'Can you do that? I realise it's hard.' Rachel's eyes scan my face.

'I can try.' I swallow.

'Brave girl,' Rachel says, getting out and pulling open the

back door. 'Now come on, let's take your mind off all this horribleness for a while and let's enjoy some positive vibes.'

Emily is already scooting through the stacked rails, looking up to smile at us as we join her. The shop has barely changed; all boho nooks and crannies with a mad jumble of colours and textures. There are velvet dresses and jackets, funky platform boots, endless strands of beads and scarves hanging on every surface. Despite myself, there is something very calming about being here in this treasure-trove cavern of dimmed lights with the drift of incense.

I stick to Rachel's side for a while and then find myself relaxing; the three of us separate, me moving around the rails in a kind of dream, allowing my fingers to enjoy the momentary textures. Not thinking too much, just staying right in the present.

I look over to see Rachel and Emily holding up a dress between them, passing it back and forth.

'What do you think of this, Hannah?' Rachel holds it up. 'Or this one?' She grabs another. 'Or possibly this?'

'Umm... Not sure.' I offer, wrinkling my nose. Part of me so wants to join in and feel normal again. 'I think you'd have to try them on. They might look different than on the hanger.'

She glances at Emily. 'Shall I bother trying it? You said you like this one best, don't you?'

'As I said, go and try them all on.' Emily points to a curtained-off corner. It's as though I haven't suggested precisely the same thing.

Rachel disappears leaving me and Emily sauntering between the racks; there's a sudden awkward moment where I know she wants to say something, but not quite knowing how.

'You fancy sitting down for a few minutes while we wait?' She gestures towards a couple of saggy armchairs. 'Shall we?' Emily moves to sit in one, leaving me no real choice but to perch on the other. She links her fingers around her knee, leaning back in the chair.

She tips her head to one side.' I know we've only just met, but Rachel has told me a lot about you. I'd love to chat with you, Hannah – and help you if I can. Would that be something you'd be up for?'

My spine stiffens a little, but I'm trying really hard not to come across as so defensive.

'I want you to know you can trust me, Hannah.'

I squirm a little.

'If you ever need to talk to someone, I'm a really good listener.'

I take a small breath. 'What's Rachel told you?'

'She's said you'd been to see Hugo Leach because you believe he was the man who attacked you when you were a student.'

I'm aware of my lungs inflating slowly.

'You see, I know Hugo Leach very well.' She blinks infuriatingly and then frowns a little. 'You know he's close to release, yes?'

'Yes.'

I can't quite glean her angle.

'So, it's quite a delicate time. Obviously there have been some pretty high-level conversations happening as he's been in the public eye.'

Delicate? I try to quell my objection to her use of the word.

'I mean, this must be so, so difficult for you and you must be having to deal with a lot, but—'

'He's practically confessed to me,' I blurt.

Her eyes raise in genuine shock.

'He's confessed? What, to attacking you?'

'Not in so many words.' I stumble. 'Not yet... But he says he will.'

'He says he will?'

I realise how weird that statement sounds.

'If I—' The rest of the statement sticks in my throat. If I what? How do I articulate the deal I've just made? No one, no one in their right mind would sit across a table from a rapist while he got off on you recounting your memory of your attack.

I am aware of Emily's patiently expectant face watching and waiting for me to explain.

'I mean, I'm thinking he will,' I start. 'If I go to see him again and let him talk freely and openly.'

The slight shadow of a frown crosses her face as the cubicle curtain suddenly swishes back and Rachel appears. She knows how good she looks as she fiddles with the tie belt of a woollen dress. It's sapphire blue, long and a kind of hippy-ish, wrapped-over style. The colour looks fantastic on her. She stands on tiptoes with her back to me so that she can see herself in the mirror and she twists her hair up, glancing at her reflection: this way and that.

'What do you think?' She looks at Emily in the mirror and then at me.

'I really like that on you,' Emily chimes in before I can even open my mouth.

'Should I get it? The other things I tried weren't up to much.'

'Yeah, I definitely would.' Emily's eyes scan back and front. 'It's so different from your usual style, and it would go beautifully with those boots you bought. You know the ones?'

'Mmm...' Rachel regards herself and then snaps to me. 'Actually, one of these others I tried, would probably suit you, y'know. Here' – she reaches back into the cubicle and pulls out a corduroy dress – 'remember how good I used to be at choosing clothes for you?' She grins. 'Look.' She flaps it out and pushes it into my arms. 'Honestly, it's so you. Trust me. Try it, go on.'

'I'm really hungry,' Emily announces. 'Shall we go and grab that lunch we were talking about? I'm famished.'

Rachel swishes past me as she goes up to the counter to pay for the dress. 'Okay?' She beams. 'You two been chatting?' Her expression is open as she flits a look from Emily to me. I manage to fix my face and nod agreeably.

'You're getting that then?' Rachel glances down at the dress she's chosen for me. 'You don't need to try it. Just trust me.' She winks. 'Like the old days.'

'Actually, both of you should wear your dresses tonight,' Emily says firmly.

'Tonight?' I look at them both.

'Rachel and Matt are coming for dinner, didn't she mention it? So, why don't you come along?' Emily looks directly at me; it's difficult to say no. 'I'm not that bad a cook, am I, Rachel? You've managed to survive every time.'

I think about the horror of us all sitting around a table. I can't imagine an evening more loaded with possible disaster. I take a quick read of Rachel, but Rachel only looks back at me steadily.

'Of course she will.' She puts a hand on the drape of fabric. I can feel the warmth of her touch on my arm. 'Like I said, it'll be just like the old days, won't it: you, me and Matt?' She giggles a little but there's a tiny flinch of desperation. If she hasn't confided the Matt situation with Emily, then I'm suspecting she's looking for a bit of moral support.

'Well, if you'd *like* me to be there...'

Rachel looks relieved. 'I'd love you to be there.'

'If you're sure that okay with you, Emily?'

'More than okay.' Her eyes twinkle with pleasure. 'It'll be a great opportunity to get to know you better.'

We step out onto the snowy pavement. A pathway down the centre has been cleared, forcing us into single file. I manage to lag behind, surreptitiously pulling my phone out and pretending to check for messages but I'm scrolling for Matt's number.

> Did you know about dinner at Emily's tonight?
> I've been invited

'Oh, looks pretty busy.' Emily stops with a hand on the door of the café. 'Maybe we should've booked.' She holds it open.

The café has that pleasant fug of steam and the damp smell from snowy coats. It does look pretty full. My phone pings.

> Yeah. Purgatory

> But thank god you'll be there as my bit of sanity.

Sliding the phone back into my pocket, I distract them by gesturing over to a tiny corner table in the window. 'Shall we grab that one?'

Emily heads over, leaving Rachel and I to stand in the queue. There's a dizzying array of fabulous-looking food banked up on display in the glass-fronted counter and Rachel gives my arm a little squeeze.

'How are you feeling?'

'Okay.'

'Was it truly awful? Seeing Leach, that is?' Her eyes scan my face. 'Did you get any of the answers you wanted?'

My mind is immediately full of the threat of him knowing where I am, and that description of the rose petals and the bath. I shiver. I suddenly don't know if I can eat a thing. I'm aware of Rachel's comforting hand in the small of my back.

'Looks like it was bad.'

'Yeah. It was.' I find I can't articulate any more than that.

'Oh god.' Rachel frowns. 'I really worry for you.'

'I think he's playing me.' I swallow. 'I definitely think he knows me too. And d'you know what, Rachel? Even if I don't get anywhere... even if he doesn't confess and not one single person believes me, the fact is, deep, deep in my gut, I know that monster will carry on where he left off seventeen years ago.

The moment he's back on the streets, is the moment he'll start again.'

Rachel blinks rapidly. 'But Emily thinks—'

'Never mind what Emily thinks, Rach,' I bite. 'I'm telling you, you would only have to sit opposite that man for two minutes to know *precisely* what he was and *exactly* how he's wired. Your gut would tell you instantly.'

She nods but I don't think she's convinced. But I am. That prison officer was right: let that filth back on the street and all that will happen is that you're lining up Leach's next victim.

I am suddenly aware of the expression on her face.

'What?' I query.

She presses her lips together before she speaks.

'Look, Hannah, you must do exactly what's right for you, but don't sacrifice your mental health in the process. Are you listening to me?' Rachel dips her head to make me look at her. 'You do whatever it takes to right the wrong that was done to you.' I am suddenly aware of the personal sacrifice that Rachel is making too. I go to speak, but she cuts across. 'This is why I'm saying talk to Emily.'

She dips her head lower until I'm forced to look her in the eye. 'Seriously. Do not take my situation into account, Hannah. We're way, way beyond that now. This thing is bigger than both of us. You're strong, you've had your power taken away from you, but not anymore, Hannah.'

The burn of tears at the back of my throat comes out of nowhere.

I sniff and search for a tissue as we shift forwards in the queue.

Rachel looks at me, defiant. 'And you want to know something else? You coming here has really made me assess things. Like about what happened in the past... what's happening now with Matt. I think what we did on that waste ground affected me more than I ever realised.' She looks away abruptly. 'Maybe it wasn't coincidence that I went to work in Children's Services. Maybe, in some weird way, I've been atoning for what we did – saving kids, when—' She hesitates and looks away.

'I understand, Rach. Really I do.'

'And I shouldn't have tried to sort the marriage out with Matt.' Her gaze turns to meet mine. 'I just felt so guilty. I've felt guilty and in reality I've been clinging onto a relationship that died a long time ago. So thank you, Hannah. Your struggles have shown me how much of a coward I've been. You think you've been running away from everything, but in my own way, I've been running too.'

She leans forward and gives me a little kiss on the cheek.

The sensation both shocks and delights me. Whatever I'd been going through in my head, suddenly stills and calms. I realise, in that moment, Rachel and I are bound in a way that can't be broken. We've shared something that changed both our lives forever, and somehow, in the midst of all this horror, we've found each other again.

'Hello, ladies, what can I get you?'

I look up to see a bubbly, round-faced woman behind the counter. She has flour dust on her rosy cheeks as she sweeps a stray curl out of her eyes with her forearm. Rachel points out an oval earthenware pot oozing with cheesy cannelloni.

'Three of those, and a green salad for us all to share please.'

Rachel gestures to where Emily is sitting. 'We're just over there in the window.' She points over. Emily is on her phone. She catches my look and puts it down as we squeeze our way back through the tables.

'There,' Rachel breathes as she pulls out her chair. 'I've ordered for all of us. Did you want to ask about wine?'

I go to sit too but realise there are only two chairs.

'Ah yes, sorry,' Emily says distractedly. 'I didn't like to go in search of one in case I lost the table. Are you able to grab one from somewhere?' She casts over at the other tables as Rachel hands her the wine list and suddenly that old feeling of being forgotten washes over me. I try to fight it as I attempt to scout pathetically from table to table, interrupting conversations and muttering, *Sorry... sorry, is this free? Sorry,* as people shake their heads and hang on to their chairs. Finally, I locate one, bumping it over awkwardly and finding myself crammed into a corner.

'Isn't this nice?' Emily lifts a hand to pin up a stray tendril of hair and a load of sliver bracelets jangle down her arm. 'I love spending time chatting over food. We don't do this often enough, do we, Rach?' She smiles at Rachel and then turns her attention to me. 'Rachel mentioned you're a teacher.' She cups her chin in her palm. 'And you were at a Ministry of Justice conference for young offenders? I get to know what's taking place locally.'

I begin to panic slightly.

'Oh yeah, I've done bit and pieces here and there.'

'Oh, I think it's fascinating.' Emily's eyes widen. 'That's definitely part of the correctional service I'm interested in exploring further. Maybe you'd talk to me about it tonight?'

A harassed-looking waitress appears and saves me from further exploration on the subject. Rachel and Emily begin to discuss wine as I glance over at the window. Its steamed-up pane filters the passers-by into a blurry rush. I have a clench of terror at the thought that Leach will be out there one day, walking amongst young women, choosing his next target. Leach with his dirty mind and thoughts about me... memories about me...

'Didn't you—?'

I realise that Rachel has just spoken to me.

They're both sitting looking expectantly.

'You were saying earlier you thought it would be good to talk to Emily, didn't you?' Rachel is trying to be encouraging. Emily's bush-baby eyes regard me sympathetically.

'As I said before, I know Hugo very well.' She traces a line on the tabletop; I am instantly reminded of his finger doing the same. My skin crawls.

'And he was receptive? I mean, he was willing to talk to you?'

I watch her carefully. 'He was prepared to talk to me, yes,' I say levelly.

'Right, right.' Her head bobs about in that patronising way. 'And did you come away feeling you had some answers?'

There's a thump of angry blood in my ears at the memory of his sickening face leering across the table. The smell of the place. The taunts as he offered me his 'deal'.

Emily crinkles her eyes at me. 'Maybe it would be helpful if I share a couple of things that might be useful to you going forward, Hannah?'

I want to wipe that smile off her face.

'The work I do, the *really* important part of the work' – Emily looks at me to emphasise the point – 'is to enable offenders to talk openly about the crimes they have committed. To admit what they've done, in simplistic terms. But what's not so simple is to get them to understand and accept the pain and suffering they've caused, but most of all, most *importantly...*' She does that crinkly eye thing again. '...is for them to empathise with their victims. To regret and be deeply shamed by their past actions.'

She leans back as the wine is delivered over her shoulder.

'And you believe that Leach is deeply shamed?' I watch her face.

She tilts her head in a patronising way. 'Believe me, unless I was totally convinced of that with *any* offender who attended one of my courses, he would *not* be getting out.'

This unshakeable confirmation of her own blindness almost takes my breath away.

'Of course, many of the offenders are also required to attend drug rehabilitation programmes too, as we often find that that many crimes are fuelled by addiction.' She holds up a placating hand. 'Not that drug use by an offender excuses his crimes in any way at all... but it does go some way to explain and mitigate behaviour.'

All I can see in my mind's eye is that sick face hanging in front of me, smirking as he made his sly, smutty jokes, power-crazed and hungry for his next fear fix.

'So often,' Emily continues high-handedly, 'these offenders, in layman's terms, are "not in their right mind" when they commit their offences, and this is what the Parole Board looks at. My job, in running these courses, is to inform the Board how receptive a prisoner has been to changing, and how willing he is to address his offending behaviour.'

My every nerve ending is on high alert.

Slowly she picks up her glass and takes a sip. 'Can I just ask – and I'm sorry to be so direct, Hannah, but what is it that makes you believe it was Hugo who attacked you?'

I watch her throat lift and fall as she swallows. The action is so casual.

'Hannah's done a lot of research,' Rachel puts in quickly in my defence. 'She's drawn parallels between what happened to the other women and what happened to her.'

Emily's eyes graze my own. 'And did you confront him directly?'

'I did.'

'That's very important if you're going to get any kind of closure.'

How I hate that word.

'But I'm assuming as you're here and not at the police station, you realised—?' She waves the wine glass.

'We've agreed we'll speak again.' I lick my lips.

'So, he really is trying to help you.' She sits back a little in her seat.

Rachel gives me an encouraging smile.

Emily nods, putting down her glass with a satisfied smile. 'This tells me such a lot, Hannah. This really illustrates how far Hugo has come. It demonstrates a maturity and an empathy that he just wouldn't have shown years ago.' She blinks rapidly, turning her phone over on the table. 'Which is why I'm prepared to share something with you.' She picks it up and scrolls through the screen. 'Hugo has spoken to his casework officer about all this, who in turn, has spoken to me.'

There's a quick sip of air that inflates my lungs.

'He mentioned that he'd agreed to help you.' She looks up from her phone. I'm aware of Rachel's eyes flitting, anxiously between us.

'He wanted his casework officer to know that he was open to any questions you might have: that he actually *wants* to be confronted and challenged. He really is *owning* his offending behaviour. It's so, so beneficial. It's a *very* positive sign that he's been successfully rehabilitated.'

That night, that party.

The horror.

Sanitised and condensed into palatable words: *owning*, and *offending behaviour*.

I observe myself sitting at this table as though far away. I'm aware of Emily talking on and on. Rachel is replying, but I can't hear either of them. I want to grab hold of the table edge and heave – watch their shocked faces turn to me in horror at the crash of broken glass and the splintering of wood. But I contain the fury to allow my tongue to articulate the words.

'There will be more victims, Emily. You must know that. You won't stop him.'

My voice sounds reedy, as though someone else is speaking.

Emily looks a little taken aback but then gives me her warmest smile. 'I know you must doubt the rehabilitation process, Hannah. I do understand your fear.'

I look into her gullible, ego-driven face, aware that she is playing with a darkness, believing that she can control it when all the time, it's controlling her.

I can't even begin to explain it. I know that darkness. I've seen it. I've felt it inside me. I knew the poison of it is still in there eating away at me.

'Which is why, in the light of all this, I'm hoping you'll agree to this meeting his caseworker is suggesting. You, me and Hugo. I'm thinking if we could sit down, the three of us, in a properly managed setting, so that you feel really supported, Hannah' – her hand hovers above the tabletop – 'and you get to speak to him, make him hear what you need him to hear, ask the questions you need answers to – it would be hugely beneficial to both you *and him.*'

'Who suggested this... this idea?' I ask carefully. 'Was it you? Was it the casework officer?'

There's the minutest shift in her seat. I know exactly who suggested it. I know exactly who would want an audience for his next performance where he'll make me dance and squirm and all for nothing. I know that now.

'It was a joint solution,' Emily says.

I can only stare at her.

'You see, Hannah, I think he genuinely wants to help you to move forward.' She looks at Rachel to draw her into agreement. 'It's a way that he can do something good, you see. A way of making reparation for the past.'

The waitress appears again with a tray of food and begins sliding it onto the table.

Rachel and Emily begin moving glasses and cutlery around on the table to make space for the salad, passing the serving spoons between them. I'm forced to eat, taking a mouthful of pasta, feeling the thickness of the sauce coating my tongue and making me gag.

I can't do this. I can't listen to any more. I'm aware of the hubbub of chatter around me, the scrape and chink in a cacophony of endless noise.

'Do you know what?' I remark loudly, and they both stop talking and look at me.

'I'm beginning to think you're right,' I say, bringing the glass to my lips with a grateful look. I want them to think they've convinced me; that I've seen the sense of what's being proposed. *Yes, I'll put myself in expert Emily's hands.* But all the time I'm thinking quite the opposite.

He says he knows where I am. Well, I know where he is too; he's in prison, and in prison is where I want him to stay. I'll go to their meeting, I'll play their games – but only to get what I want. How much would it take to get questions asked about a high-profile prisoner? How many journalists would I need to speak to, to create enough of a story that releasing him becomes a problem? I might not be able to stop it, but I can make it more difficult.

Leach thinks he's clever, but I'll be cleverer – I'll dog him like a shadow. I'll be there, always in the background; follow him to the ends of the earth and make his life a living hell. And hell is where he belongs.

TWELVE

'You'll come to mine around seven then, yes?'

'Yep, perfect. Looking forward to it.'

Emily swings the door shut and lifts a hand as Rachel turns the car around and we head home. I'm aware that Rachel has gone very quiet.

'You okay?' I glance across at the side of her face.

'Not really.' She shakes her hair from her eyes for a moment. 'But you've got enough on your plate right now without me adding to it.'

I hear her phone vibrate quietly in her pocket, twice, but she makes no attempt to look at it. I don't ask why: I'm guessing it's James.

We pull up in the road away from the house and she kills the engine. She sits with her hands in her lap for a moment, not moving.

'You don't want to go back in there, do you?' I say quietly.

She looks round at me. I see her eyes are red-rimmed.

'Oh, Rachel,' I start, but she shakes her head quickly, biting her lip.

'What I said before is so true, Hannah. I've been such

coward. I haven't told anyone about what's happening with me and Matt. Emily thinks she warned me off James and it's all hunky-dory at home again.' She closes her eyes. 'And I haven't disabused her.' She presses her fingers into her forehead.

'I mean, what's happening to me is nothing, *nothing* in comparison to what you're facing...' She chews her lip. 'But the thought of facing Matt and talking through it all.' She turns her pained eyes to me. 'If he's seeing someone, I just need to know. I just want all the lies to stop.'

My stomach instantly clenches.

'And then there's Emily...' She sighs. 'I haven't told her the full truth either. I promised that I wouldn't see James, and I'd block his calls, but' – she looks up, staring out into the road at nothing – 'I just can't stop thinking about him. Every time there's another row with Matt, I'm reminded—' Her voice falters.

'How happy you could be with someone else.'

Her phone buzzes again. I glance at her pocket, but she only gives me a watery smile. 'I've stopped checking to be honest. She's right, I should block him, but I can't bring myself to. See? I told you I was a coward.' But then she shakes her uncertainty away. 'Seriously, Hannah, ignore me.'

'We're in this together, Rach.' I reassure her. 'We'll get through it. Both of us.'

She gives me a shaky smile as we clamber out into the dirty slush of snow. She squeezes my hand as she pushes open the front door.

There's an eerie silence. Rachel peers around anxiously, listening for Matt as I shrug off my coat.

'He's probably holed-up in his office.' Rachel sighs. 'He hasn't replied to my text reminding him about dinner at Emily's tonight. That probably means yet another argument.'

I don't say anything, wondering how on earth I'm going to get through it.

'I'll go and get showered.' I pluck at my clothes. 'I can still smell the prison on them. Sorry, I'll be down in a minute.'

I head up the stairs. My head is buzzing. I think of this meeting with Leach – how I'll play it; then I think of Emily and how she might try to discredit me; and then what Rachel's just told me. And then, I look up...

The door to my room is not as I left it.

My hand pauses, hovering in the gap, knowing it's just too wide, and I peer inside into the darkness. My spine tingles knowing there's someone there. For a second, I can't move.

'Hanny?'

I nearly leap out of my skin.

'Matt!' I hiss. 'What the hell?'

Glancing quickly behind, I close the door quietly and stand there blinking into the shadows. I can make out the hump of the duvet in the darkness. He shifts a little, the side of his face appearing over the edge.

'Sorry, I shouldn't be in here,' he mutters as he pushes away the cover and struggles to sit up. 'I missed you so much, so I came in to lie on your bed... Does that make me sound crazy?'

'You can't be in here.'

'I know, I know.'

'You can't do this, Matt.'

He pushes back the covers. 'Tonight. We'll get through tonight, Hanny, then I'll tell her. I'll tell Rachel what happened and how I feel about you.'

'No.' It comes out fiercer than I'd expected. 'No. You can't, Matt.'

'You don't want me to be truthful?'

'Look, it's not that—'

'So you do, then?'

'Matt, stop it. There's nothing to be gained from all this.'

'You don't know what's going on, Hanny. I can't carry on living here.'

'Matt—'

'No. Look at this. This came.' He reaches down beside the bed and pulls up a jiffy bag. 'Here.'

He chucks it towards me. The end of the package is open. I take it tentatively, turning it upside down to shake the contents out.

It's a scarf. Silk. Expensive. The colours almost glow in the dim light, radiating pink and gold, flashes of silver, tiny spotted pools of sky blue. It almost feels warm and alive in my fingers as slithers, slippery and lithe.

I turn the parcel over.

You're Mine. I'm Yours.

I almost drop it.

'Obviously hand-delivered,' he says wearily. 'Obviously for Rachel. Obviously a gift. Her lover – that's bloody obvious too.' He breathes a sad laugh, and slumps back on the pillows. 'So now you're going to ask the next *obvious* question of if I'm so serious about my feelings about you, then why do I care? And you'd be right to, of course. You'd be absolutely within every right to feel like I'm messing you about, and totally conflicted, and generally behaving like a complete prick... Every bloody right.' His hands slap down and his jaw sets in a tremulous line. 'I just want you to know, Hannah, that I'm hiding nothing, none of my innermost feelings, however terrible they make me look. I'm sharing them – I'm being totally transparent.'

The words won't come.

'The thing is... ' I watch his face working a little with emotion. '... I really need to know how you're feeling, Hannah. For good or for bad. If I stand no chance at all, just tell me.'

He draws his knees up, burying his face in his forearms. I tentatively sit on the edge of the bed.

'It's not that simple,' I start, hesitantly. What can I tell him?

Leach? Rachel? James?... All of it?

The package lies discarded on the bed, the scarf next to it, and I'm horrified at the very sight.

'Matt.'

His face stays buried.

'Matt. Look at me. There are things I need to tell you.'

'About Rachel?' His head pulls back in anguish. Even in the dim light, I see his eyes are bloodshot, his skin is mottled into red and white patches.

'About something that happened to me. Something that involves all of us living in that house.'

He's staring at me, his expression unchanging. 'You said this before. It sounds scary. What was it? What happened?'

'Shhh. Listen... You were saying before about Alison?'

'Yeah.'

'Well, there were things I did around that time, that put things in motion – y'know, that, looking back, were the catalyst for what happened next.'

Matt frowns, puzzled. 'I don't know what you're saying, Hanny.'

'I did something petty and childish and stupid. I tried to cause a rift between Rachel and Alison. I did it because I was insecure and jealous,' I say through tightened teeth. 'I've tried to own that kind of stuff' – I shake my head in frustration – 'because it's *that* kind of behaviour that led to me being isolated, and it was being isolated—' I break off.

'You really are scaring me now.' Matt's face falls.

'Think back to the summer I left. Think back to that party we went to where I got totally wasted. Remember?'

'Yeah, but—'

I glance at the door wondering how long I've got.

'That was when things came apart. I was being shady, meddling between two women, trying to isolate them. But what I ended up doing was isolating myself. There'd been a row between them both: a row I'd set up. I tried to make Alison think that Rachel didn't care about her.'

I watch his eyes as I recount the story of what happened that day. What I did. The shame of me.

I'd walked into the hallway, hearing the raised voices, shrill from the kitchen. Alison shouting, 'I know who my friends are, and you're not one of them!'

I'd dived into my room, listening, breath held, and then Alison stomped past my door and up the stairs before her door crashed shut. Tiptoeing out, I walked into the kitchen, all breezy, pretending that I'd just come in.

'Oh, it's you.' Rachel had looked up, her face all pink.

I allowed my smile to fall. 'What's the matter?'

She beckoned to me as she closed the door. 'Alison's just gone batshit.'

'No! Why?'

'She's just stormed off shouting about all sorts that makes no sense. I have no clue what she'd on about. Firstly, she says I've been a crap friend, and I'm never there for her when she needs me.' She sighed and shrugged dismissively. 'She accused me of always choosing other people over her. Can you believe that? I mean, when have I ever done that? I've bent over backwards to include her – you know that. Honestly.'

She went to a cupboard and yanked it open, reaching for a cup.

'Seriously. I wish I hadn't bothered with her. She just wants more and more of me. It feels like she needs me to prioritise her needs in every situation, and that's just not possible. It's like she monitors me... It's like she's checking up on me to see who I'm talking to and who I'm spending time with. Jeez. It's... it's suffocating.'

'Wow! Did she say anything else?' I kept my face surprised

but impassive.

'Y'know what? I stopped listening.' She shook her head angrily. 'Everything is a bloody issue with her, isn't it?' She went over and flicked the kettle on. It immediately boiled as she threw a tea bag into the cup.

'To think I put all that effort into feeling sorry for her and now she has a go at me.' She furiously sloshed the water from the kettle. 'Thank God you live here, Hannah. I couldn't bear it if it was just me and her.' She levered open the wastebin with a violent clang, dropping the tea bag inside. 'To be absolutely honest with you, it feels like the more I give, the more she wants of me.'

I felt a quiet thrill. I'd never dreamed that Alison would have the balls to call Rachel out – but I wasn't complaining. *Thank God I lived here*, she'd said. I was someone she could rely on and talk to. *Thank God for me.*

She picked up her cup and took a sip. She'd not offered to make tea for me, but I didn't mind. *Thank God for me.*

'I'm so grateful to be going away for a couple of days to see my parents – get out of this house for a bit. Matt is doing my head in too.' She shook her curls. 'Leave them both to it.' She looked up suddenly. 'Shame you can't come with me, Hannah.'

'Oh. Well, I probably coul—'

'So maybe next time. You'd love the south coast.' She waved her cup. 'Five minutes from the beach. Talking of that, maybe I need to think about packing a couple of bikinis... Oooh, is that the time? Do you want the rest of this?'

She plonked the tea down on the table and hurried past me, leaving behind the incident with Alison and a slosh of spilled tea across the wooden surface.

I had this instant and overwhelming urge to run after her up the stairs, to tell her I could go with her if she really wanted me to; I'd only need five minutes to grab a bag. *Don't be ridiculous*, my head said. *Get a grip. She'll think you're like Alison.*

And I'm not like Alison.

I'm not like her at all.

I stood at the bottom of the stairs, listening for the sounds of Rachel moving about as she packed her case. What she didn't need right now was any form of aggravation or pressure. She needed to be surrounded by easy people – people who just had fun and a good time, but respected her personal space, too.

Feeling in my pocket, I pulled out Alison's phone and slipped it on the coffee table, pulling an old takeaway flyer over it.

I should've felt bad, but I didn't. I thought about that sneering look on Alison's face as she looked down on me, how she jeered at me in the bar that night as she picked at my clothes. How she practically accused me of stealing. I remembered the smirk as she plucked the twenty-pound note from my fingers, ordering me off to the bar.

I knew I'd moved up a notch. I knew this was me getting my own back.

I heard Rachel's bedroom door open, and then, with a shock, heard Alison's door opening too.

'Has Hannah come home yet?' Alison's voice wavered down the stairs and my heart skipped a little.

'Yes, she's downstairs,' Rachel said gruffly. 'Why?'

'Because she'll back me up,' I heard Alison say.

The skip of my heart turned to a dull thud.

I listened to the tread of their feet on the stairs. My head instantly whirled in a mass of disconnected thoughts. I glanced at the back door. I glanced into the hallway. I moved into the lounge thinking I could make a run for the front door, but it was too late.

Alison appeared in the doorway.

'Hiya,' I said brightly. 'How are you doing? Feeling better?'

'Oh I'm fine, *physically*.' Alison googled her eyes glancing back at Rachel. 'But she' – she jabbed a finger – 'won't own the fact that she's self-centred and selfish. She won't have a bar of it. She has no idea how she makes other people feel... I've told her that it's not just me – it's you too. You've felt it, haven't you?'

I stepped back into the lounge, giving myself time to think, checking Rachel's puzzled face.

'Sorry?' I looked at Alison in query.

'Being excluded. You said you felt that Rachel excluded you.'

'When?'

'Today. Earlier today. In the garden at Sanctum.'

I checked Rachel's bemused face and then looked back at Alison.

'I honestly think you've got the wrong end of the stick. I'm really, really sorry if that's how you interpreted it... I mean, that's just not true.'

Alison's eyes widened for a second and then she frowned. 'I didn't dream that conversation, Hannah. You said that Rachel dropped you when someone more interesting came along.'

'Me?' My palm flew to my chest. 'No, no, no, absolutely not. You've misheard – or misunderstood what I was saying. Honestly, hand on heart, I've never felt that way about Rachel.'

Alison's eyes were out on stalks. She stared at me and then at Rachel.

'So, all that stuff about the hospital and me not being there?' Rachel said quietly. 'What was all that about?'

'You didn't even care that I was hurt.' Alison bleated weakly, but the surge of temper had wavered into something that sounded like a whine.

'Had you *told* me,' Rachel said patiently. 'Had you told me, I would have come. Immediately. I would have dropped everything. Even in the midst of all these accusations...' Her eyes met mine.

'I couldn't contact you. She took my phone.' Alison glared at me.

But I pulled an incredulous face. 'I didn't take your phone, Alison. Why would I take your phone?' I mirrored Rachel's oh-so-patient tone.

Rachel pulled out her own and scrolled through her contacts. 'Well, let's ring it, shall we? See where it is?'

Within seconds there was the tootling jingle of her phone and we all looked down at the coffee table. Alison darted down to scrabble at the flyers as Rachel gave me a little nudge of solidarity.

Alison snatched up the phone's flashing screen, glaring fiercely at me, her glare swooping to Rachel and back again. 'I knew I didn't like you. I knew I didn't trust you from the moment I clapped eyes you,' she snapped. 'The fact is, you two deserve each other. I hope you're both very happy together, now that you've got what you want.'

Her eyes bored into mine, the tears and hatred springing there as she flew out of the room and up the stairs, her bedroom door slamming with such a crash, all the windows rattled.

Rachel turned to me, wide-eyed, genuinely shocked.

'What on earth was all that about? Do you think she'll calm down and apologise? Gosh, what an outburst. She'll get over it. Anyway, I'm off to finish packing.'

Part of me felt bad, but part of me definitely didn't.

Ten minutes later, I heard the slam of the front door, sending me running to the window to watch Rachel hoisting her bag onto her shoulder, her hair lifting in a great blonde coronet around her head, as a wave of loneliness surged over me. A weekend all alone. I looked around my room, at all the little things: a funny postcard she'd given me that I'd stuck on the wall, the daisy chain that I'd dried and hung on the mantel-piece, reminding of our day at the river. It all felt odd and empty; the silence in the house oppressive and ugly.

I turned with a sigh, and then I saw it. Over the bottom of

my bed, she'd draped a silk dress with a Post-it note poked onto the hanger.

For you. My amazing friend.
Thank you for being there for me.
Find urself some fun XX :)

I'd stood in front of the mirror holding it up. A paisley pattern, pure silk of mustard and red. Very, very pretty. Cinched in under the bust and a full swinging skirt, perfect for me in every way.

I am aware that Matt is listening carefully as he hugs his knees closer to his chest.

'Yes, I remember.' He nods. 'I remember now. Rachel wasn't around. My mate Chris texted me and told me about some party. We went, didn't we? You and I?'

Flashes of that afternoon come back to me: me wearing that dress, Matt's invitation. I remember feeling bad about Alison and creeping up the stairs and pushing a note under her door telling her where we were going. She didn't respond. I didn't blame her.

'Alison didn't want to come with us, then?'

We made our way through the overgrown front garden of the house, the music booming from the back into a hubbub of bodies. White and blue lights bobbing in the trees. A warm summer breeze lifting the skirt of my dress, sticking it to my thighs.

'No, she was staying in tonight, I think.' My face reddened furiously. 'I'll go and find us some drinks.'

And I'd walked off alone into the unknown, away from Matt, away from safety, no Rachel. No one who could protect me at all. And I'd found that drink and I was dancing, only the drink was drugged and then there was just the trees and the bushes.

And the darkness.

'Do you know who it was?' Matt's voice is hard, but I hold up a hand to shield the question.

'I was drugged, Matt. I wasn't drunk like you thought.'

'Jesus, Hannah.' He runs his fingers through his hair. 'Did you go to the police? What the hell happened?'

'I believe it was Hugo Leach.'

His hands pause in shock.

'It changed me, and it changed my life from that moment on. I was encouraged by a counsellor not to run from my feelings anymore, but to confront them. I started doing research – about what happened to other women in the area. I know it was him.'

'How?'

'Because I went to see him, Matt. In prison. And he sat across a table from me and practically told me as much. And that was the reason I disappeared, Matt. That was the reason I jacked in my course, and never came back.'

'Jesus, Jesus, Jesus.'

'He was there, that night at that party. He was baiting me; toying with me. Now he wants to terrorise me. He told me he could find me. *Here*, I mean. *This house*. He wants me to know he can find me whenever he wants.' I glance down at the scarf.

Matt blanches. 'You're saying he sent this?'

I gingerly poke at the wrapping. 'See that writing? Well, the other night I found something outside. Remember I asked you about a snowman and you said it was kids from next door?'

Matt's horrified eyes search my face.

'There was a... a heart thing, with writing on it. You picked it up. It said, *You're Mine*. Remember that? You threw it away.'

Matt's expression doesn't alter. 'But it can't be, can it?'

I'm beyond frustrated and I throw my hands up. 'Don't look at me like that. You think I'm paranoid, don't you?'

'I'm sorry. I'm sorry. It's just... Well, it makes no sense, Hannah.'

He's right, I sound crazed. I feel manic and paranoid.

'Look, Matt, I know how this sounds. How could a man behind bars organise all this?' My hands rise and fall in frustration. 'But he told me: he said that he was having "days out". Preparing himself for the outside world. How do we know he's not doing stuff when he's out? Emily said—'

'Emily?' Matt's jaw juts in anger. 'What the hell has she got to do with it?'

'She's been working with him. She's running some rehabilitation programme.'

Matt's head swings slowly in disbelief and he closes his eyes. 'Let me guess Emily's angle. Miraculously, with her intervention, a convicted sex offender and serial rapist has "seen the light" and the error of his ways.' He shudders with anger. 'Christ, I've heard her spouting her clap-trap theories so many times before, it sickens me. She's one big ego, that's all she is, and yet Rachel seems to hang off her every word.'

'She says she'll help me. She believes I should talk to him.'

He pauses, scanning my face. 'Hey, you're not thinking of going along with all this, are you?'

'She's talking about setting up some kind of meeting with his casework officer.'

Matt takes a moment, his discomfort etched on his face. He reaches to take my hands. 'Don't do this to yourself Hannah. Nothing good will come of it if Emily's involved. You've been through enough. You have to find a way to move past this horror, not drag it all up again.'

'But I can't, Matt!' I explode. 'I can't. I've tried. Don't you think I would if I could?'

His grip tightens angrily. 'I blame myself. You weren't able to come to me. You didn't feel safe enough to confide in me. I would've gone out there and found the guy. I would have gone out there and—'

But I cover his fingers with my other hand 'And I blame myself too. If I hadn't created a drama with Alison, if I hadn't gone to that party, if I hadn't worn that dress, drunk that wine, danced the way I did... There's no blame in the world that I haven't tortured myself with already, Matt. The fact is, you couldn't've done anything. I couldn't've done anything. It's not you or me who's to blame. It's him.'

He frowns, the pain creasing his face. He brings a finger up to stroke my cheek. 'My poor, poor Hannah.'

'Don't say that, please.' I snatch my face away. 'That was it, that's what I couldn't tell anyone. I couldn't bear to be a victim then, and I can't bear to be a victim now. I have to stay in control of this thing, Matt, it's sucked the life out of most of my past. I won't allow him to destroy my future as well.'

I feel the hair on the nape of my neck tingling with rage.

'Which is why you can't let Emily in, Hannah. Trust me, that woman will stage manage any meeting you have to suit her own needs. She'll need Leach to be her success story. He's the name that she'll get to write all the books and the papers about. He's the one that'll give credibility to her pathetic rehabilitation courses. She'll use him and his crimes to promote her own career. She's the worst kind of parasite.'

'But I need to go to that meeting Matt. I need to find out what their plan is with him. I need to know the names of the people who are dealing with him. I need to know the depart- ments who have written reports on him. If I want to challenge the decision to release him, I need to be armed with as much information as possible.'

'You'll challenge his release?'

'In any way I can. I may not be able to prevent it in the long run, but I can put spanners in the cogs. I can spin this thing out. I can make it difficult by telling my story to anyone that'll listen.'

'Wow!' he says, his mouth twitching with pride. 'Wow! You are one ballsy bitch.' He grins with admiration. 'Of course I'll be there backing you up all the way,' he says, entwining my fingers in his. 'You'll never have to face anything on your own ever again.'

I feel the tears smart.

'Just tell me one thing, Hannah.'

'What's that?' I look at him.

'Do I – do we stand a chance? I mean, I know not right now, but in the future. You and me? Is that possible?'

I look into his face, his kind, gentle, impassioned face. Would that be possible? Could I let myself be vulnerable? Take a chance?

You could, my head says. *You could have a whole new life.*

'Maybe,' I say shyly.

'Really?' His eyes light up for a second, but then he grips my hand even tighter. 'This is such a dangerous game to play though, Han.' He turns my palm over and traces a line with his other finger. A shiver thrills through me. 'Even with me at a hundred percent, I'm truly scared for you.'

'I know, but for me it's not a game, Matt,' I say quietly. 'And I'm really not playing; I'm actually deathly, deathly serious.'

I listen to Matt's footsteps as he makes his way downstairs.

Something has just happened between us, but I'm not sure what.

I hear him in the hallway talking to Rachel. I take a

moment; the duvet is a rumpled mass, and when I slide my hand beneath it, the residual heat of him warms my palm. I briefly close my eyes. How I would love to just curl up in the dip he's left and pull the covers over my head. How easy it would be to hide: shut it all out with the darkness and not face any of it again.

But I can't.

Checking the time, I grab a towel and go straight into the bathroom, locking the door and turning on the shower. Stripping off my clothes, I step into the hot stream. The water feels so good. I want to stay uncontaminated and washed clean of everything that's happened today. Despite the heat of the water, I shiver, soaping myself quickly all over... and then again, and again... Rubbing my palms together to scrape under my nails, lathering off the last remnants of stink of that prison and him, watching it all swirl away down the plughole.

Drying myself, I stand in front of the steamy bathroom mirror above the chest of drawers, face pinkly scrubbed and shining, feeling a tiny creep of something that could almost be the 'real' me fluttering deep inside. I think of the dress hanging in my room waiting for me – the one that Rachel chose.

Emily thinks she's in control, but she's not. The trembling wings in my stomach move up to around my heart. I'm close, so close to getting what I want it scares me. I have leverage on Leach that Emily knows nothing about. She can try her damnedest, but ultimately, she can't stop me. I feel that beating tremble growing tiny wings.

I come out of my room, smoothing the front of my new dress. I've only taken the first two stairs when I'm aware of raised voices. Matt and Rachel. I can't hear what they're saying but I know it's not good.

They both stop as I walk into the lounge. Rachel turns in a

swing of her blue skirt. She looks magnificent.

'Wow, Hannah. Stunning,' she enthuses. 'I said that would suit you, didn't I?' But I sense the strain on her face.

Matt is leaning on the doorframe to the kitchen. He has his arms tightly folded, and he's hunched, miserably. He's staring at the floor as though afraid to look at me.

'Did you think to pick out some wine?' She glances at his folded arms. 'Clearly not,' and then tuts, stalking away into the kitchen.

Matt doesn't raise his head. He just looks hunted and furious as I try to catch his eye.

I listen to the crash of cupboard doors and then the rustling of plastic bags.

'What's going on?' I whisper, but he refuses to engage as Rachel swoops into the room again.

'He's decided to investigate what's really going on, Hannah.' She glares scathingly. 'So, what do I find him doing when I walk in the room?'

I glance at Matt.

'Checking my phone, that's what,' she spits. 'How dare you. Seriously. How dare you look at my private messages.'

Matt only glowers back at her but has the grace to look uncomfortable.

'It's because of the way you behave.' He folds his arms defensively.

I shoot him a look.

'The way *I* behave,' Rachel retorts. 'That's bloody rich coming from you.'

'You and your new sidekick, Emily,' Matt says stonily. 'Covering for you, backing you up. Why can't you just be honest Rachel.'

'I think, what you mean is, Emily challenges the way you talk to me, and you really don't like it, do you? Emily stands up for me. She's a very loyal friend.'

She sweeps past him to pick up her bag, her eyes catching mine as I stand there awkwardly.

'Loyal? You're seriously going to lecture me on loyalty, are you, Rachel?' Matt says to no one in particular. 'Like, this is seriously ironic. You really want to open up that particular can of worms? Really?' His eyes track her as she disappears out of the room into the hallway. 'I don't think you're in any position *at all*, do you?' he hollers after her.

'Matt. Don't,' I whisper, terrified at what he might be about to say next.

'Wow, this is going to be one fantastic evening,' he mutters. 'Thanks for dragging me into it.'

Rachel appears in the doorway, slightly breathless and pink-cheeked.

'Ready?' Her eyes look wild as she turns to the front door, flinging it open and trudging down the path. I meekly follow, the door slamming behind us, and Matt strides on ahead.

'I'll drive.' He jangles the keys from his pocket. 'I'm really not in the mood for drinking anyway.'

'Good idea. You do that,' Rachel spits, 'as you'll be driving yourself to a hotel this evening.'

'A hotel?' He glares at her in the mirror, flabbergasted. 'What are you talking about?'

'We'll be staying at Em's.' She holds up a weekend bag as evidence as I stare at her in stunned silence, but he only shrugs aggressively. 'You are welcome to do as you like, Rachel, but you're not dictating terms to me.'

It's as though both of them have forgotten I'm here.

I get into the back and we drive in silence, the snowy road picked out in the car headlights, the fine rain needling through the night.

'You really don't have to bother coming. You can just drop us off if you like.' Rachel's voice resonates loudly into the quiet.

I snatch a look at Matt's face. He stares moodily through the windscreen, the wipers shrieking back and forth. He doesn't answer.

'So, just out of interest, what were you hoping to find on my phone, Matt? Something to make your own guilt feel better?' she pokes.

His jaw works angrily.

'The fact is, we both know we're done, Matt. That was about the last straw. I'm done, I'm finished. I don't want you anywhere near me.'

Silence.

'Did you hear what I said?' She turns her face to him. The solid jut of his profile says it all as it turns towards her.

'You dress it up as something else, but you're a liar, Rachel. You're a user. You betray people's trust. You're flaky and a mess but fundamentally you are so self-absorbed, you—'

'Stop the car,' she blurts suddenly.

'What?' He snaps a look at her.

'Stop the car. I want to get out. I want out of this whole bloody thing.'

'Don't be so totally ridiculous.'

Her hand shoots to the door handle. 'I said, stop the car, I want to get out.'

I watch nervously as Matt's head swings round; I see his face drop in shock as a whistle of wind eases through the gap of the opening door.

'Rachel. What the hell?'

'You can either let me out, or I'm getting out right now!' she shouts. 'I'm not putting up with this. Christ alone knows why I even agreed to get in the car with you.' She grips the lever with both hands,

'Rach—' I hear myself begging. 'Rach, please don't do this.'

But she only cracks the door wider. The wind whips my hair from my face.

'Whatever it is, Rach, we can sort it out,' I shout back,

suddenly terrified as I feel the car begin to pick up speed. I hold on to the safety belt, as the car begins to slew a little on the icy road. I see the rage glistening in her eyes as she rounds on Matt furiously, grabbing the door handle with both hands as she slams it shut.

'You bastard,' she mutters. 'You bastard...'

A tiny grimace of a satisfied smile picks at the corners of his mouth, but he says nothing, relaxing the acceleration, indicating to turn left and then right and I realise we're heading onto a housing estate of thirties-style houses. The car hasn't even stopped at the kerb before Rachel is fishing for the safety belt catch.

Heaving open the door, she stops to looks back at me. 'Are you coming?' she pants.

'I think I just need a minute,' I lie. 'I'm feeling a bit queasy.'

'You really don't want to stay here with this maniac.' She shoots Matt a filthy look.

'You go on ahead,' I urge her. 'I'll be there in a sec. I just need to get myself together.'

'You sure? Careful he doesn't kidnap and try to kill you,' she snarls.

'No, honestly, Rachel. Just a couple of minutes.'

She nods smartly and strides off down a pathway towards a house where the curtained windows cast a warm glow into the snowy front garden.

'You okay?' Matt breathes, his leather jacket creaking as he turns to look at me. 'I'm sorry about all that. I don't know what came over me.'

I allow my lungs to deflate with the tension. 'So, what the hell was all that about? Why were you looking on her phone?'

Matt rubs his hand across his face and then lets out a long, defeated sigh. 'Dunno. Maybe I wanted to force the issue. Start the argument. Get it all out in the open for once.' He stares moodily out towards the snow-laden house.

'Did you tell her about the scarf?

His expression doesn't alter. 'No, I didn't. There was no point. She'd only lie and then wriggle out of it by ganging up with Emily once the pair of them had had a drink. I spared myself the humiliation.'

There's a pregnant pause.

'You know what's happening right this moment in that house, don't you?' He twists round to look at me. 'Right now, Rachel will be presenting me as a controlling asshole who invaded her privacy. She'll be rehearsing the whole drama. It'll give them both time to work out their strategic plan of attack.'

'Then don't do it.' I'm quite definite. 'Don't go in there. Why put yourself through it. I would never have let you agree to come if I'd known how bad it was. Don't worry about me, honestly. I'll be fine.'

But he only puts his hand on the door. 'Oh no, Hanny. I'm coming. I promised you earlier and I meant it. You're not facing any of this on your own. You think I'm going to be dictated to, do you? No, absolutely not. Not with that pair of she-wolves. No way.'

He pushes the door wide and my heart thuds with anxiety.

'No, Matt. Please. There'll be another scene.'

'Then bring it on.' He slams the door and begins to march up the path. 'Come on. It's beginning to freeze out here. Be careful where you're treading.'

I have no option but to slither after him. Matt reaches up to the bell and we wait for what feels like forever before the door opens wide.

'There you are.' Emily beams happily, seemingly unaware of any drama. 'We thought you'd got lost parking the car.' She stands back to let us in, her eyes sliding away from Matt and settling forcefully, eyebrows raised, on me as she takes my coat, hanging it on the newel post at the bottom of the stairs.

'I'm so pleased you could come tonight. Really looking forward to chatting with you.'

I flicker a slightly nervous smile.

'And how lovely that dress looks on you,' she gushes. 'Rachel's so good at spotting what suits us, isn't she? Anyway, come on through; we've already cracked the wine open.'

She leads us into a lounge. A wall of heat immediately hits me. An ornate enamel woodburning stove glows orange over in the corner. The walls are bedecked with rugs and African wall hangings. Rachel is sitting on a couch and looks up as we walk in. Her face is a mask of politeness.

'Wow, what a lovely house,' I exclaim, trying to break the tension.

'You like it? Oh, thank you.' Emily gestures Matt to the sofa. 'Come and see the kitchen. I've just shown Rachel all the building work I've had done in there.'

I shoot Matt a panicked look, but Emily is insistent.

'Rachel had a hand in the colours I chose, of course.' She giggles. 'But come and have a look.'

The invitation clearly doesn't extend to Matt. *She's been primed*, my head says as I'm forced to trail obediently after her and he closes the door firmly behind us.

I glance nervously back but have a feeling this will have to play out.

'Here.' She hands me a glass of wine. 'So, what do you think?'

The kitchen is a mass of colours. A range of Victorian tiles cover a wall above the wooden counter and a huge cream aga sits in a brick inglenook.

Emily goes over to pick up a bowl of spliced carrots and a pot of hummus. 'Between you and me, I thought we'd leave them alone for a bit,' she lowers her voice. 'I heard there's been a bit of a row... Have a seat on this stool. We can say we were talking renovations.' She giggles again, but it feels forced.

She takes another bottle of wine and pours some into her own glass before settling herself to sit opposite.

'I thought it would be nice to chat, just the two of us. Get to know each other a bit better, eh? What do you think?'

Something feels a bit off; I'm not sure what.

'That conversation at lunchtime intrigued me actually. Given that our professions are aligned, I'd be really interested to know more about the young offenders you've worked with. How successful you've found it.' Her head tips in that infuriating way.

'Oh heck, we're going to talk shop then?' I watch her lining up the base of her glass with the join in the worksurface.

'If you wouldn't mind? I don't want to grill you or anything. Just the basics, so I can understand.' She taps the stem with a fingernail.

I hesitate. 'I don't think you'll find my experience very interesting.'

'It might be to me.' She rests her chin on her hand.

I take a sip from my glass. 'Well, to be perfectly honest with you, I'm on leave at the moment, so I'd really like a break from talking about it.'

'From talking about—?' She frowns.

'What I do.' I bring the glass to my lips again, grateful to cover my face.

'You mean, what you do as in, what? You mean, not tell the truth?'

A stone plummets in my gut.

'Sorry?' The glass freezes mid-sip.

'When you say "to be perfectly honest", you're not actually being perfectly honest, are you, Hannah?' She settles her chin more comfortably and gives a me little smile.

I am aware of my cheek muscles beginning to tremble. My lips won't hold still. I have this overwhelming need to swallow... And then swallow again.

'I am, as I said, genuinely interested in the work.' She plants a forefinger on the table. 'I do believe passionately in the rehabilitative process, and so working with young people and turning their lives around is a dream job for me.'

Her mouth flickers earnestly. 'And I really thought, given that you're on the inside of that process, I would put the feelers out. You'd be a good contact. You know how it is in the field: someone always knows someone who knows someone.' Her finger taps the table. 'Only in your case, they don't.'

I can't speak.

'I've only managed some preliminary enquiries, but in these days of staff databases and security checks, it's pretty conclusive. No one knows you, Hannah. No one's heard of you. You don't appear on any security check document, or on any database for the Prison Service teaching staff. Don't you think that's odd?' She frowns in query.

'Not really.' My voice squeaks and I cough.

'And why's that?'

'Because I don't work for them anymore.'

'Okay.' Emily glances at the door. 'I guess you're having a hard time, so maybe it's understandable, but I'd love to hear your story... Oh, by the way, I haven't mentioned any of this to Rachel – yet,' she adds pointedly.

I wait. The seconds tick between us as she observes me, in that awful quiet way of hers, taking me in until I don't think I can bear it any longer.

'I got suspended.'

'From?'

'I got a job with Social Services.' I address the worktop.

'You were a Social Worker?'

'I worked in the office,' I say in a small voice. 'I was an administrator.'

'So, why couldn't you tell people that?' She's exasperated. 'Why couldn't you tell Rachel that?'

I open my mouth to speak. I manage a tiny breath.

'Because I got suspended. Because I was embarrassed.'

'Oh.' She sits back. 'Why, what happened?'

'I was really good at my job. I handled the casework files. I was so good, that when one of the social workers went off sick with an emergency, my boss said I knew so much about the case that I should handle it and she'd sign it off.'

'Uh-huh. Go on.'

'And this went on for ages. My boss even suggested I did the training, so I started doing voluntary work.' I swallow awkwardly. 'And that's when I did teaching work with kids on exclusion, and in care, and in secure units.'

'And the suspension?'

I swallow again. 'There was a boy, Harry. He had just turned eighteen, so he had to leave the care process.'

'And you were working with him?'

'I had been.' I nod miserably. She thinks she knows where this is going, but she doesn't.

'It was about four months after he left the care home. I was walking in London, in Camden, going to a meeting when I saw him. He was on the streets. He looked terrible. I asked him if he was using and he said no, he wasn't, he was just hungry.' I pause, not quite daring to look up. 'So I didn't go to my meeting, I took him for something to eat instead... He told me all kinds of appalling things that had happened to him: that he was being pressurised by dealers, pimps, that he couldn't sleep at night in case they found him.' I pause for effect. 'I don't know what made me do it, Emily—'

'Do what?'

'I took him home with me.'

I can feel the judgement coming at me in waves.

'Home?'

I nod desperately. 'That's how I got suspended. They found out.' I lift my face, imploring. 'I know. I know what you think, but the thing is, Emily, if I hadn't taken him in, what else was he supposed to do? You know how hit-and-miss support services are. And even if he'd found a place to stay, there's no guarantee he would've been safe. So his only choice was to go back to the streets, and Christ alone knows what might have happened. I couldn't just stand back, could I? I was unable, in conscience, to turn my back on him and walk away.' I can't bring myself to look at her.

'And I'm guessing this became... well, umm... romantic?'

'I know how it looks, Emily. I know how it sounds, but he was kind, and thoughtful, and decent, and because I gave him an address, he got himself a job. That has to be a good thing, surely?'

She shakes her head, dumbfounded. 'They'll sack you, you know that?'

'I know what's coming, Emily.' I hold my hands up in surrender. 'It's all a hot mess, and I'm a total screw-up – I *know* that. And I know I can't go on being those things. I take full responsibility and I'll pay whatever the price.'

I hear her take a breath. 'Do you think any of your actions were influenced by what was happening with your own mental health, Hannah?'

I prickle as she slips so easily into patronising mode.

I take a deep breath and let it out slowly. 'Maybe. Who knows what I was thinking. Perhaps carrying this terrible thing around with me all these years finally caught up with me.' I shrug, slowly letting my shoulders drop. 'All my poor decision-making, my self-destructiveness... All of it.'

'How much of this have you told Rachel?'

I look up quickly. 'None of it.'

'Why not?'

I scramble for an answer. 'I thought she had enough on her plate,' I say lamely. 'And what good would it have done?' I hold out my palms. 'This is why I need your help, Emily.' I watch her face as I play to her ego. 'This is why I need to talk to Leach. I need to get my life back.'

There's a sound from the lounge and Emily glances round.

'We'll talk soon, yes?' She gives me a look. 'I suspect those two are wondering where we've got to.'

'Sure. Absolutely.' I slip off my stool. 'Thank you, Emily. Thank you for being so... so understanding.'

'No problem. I'm just going to check on the food and I'll be right in.'

I want to be out of there so badly. I take a step to the door, pushing it open, relief flooding through me; the sight of Matt standing there, looking worried.

'You okay?' he mouths.

I nod and look past him.

'Where's Rachel?' I whisper.

But he only shrugs towards the door. 'Surprise, surprise, lover boy has been in contact again. It's bad news by the look of it. Maybe his wife has found out. She's just stormed out in floods of tears. Don't ask me where.'

I glance back into the kitchen. Emily is busying herself sorting out the dinner as I slip past Matt and peer out into the hallway.

'Rach?' I call softly. 'Rach? Where are you? Are you okay?'

I hear water running in the downstairs cloakroom and then the toilet flushes. The bolt slides back and Rachel appears, her face puffy with tears, yet strained white.

'God, Rach.' I take a step forward to comfort her. 'Are you okay? Matt's told me what just happened?'

'What did he tell you?' Her hand stops in shock.

'That he saw James's message.'

'What?' Her face drops.

'James just contacted you?'

Her eyes widen. 'I don't know what he's talking about.'

'He's probably guessed who it was,' I say ruefully. 'He

knows there's someone.'

'Really?' She gives me an angry stare. 'Really? That's what he says he thinks, is it? 'How bloody ironic.' She laughs sadly. She holds out her phone so that I can see, scrolling through the screen.

'Here, look – and here, and here... Loads of them,' she snaps. 'Message after message. My god. The bastard.'

It takes a second for my brain to register.

'I don't understand, Rachel. Who are they from?'

But she only stares down at the screen in disbelief. 'I have no idea how she's got my number.'

'She? Who?'

Rachel looks up at me, her eyes red-rimmed with fury.

'Who do you think? Matt's girlfriend of course.'

The air leaves my lungs as though I've been punched.

But she doesn't notice my reaction.

'I heard my phone go off. Matt demanded to see it, but I told him no. He threatened me, grabbed it out of my hand, but I got away from him and locked myself in here.'

She must have this all wrong, she must have.

'Dunno what I'm so upset.' She shakes her head. 'It's not like I didn't know about this girl, is it?' Rachel says quietly. 'That's who I'm assuming, anyway. She's begging me to say nothing to Matt, but she says she wants to meet me. She says she has things she wants to tell me.'

There's a swell of anger, hurt pride and a whole host of conflicting emotions.

'You okay, Hannah?'

A weird, slow-motion undulation of the floor makes me stagger as I reach for the door frame and a burn of pain sears through my heart.

'Hannah?'

Rachel's face comes close to mine. 'Hannah? Hannah? Are you alright?'

THIRTEEN

'She's not, is she?'

I am aware of Emily's grip on my elbow as she guides me into the lounge.

'You weren't feeling well in the café earlier, were you?' Rachel's voice sounds as though it's coming from very far away. 'Does she need to sit down?'

'I'm fine, I'm fine,' I hear myself saying. I can't look at Matt. I am aware of his outline over by the window, silhouetted against the curtains. The shock and the rage of blood fizzes in my ears. I can't think straight. I can't function properly.

'Actually—' I hold myself together just enough. 'Actually, maybe I need to go home. You're right. I'm really not feeling well.'

'Would you like to go and lie down for a bit?' Emily's hand is on my elbow, steering me towards the sofa. 'Maybe that would help?'

'No, thank you though.' My eyes cast around for my jacket. 'I just need my phone to call a cab. I think I left my coat at the bottom of the stairs.' I make a grab for the doorhandle. 'I'm so sorry about this. I don't want to ruin your evening.'

'I'll take you home,' Matt says suddenly, patting his pocket.

'No.' It comes out louder than I mean it to. 'Definitely not,' I say stiffly. 'There's no point.' My meaning is clear, but Matt only pulls out his car keys.

'You'll wait forever to get someone to pick you up on a night like this. Come on, I'll take you. It's no problem.'

My head is spinning. *No problem?*

'I need air,' I say suddenly. 'I'll ring for a taxi and wait outside.' I'm pulling my coat on.

'Outside?' Emily is aghast. 'You can't be outside, Hannah, you'll freeze to death. That's crazy, Matt will just take you home. It's no big deal.'

The panic at the thought flutters high in my chest.

I'm caught. Trapped. I can't get out of this, and I know it. I can't bring myself to look at him, but once I'm out of this house he can do what the hell he likes.

'Okay,' I say stubbornly. 'Then you can take me home.'

'Hallelujah,' he says. 'Right. I'll say goodnight, Emily, and thank you for the invitation.'

Emily rubs my shoulder, patting me. 'It's all going to be okay, Hannah,' she says meaningfully. 'I'll be in touch about this meeting at the prison. Get a good night's sleep and we'll speak in the morning, yes?'

I manage a half-hearted smile as Matt and I walk in stony silence back down the path towards the car. The immobiliser flashes orange into the darkness as the light from the front door disappears behind us.

'You okay?' Matt looks at me across the roof of the car.

I don't think I can answer. I walk around to the passenger side knowing the last thing I'm doing is going anywhere with him.

'I said, are you okay?'

The fury erupts.

'You... you *bastard*,' I splutter. 'You really are. You really are an absolute and total piece of work.'

He recoils in shock. 'What?'

'Ohh. Don't even go there. Seriously,' I say, swallowing and looking away again. 'Who the hell is she?'

'Hannah. You're not making sense. Who the hell is who?'

But I am so beside myself I can't speak properly. 'Jesus... You... you...' I raise my hands. 'No, I'm not doing this. I'm really not.' I begin to walk away.

'Hannah.'

'No. Leave me alone. I want nothing to do with you. I've had enough.'

'Hannah, wait.'

I don't care that he's close behind me. I start to walk, my feet slipping and sliding on the ice. I feel stupid in my too-thin dress and unsuitable shoes. I look stupid. Christ. I *am* stupid. I've allowed myself to be duped and played like some pathetic—

'Hannah. Don't do this!'

I tuck my head down resolute and determined as I pick my way along the street as fast as I'm able. I have absolutely no idea where I'm going. I have no clue what I'm going to do next. All I know is, I want out of here.

Matt catches my arm, swinging me round. My feet slither as I try to wrestle my arm away.

'Get off me.' I manage to yank free his grasp.

'Look, I don't know what you think is going on, but—' He snaps a furtive glance about. 'We can talk in the car, yes? Privately. Not like this.'

'I'm going nowhere with you. Absolutely not.' I raise my voice again.

'For god's sake, Hannah. Shh. Anyone could hear you.' His eyes flicker nervously. 'Look, if you won't get in the car, then let's find somewhere. We'll talk, yes?'

'I've got nothing to say.'

'Well, there are things you clearly need to hear. Come on, let's go this way.'

He takes me down a side street, a cul-de-sac of houses that peter away to a footpath leading to a park. The sodium street-lights offer an eerie orange glow that illuminates nothing. The roads to left and right are swallowed by the shadows. The trees guarding the black gates are silhouetted against a black sky.

My feet falter. 'You want to walk through the park in the dark? Are you mad?'

'No, look, there's no one about. We can go and sit over there. Someone's cleared the swings, they'll be dry.'

The children's play area lies quiet beneath a snowy blanket; the see-saw is lined with thick white, but the swing seats are clean. Snowmen of different shapes and sizes sit in a ring, leering like horror-story Humpty Dumptys. I shiver at the memory.

'Here—' He holds out the chain of a swing and I tentatively sit, easing myself back. He sits on the one next to me, knees together, hands clasped, readying himself.

'You're going to have to give me a clue what's going on here. What on earth did Rachel tell you?'

I stare blankly out in front of me.

'I challenged her over this James bloke.' Matt sounds flat and calm.

I don't speak.

'I asked her about the scarf. I called her out. I told her I knew what was going on.'

A slight breeze shakes a pattering of snow from the lower branches of a tree. The icy particles glisten like a shake of glitter on thick paper.

'I said I knew she'd been seeing someone behind my back. I said I believed she was still in contact with him. I said she was treating me like a dumbass, and it was humiliating. At the very least, she owed me the truth.'

I force my neck to crick around towards him. He's bowed in the seat, shoulders stooped, hands clasping and releasing with anxiety. The pale skin of his wrists glow in the moonlight.

'She tried to lie to me, repeating all the guff she'd spouted before about this bloke of yours that's supposed to have tracked you down. She said she had no idea about any scarf. Then she tried to make out that I was paranoid... So, I went over to her and demanded to see her phone. She said I was threatening her. I made a grab for it and she bolted.'

His hands twist in his lap. I can't read his expression.

'It's the truth, Hannah. I swear it.'

I can't speak for a moment.

'And the woman and the texts?'

'What woman? What texts?'

'The one you've been seeing. The one who contacted Rachel and wants to see her.'

His face crumples. '*What?*' he sounds genuinely appalled. 'That's what Rachel told you?'

'Yep.' Tears burn tight in my throat. *I shouldn't have allowed him in. I shouldn't have.*

He lets out a little wheeze of laughter. 'My god. New depths, even for Rachel.' He shakes his head. 'So, you saw them? You read them?'

'What?'

His eyes are steely. 'I'm asking, did you actually read these texts for yourself?'

I falter. 'Well... No... Not exactly. I saw the screen with—'

'You saw the screen,' Matt says slowly. 'Right. Well. That's evidence enough, isn't it? For my conviction, I mean. You saw a screen full of texts. Wow!' He lets out a whistle of air.

'I mean, why would she say it though?' I can hear the pitch in my own voice. 'I can't see why she would unless it was true...' I peter off.

'Hannah. Look at me,' Matt says suddenly. He sounds so different I find my eyes being drawn to him.

'No, seriously. Look at me properly. Even if you don't believe a word I say and you totally believe Rachel, would you just hear what I have to say?'

I nod dumbly.

'What I am about to tell you Hannah is the truth. There is not any "woman" I've been seeing. I challenged Rachel. She said she had proof on her phone. I asked to see it and of course she refused to show me. We argued. I grabbed her phone for a second and there was nothing there. Like, *nothing*. Do you hear that? I don't know what game she's playing, but she's desperate, Hannah. Desperate to be seen as the good guy because she knows she's doing wrong, so she's trying to paint me in the same light too...' He holds up a hand. 'And before you say anything, there is only one question now I need an answer to, and that is: do you believe me?'

I look into his quiet, patient eyes softly shadowed in the darkness. I'd like to believe him, yet do I? I don't know what I think about anything, anymore. This web, this tangled knot of lies, deception, half-truths, fury, fear, sadness, washes over me in a tidal wave of weariness that makes me want to curl up in one of these piles of snow, bank the drift around me, and close my eyes.

'I just want to go home, Matt.'

'*Arrgggh. Hannah.*' He beats his fist on his knee and makes me jump. 'Then ask her,' he says furiously. 'Ask to see the message, or listen to it, or whatever she's claiming. If she refuses, then you'll know, won't you?' He reaches out to grab my hand, but his hand stops, midway. He suddenly snaps round.

'What was that?'

I can't see anything, just the weak orange glow of the street-lights illuminating the way to the park entrance.

'I thought I saw someone, that's all.' He looks around again.

'What?' My heart skips a little. 'Where?'

'Over there.'

He points and I think I see it too; it's quick – definite. And then nothing. Another flurry of snow falling perhaps? An animal shifting from the shadows.

'There's someone watching us,' he whispers.

'What?' My skipping heart jags up a notch, my eyes widening, trying to absorb the darkness and make sense of it.

A shadow over by the gate moves a little. 'There they are,' I whisper back. 'By the entrance.'

'I can't see them now.' He shifts, standing. 'Maybe I was wrong, maybe I was imagining it.' He breathes out slowly into the cold air, reaching for my hand to pull me towards him. 'Hell, I think we're both strung out after all that's gone on. Come on, let's get back to the car.'

I let him lead me back towards the gate, but the hair in the nape of my neck is prickling up and down. He has my hand clasped tightly, but I keep my eyes fixed on the place where the darkness moved. I don't feel safe. The snow at our feet is lit in an eerie light that dissolves into black pits of nothing. Anything, anyone could be hiding there.

'Can we walk quicker? I just want to get into the light.'

'I'm with you now, Hanny. Nothing's going to happen. Trust me.'

We reach the road where the houses send their cosy comforting glow from behind tightly drawn curtains onto the pavement. A car turns into the street. I instantly feel better at the growl and crackle of the tyres as the brilliant sweep of car headlights come towards us. I glance away from the glare, casting a look behind me. And there it is. A figure, hunched over, lifts its white face that flashes pale in the passing light and then there's nothing but a shroud of blackness.

FOURTEEN

I can't stop shaking.

I don't even wait for Matt to get out of the car before I'm walking up the path to stand in mute shivering silence while he finds the front door key and lets us both inside. I go straight upstairs, not even pausing to say goodnight. Once in my room, I grab my case and wedge the handle under the doorknob. I go and sit on the side of the bed without even taking my coat off.

Am I being followed?

But who by?

My mind races.

The stairs creak and I glance anxiously at the door. I don't want to talk to Matt. I don't want to talk to anyone. I sit, breath held, as he passes my bedroom door. There's the sound of running water and then a squeal as the bathroom door opens. I'm aware of him pausing on the landing for a moment, but then moves quietly away. And then there's silence.

Will Emily tell Rachel what she knows about me? Will she set up this meeting at the prison to trap and expose me? Will she ring around Social Service departments until she finds my boss and tell him what's been happening? My head spins with it. Rachel will believe her. Rachel might think I've lied to her once before, so why not again? But then again, is Rachel telling me the truth? Why would she tell me that she's been contacted by some woman that Matt is seeing, if it's not true? Is Matt lying to me?

It's like sitting at the centre of a maze. I'm completely alone with no one to turn to. I am surrounded by high hedges, each one leading to another dead end. Each one another trap. I can't go back there. I can't go back to that place where nothing is real – and I can't breathe. I'm not going back.

My phone lights up.

Emily.

There's a patter of heartbeat. It's a message:

> Hi Hannah. Hope ur feeling better? I'm in the prison tomorrow morning and I'd love to introduce you to Geraldine (Leach's case officer) if you happened to be free? We can then discuss setting a date for a meeting maybe? Does 9ish suit?

I reply, saying that I'm feeling better and have gone straight to bed. I tell her I'll come to the prison tomorrow, and thank her very much for helping me. I apologise for messing her evening up. She replies.

A vague dread thrums. I'm aware of her tentacles manoeuvring me into a corner. She's taking control. Leach will be taking control. Between the two of them, it's like a pincer movement.

Sliding the phone onto the bedside table, I turn the light off, still in my coat, and lie down in the darkness. I stare up at the ceiling as my mind runs way with me, churning anxiety over and over, my senses all on high alert.

There was no one following us tonight.

There was no one outside the house leaving snowmen.

The *You're Mine* heart was just a coincidence.

Wasn't it?

So why is my gut screaming that something really weird is going on here?

It can't be Leach.

He can't possibly know where I am. He wouldn't be able to get hold of any information that would link Rachel's address and me, can he? The only possible link between the two of us is—

Emily.

My mind turns over and over.

Emily.

She wouldn't though, would she? She wouldn't jeopardise her career by giving information to a man like Leach, surely? I picture myself walking across that snow-laden prison car park towards Rachel's car and suddenly it dawns on me as my mind trawls back: those dead eyes of windows from the cell block staring down at me. I remember wondering what horrors might lie behind them?

What if one of those horrors was Leach?

I have this vision of Emily walking across that car park. Emily getting into Rachel's car. What if he saw Emily and Rachel together? How far is his cell from the Visits Hall? How long did it take me to get back through the prison? Longer than for him to be staring out of his window? Could he have been watching me get into Rachel's car? Could he have been in town that day and seen the car outside the café? Am I making connections that are impossible?

A car headlight illuminates the ceiling for seconds and then disappears in a corner. The central heating clicks and cools. I imagine what tomorrow might look like. The horror of being on Emily's territory with Emily's already primed colleague, the two of them setting the stage for the drama that Emily is busily writing the script for.

Emily writing the lines, but with a master playwright dictating the words.

All of them against just one of me.

I feel the snare grip and tighten.

FIFTEEN

A gauzy grey dawn beads the edge of the curtains. I have that sticky, dulled feeling of having slept fitfully, fully dressed, exhausted but simultaneously wired into wide-awake queasy anxiety.

I listen for sounds that Matt is up, but the house is silent.

I need to get out of here,

Slipping quickly down the stairs, I pull the front door closed behind me, glancing back fearfully in case the rumbling of my car engine brings Matt peering out of the window.

The sky is still laced with darkness. There's a feeling of something deep unravelling inside me – an unspooling that I can't stop. I've set this thing in motion with Leach and with Emily's help, he's grappling control back.

But I'm not going to let him.

The car whines on the snowy road.

Not this time.

The tunnel of dark road is sweeping me towards the edge of a precipice.

Not now I've got this far.

I turn into the prison grounds. It's still very early. The perimeter arc lights, silent sentinels, cast deep shadows over the rolls of razor wire. I step out of the car and pause a moment. I'm alone, watching the lighted fishbowl of the gatehouse showing the staff going about their business, catching each other up, chatter as they pull the jackets tighter around them in the cold morning.

I begin a slow walk down the path to the fate that awaits me.

'Gosh, you're keen, aren't you?' A voice behind me makes me spin round. It's the female prison officer who escorted me yesterday, bundled up in a scarf and coat.

'Oh. Hi.'

'What are you doing here at this hour?' She grins kindly.

'I think... Well, I'm... I'm supposed to be having a meeting with Leach's casework officer.' My brain stumbles. 'But you're right... Um... someone offered me a lift and so—' I wave pathetically at the cars coming into the car park.

'Oh, okay. Well, they won't just let you in at this time, and you can't stay out here, not dressed like that.' She eyes me and I realise the dress and coat from last night are completely unsuitable.

'So, you'd better come in with me. I know Geraldine, Leach's casework officer. Her office is on my wing. She won't be in yet, but we can probably find you a cup of tea while you wait. I'm Annie by the way.'

'Oh, I'm Hannah,' I mumble. She chatters on as we walk, telling me all about having to exercise her dog before she comes into work, asking me about any pets I have as she leads the way down to the main entrance. I chat on about my flat and my neighbour who is looking after my cat and all the while I can't quite believe I'm actually doing this.

A band of anxiety tightens as we go up to the Perspex screen at the front desk where an officer takes my ID to book me in. I'm aware that Annie is still talking away happily, but my head is full of what I'm about to face. She pulls out her key tally to collect her keys, and unloads her bag onto the scanning conveyor belt, gesturing for me to do the same.

She unlocks a gate and we take a route I partly recognise from yesterday, but this time we head towards the prison proper. This is Leach's territory. The wings loom up on either side of us, the exercise yards out front, grim and garlanded with hoops of barbed wire.

She takes me through a single barred gate and then through a wooden door. Each one closes behind me taking me further and further towards the place I don't want to be.

We come out into a circular concourse where Annie unlocks a gate next to a plaque marked *A Wing*. The noise level suddenly ramps up by several decibels.

'I'll have to leave you in a wing office while I help out with unlocking and breakfast,' Annie explains. 'But I'll find you a cup of tea and maybe a few rounds of toast. How does that grab you?' She beams as she opens the last of the doors and the volume level shoots up in a cacophony of hooting and hollering.

'I'll put you in here until Geraldine gets in.' She raises her voice over the din, gesturing me to an office with the sign *Casework Room One*.

It's plain, with a simple desk and a couple of chairs, and some other comfy chairs pushed against the far wall.

'I'd say make yourself comfortable, but—' She pulls a face, looking around the room. 'I'll pop a note on Gerry's desk telling her where you are. Tea okay?' She raises her eyebrows. 'Milk? Sugar?'

'Just milk, thanks.' I smile gratefully. 'This is really kind of you. Thanks so much.'

'Well' – she wrinkles her nose – 'the truth is, when you said you were working for one of Leach's victims, it struck a chord with me. If I can help in any way at all, I'm happy to.'

She glances at me with a cautionary look. 'He's as slippery

as an eel and as devious as hell. These lot get drawn in by him.' She pecks her chin towards the wing. 'Don't let that happen to you.' She goes to pull the door closed but then pauses. 'What time did you say you were meeting Gerry?'

'Oh, I'm not sure exactly. Emily Travers set it up. She mentioned nine.'

'Okay. Cool. It's just I know Leach watches everyone coming onto this wing. He seems to have a way of finding things out and if he gets wind that you're talking to his case officer, he'll try to muscle his way in here to find out why.' She rolls her eyes. 'But don't worry, I'll keep an eye out and make sure I get to him first.' She assures me. 'Right. What was I saying...? Oh yes, toast. I'm on to it.' And she disappears, leaving me with the cacophony of sound still in my ears. The gut-trembling knowledge, the absolutely awful thought that Leach is somewhere on this wing, and has clocked me already.

I keep glancing at the door. Every time I hear a voice coming closer, my heart rate climbs wildly upward. I look around at the various chairs, manoeuvring myself so that I'll see him before he sees me.

'Here we—' Annie stops abruptly in the doorway with a mug and a plate of toast in her hand. She looks around to find me behind the door. 'Heck, what are you doing there?' She puts the plate down on the table.

'Sorry... sorry...' I mumble. 'I'm actually fine. I'm just feeling a bit headachy and weird. Honestly, I'm good.'

'Mmm.'

I can see she's not convinced. 'Let me go and find you some paracetamol. I've got some hidden in the main office some-where, hang on. Two secs.' And with that she's gone. Pressing the tips of my fingers to my forehead, I take a couple of deep breaths, counting out slowly as the door opens and she's holding out her hand.

'That was—' I start.

But it's not her.

Leach is standing there, his outstretched hand so close I can smell him.

'Not even a handshake then?' His eyes crinkle.

I'm paralysed. I don't think I can think, or act, or scream.

'You're not supposed to be in here.'

I try to keep my voice steady as I stare at his sun-kissed skin and nails, all soft and doughy.

'And yet, here I am.' He runs his tongue along his top teeth. 'I had an inkling I might see you, Hannah. Now how did I know that?' He presses a finger into his chin. 'Oh yeah, I have the gift of second sight.'

We both glance at the door, but his smile only broadens. 'Officer Annie Bridges is dealing with a bit of an emergency down on the Ones,' he explains, 'so all the staff are a bit distracted right now. She may be a little longer than she intended.'

I can't move. My spine is stuck rigid to the back of the chair. Leach reaches behind me, leaning in so that the skin of his arm brushes the side of my head. There's a warm sickly stink and I almost retch. He pulls a chair around, settling himself so that his knees are almost touching mine. He takes a deep breath in.

'Mmm-mmm.' He moans, whispering: 'This is so what I came for. I told you, it's your fear, Hannah. Its perfume. Mmm-mmm, it's like nectar. I've been remembering actually, Hannah. I've been remembering that first time. You're like a drug to me, Hannah – you're like that hit you get that first time you use... And that first time for us, Hannah... It was magic, wasn't it? Do you remember? I do. You were dancing, whirling round and round – it was like the Dance of the Seven Veils. I came up behind you and grabbed you, caught you off guard, and your eyes slammed open in shock and I got a hit of it right there and then.' He closes his eyes briefly and then they drop open again suddenly.

He goes very still.

'Cat and mouse, Hannah.' He snickers. 'I grabbed you, and then I let you go. You turned around and around in shock.' He pauses. 'The expression on your face, the tiny pulse in your neck... Oh I wanted you from that second. Do you remember that moment, Hannah?'

My head flounders, panicking, trawling through this flick-book of memories. *Do I?*

'Then you staggered away into the darkness into all those people. You felt safe there, didn't you, Hannah? So when someone casually offers you a drink, you take it, don't you? Of course you do. All I had to do then was wait... Circle and wait.'

My head revolves slowly with his words. This is what I came for. This is what I've wanted.

Yes, someone put their hands on my waist. A few seconds of touch, that's all, before whirling me off like a spinning top into the darkness.

The sounds of lots of people: girls and boys laughing. Safe. Relax again. A girl smiles, 'Have a drink,' she says. Trying to dance again, feel that feeling again, but the grass beneath my feet becomes unsteady, undulating...

Leach brings his fingers to flutter at his top lip, breathing deeply, eyelashes fluttering. 'Do you know how many years I've spent trying to create a memory of that smell, Hannah? I've lain in my cell trying to conjure it up. It's been there, always just out of reach on the periphery of my senses... But now—' His fingers tiptoe across his top lip. 'Here it is, where I can almost touch it.' The eyes slam open like shutters. 'So.' His voice goes hard. 'I've given you something, a taste of what I know – and now a deal's a deal, Hannah. Now it's your turn. What little something have you got for me?'

The door bangs back.

'Leach.' Annie stands there in shock. 'Get out of here, now.'

He rises slowly, the chair screeching back, and he saunters casually over to the doorway.

'I assumed Hannah wanted to see me one last time.' He's all young, innocent-eyed with innuendo. 'She's come so early, I just assumed she was keen.'

'I said out.' She glares at him. 'Now.'

He twinkles his fingers in the doorway as it closes behind him. I don't know where to look. I don't know how to feel. I don't know if I will ever breathe properly again.

Annie crouches at my feet, putting her hand on mine.

'He didn't touch you, did he?'

It's as much as I can do to shake my head.

'You look totally freaked out. What the hell did he say?'

I can't repeat it. I can't repeat any of it.

The pressure on my hand intensifies.

'Can I ask you something?' Her eyes search my face. 'This victim you mentioned... I was just wondering – and tell me to mind my own business – but was this person you spoke about, was it you?'

My silence says everything. I look up at her.

'He's just confessed to raping me.' The words sound alien as they leave my lips. 'He's just told me he stalked me at a party. I was only eighteen. He told me how he set it up, the spiked drink, everything.'

'Oh my god, Hannah.' Annie's face is pale. 'He just came out with it, just like that?'

I swallow at the thought. 'He said...' I can barely form the words. 'He said he would tell me what had happened... He got off on my being afraid. It turned him on.' I pause. 'And he was right, I was afraid the moment he set foot in this office. I gave him precisely what he wanted.'

Her jaw drops.

But not everything, the voice in my head reminds me.

'That's sick.' She's horrified. 'That's seriously sick.'

She gives my hand a little squeeze. 'I can't tell you how brave I think you are, coming in here, fronting him out. I watched you with him in Visits yesterday. I saw he was trying to intimidate you. Seriously, you've got so much bottle.' She strokes my knuckle. 'You're so together and so strong, Hannah.'

'I'm not together and I haven't been coping.' I shake my head in blank fear. 'I think I've been going mad actually.' I close my eyes and swallow. 'All kinds of weird stuff have been happening – I've been so paranoid. He threatened he could find me whenever he wanted – but that's impossible, isn't it? The fact is, I don't know what to believe could be true and what's his way of intimidating me... I haven't been able to tell anyone. They'd think I was literally going mad.'

She pats my hand, reassuringly. 'Well, you're not going mad. You're absolutely not, my love. It's totally unsurprising after what you've been through... No, no. There's no way Leach would get access to anyone's personal details and find you, just like that. People who work here are really careful about addresses and phone numbers. They aren't that stupid, they're—'

Her words float into the air around me as something quietly dawns.

Emily.

Emily's not stupid, but she'd do it to frighten me off.

'Are you thinking about going to the police with all this?'

'All what?' a voice says.

We both snap round. A woman is standing in the doorway. Her face is stern and unwelcoming.

'Gerry.' Annie gets up. 'Hope you don't mind, but I brought your visitor in. I didn't want to leave her out in the cold.'

Gerry's eyes switch to me and then back to Annie.

'Visitor?'

'Yeah.' Annie looks to me and back again.

'You know she's not a visitor of mine, don't you?'

'Sorry?' Annie glances at me, confused.

'I had a call from Emily Travers last night saying she was being harassed by this friend of a friend who was engaged in some kind of attention-seeking stunt.' Gerry looks at me. 'Can I just ask, for the record, were you approached by the newspapers, or do you plan to go to them with this story? That's what you're planning to do, I understand?'

'I—'

I look at Annie who is standing there, looking stunned.

'You of all people should really know better Ms Bridges,' Gerry says sharply. 'You're always banging on about staff not being switched on enough.'

Annie instantly colours.

'You are fully aware we get a raft of attention seekers with high-profile prisoners. Particularly as they get closer to their release date.'

'Attention... attention seekers?' I stammer.

'Yes, the kinds of people who would target someone like Emily, inserting yourself into her life. You've been clever, I'll give you that, inveigling your way with one of her friends first.'

'Inveigling?'

'Emily is a smart cookie though. She sussed you were a bit of a fantasist from the off – she had no idea what you were planning, but of course she's very familiar with women who are obsessed with offenders.'

'Obsessed with...? Emily?' I start. 'Emily said that? About me?'

'No. Emily is too nice to be that blunt – I'm the one who's saying it. But Emily's blown your cover, Hannah – oh, that is your name isn't it?' She gives me a mock-query frown. 'Or is that another one of your fabrications?'

I can feel the back of my throat tightening and a burning sensation behind my eyes. I can't look at Annie.

'Ah, Mr Jacobs.' Gerry turns as an officer passes by the door. 'Are you going anywhere in the vicinity of the Gatehouse?'

'I wasn't, but I can do.' The officer looks around at us in query.

'I wonder if you'd be so kind as to escort this person back from whence she came.' Her sarcasm isn't lost.

'Err... Yep... Sure. No worries.' He extends an arm towards me. 'If you'd like to come with me?'

I find myself stumbling out of the office, as he strides away, leaving me embarrassed and stunned beyond belief. He swings the wing gate wide leaving me no option.

I grabbed you, and then I let you go.

Leach's voice is in my head.

You turned around and around... Do you remember that moment, Hannah?

I close my eyes. I do, I do.

Then when someone casually offers you a drink, why wouldn't you take it? Of course you would. All I had to do then was wait...

My eyes spring open in shock and I stutter to a halt.

'This way, please.' The officer is holding another gate open.

Who offered me that drink?

'You've not crossed swords with Geraldine before then?' He gives me a smirk.

'No.'

My head is full of images of trees and lights and there's the feel of grass between my toes. People all around me are laughing. It feels like a dream. *Was it a dream?* Why can't I remember every terrible, terrifying moment? *There's a fog of shifting images; a fog I can't get through.*

'Ah.' He raises an eyebrow. 'You might've caught her on a bad day. She's just had to run the gauntlet of journalists – they're out there like a pack of hyenas.'

I'm punched back into the present. 'Out there? Out where?'

'Yeah.' He grins. 'They're waiting for Leach to be released this afternoon. That's the time we told them.' The officer laughs. 'But they might discover they've had a pointless journey.'

He's not picking up on the look on my face.

'I escorted him down to be discharged, not ten minutes ago.'

'What?' I'm almost reeling.

'Yeah, the journo hyenas are waiting out the front gate, but the staff managed to slip him out the back.'

SIXTEEN

I'm numb, and not just with cold.

The prison security door swishes closed behind me. The scene out front is like something from a movie. Lines of vans and cameras, and men holding microphone booms stand there, sipping their coffee and stamping their feet on the frozen ground. A couple of them glance round at me, but I'm clearly of no interest.

A thick frost has already formed on the windshield. I sit, cocooned, the ice blooming in flowers all around me. My head feels thick and full. Ramming my hands into my pockets, I huddle deep into myself, burying my chin and wanting it all to go away.

Something crackles against my knuckle, and I pause, my fist opening and my fingers closing around the thing in my pocket.

It's a piece of paper; I recognise it as my piece of paper as I unfold it and read the words: I have your DNA written in my handwriting on one side.

But then I turn it over.

And that night I took your heart and soul, is written on the other.

I instantly drop it, my fingers fumbling.

He did it. He did it... It was actually him.

Hands shaking, I try Rachel's number, but there's no answer.

'Rach, can you ring me please? It's Hannah. Please, Rachel. As soon as you get this.'

My head buzzes, whirling giddily with it all. I have to talk to someone... *about this, about Leach, about Emily... Emily... Leach...* I wish I could speak to Rachel. I wish she was here right now so that she could tell me that it's all going to be alright, and my head will stop spinning.

Be careful what you wish for, Hannah. That voice in my head slamming me back to that night.

I might have Leach's confession, but whose voice spoke those words? Could they have seen what happened? If I can remember, maybe they can help me?

I was gulping down alcohol – anything that came to hand. Anything I could find, I didn't care. I wanted oblivion, not bothering what form or shape it took. I just *wished and wished and wished* to not be feeling what I was feeling. Something had really upset me, I do remember that... *Yes... Yes...*

I remember dancing. There was a boy, wasn't there? Where did he go? *Whirling round and round...* I remember the feel of someone else's hands on my waist. *Did someone whisper those words in my ear?* The revulsion of that thought shudders through my spine. I pulled away, running out of the room, off into the darkness of the garden where the sounds of laughing voices wound through the trees; the bobbing lights casting multi-coloured shadows through the leaves, silvering them into weaving strange lights.

Why was I running?

My head trawls back to that night and a memory hits me – one that I had blotted out but now brings with it a feeling that is so familiar, it hurts.

I remember.

It slams into me like a brick wall.

It was Rachel.

I'd left Matt, hadn't I? And gone in search of wine. I remember picking up plastic cups from a long trestle table laid out under the trees and glancing round as I did so.

I caught sight of someone who looked just like her.

But it couldn't be Rachel, could it?

She couldn't be here – she was on a train going down to her parent's house. She'd packed her bag... So I'd forgotten the wine and moved to where I could get a better look.

But it *was* her.

And then the realisation that something must've happened, or she'd changed her mind, and heard about this party and decided to stay after all...

I remember my sudden surge of happiness as I walked quickly across the grass towards her. She was half turning away from view, glass in hand, laughing as I momentarily lost sight of her behind a line of bushes. Putting my hand out, I plucked a stem, aiming to step casually into their circle to surprise her, but as I did, her amused voice rang out, cutting through the background noise like the swish of a knife.

'*Hannah?* You mean the girl who shares my house?'

My hand paused.

'I know what you're going to say, but she's just a bit needy and insecure, that's all. I honestly feel sorry for her.' She paused. 'I know, I know... you don't have to tell me, I'm aware she can create a weird vibe with people sometimes... You have no idea what's wrong, but my god, you know that something is.' She laughed. I couldn't see her mannerism, but then I heard her sigh. 'It's a lot of pressure trying to second-guess what might have upset her. It's exhausting, but it's not like she means to be odd.' I imagined her shrugging. 'She just doesn't know how to articulate how she feels – hence creating the weird atmosphere is the only tool in her box to show how unhappy she is.'

'Sounds like hard work to me,' a male voice said, laughing.

A chill pooled into my gut. I was frozen, desperately wanting to turn away, but sick to hear more.

'I feel bad though.' I could just see the side of Rachel's face as she looked around the circle. 'She could make friends, but somehow she manages to create friction amongst them. She always needs people to take sides.'

'She's done that with you?' the male voice chimed in again.

'Mmm-mmm.' She sighed again. 'You know the other girl who shares the house – Alison, yeah? Well Hannah created a whole load of drama with her, telling her stuff – about how she felt that I'd excluded her, chosen to spend time with other people, and generally been a shit friend – and then, when I tried to speak to her, absolutely made out she hadn't said it. Practically called Alison a liar. It's all very odd. It's a way of getting me to choose her, I suppose. A kind of massive insecurity...'

'Sounds like she's got real problems,' the man's voice piped up again.

'I think she has. It's all very sad.' I imagined the hopeless shrug again. 'I just don't know what to do about it. I mean, it's all got a bit weird and nasty. I went back to the house when my train got cancelled and that's when I found Alison in her room, crying. She said that after I'd left, Hannah had gone up to her room and said to her, "You have to remember, Alison, with Rachel, I always get what I want."'

'No.' It was a woman's voice this time. 'Wow! That's too much. That's all so extra, you know? It's very, very intense, isn't it?'

'God. You do attract them, Rach,' someone said, and suddenly they were all laughing. Laughing at me. I was the joke. *Is that how they saw me?*

Horrible people, all of them, saying stuff so they could make Rachel question her relationship with me. Yes... that's what it was... They wanted to drive a wedge between me and her and make me look like someone I was not...

I wanted to run away right that moment. I wanted to disappear and hide so that none of them could ever find me again, but I found couldn't move; I was paralysed. Their laughter peeled out, ringing gaily over the line of bushes, getting louder, making me realise they were coming towards me. My feet galvanised into action. I floundered across the grass into the darkness where no one could find me, her words ringing in my ears, the laughter of the group...

Pity.

The worst feeling.

Rachel pitied me. Alison had lied about me. I didn't go to her room. I would never say such things. They were painting me in such an awful way. I wasn't needy and I wasn't the terrible person they were making me out to be. Why would they say such things?

My feet caught on the uneven ground making me stumble. My breath came out hoarse and ragged into the night air as I plunged further away from them, heartbroken and reeling in disbelief.

And there was the house with the French doors laying open, the light so inviting, where new people shouted and shrieked with laughter, dancing, having a great time... And I wanted to be like them... Leave all those old people behind. Find myself some new friends, ones who would never judge me, who would see me for the kind and caring person I really was... And so I threw myself into the midst of them, finding half-empty cups of whatever and downing it, not caring, and dancing like some mad thing... plastering a smile across my face that told anyone who was watching that I was the kind of person they'd want to be around.

But who was watching? Watching what was happening... Taking the opportunity when it presented itself?

Some long-buried memory threatens to step out from the shadows. From the corner of my mind's eye, I turn my head a little to see the face.

A hand offered me something... And a voice...

Not a boy's voice like I thought.

A girl's.

Alison?

But she wasn't there? She was back at the house sulking after the argument – she wasn't at the party.

I see her mouth smiling at me in the darkness as she offers me a drink. She's saying something; I can see her lips moving but I can't quite make out the words...

And then I do.

'Please, Hannah. Honestly, I don't hate you. I understand why you feel the way you do... Everyone feels the way you do sometimes. Everyone gets insecure and a bit jealous. Everyone gets things wrong with friends sometimes. Don't feel bad. Here – have a drink. It's some kind of cocktail, I think. Think of it as a peace offering.'

I stared down at the plastic glass in her hand.

'We were both upset, that's all. It was all so stressful with the Sanctum House stuff, wasn't it? We all say things we don't mean when tempers flare. I want us to all be friends, Hannah. We can put this behind us and move on. What do you say?'

I looked up into her face. Did I even trust her?

'You told Rachel bad stuff about me. You said, "I always get what I want",' I said to Alison heatedly. 'Why did you tell her that?'

'Because you're always manoeuvring and manipulating and working out ways to do just that. You don't need to create all that drama. Why not just be straight? Say what you'd like people to do – say what you need. Be open.'

A prickle of irritation scoured the nape of my neck.

'Oh, I wish I could be more like you, Alison.' I know I sound sneering. But it's because I'm hurt and bruised and angry. 'You seem to have it all sussed.'

Alison only regarded me gently but pointedly. 'Be careful what you wish for, Hannah. You really don't want to be like me. Be more of yourself, Hannah – but a softer more relaxed version. Chill out a bit. Give yourself a break. I'm not the enemy. I could be your very good friend.' And she thrust the drink into my hand, making me take it. 'As I said, it's a peace offering.'

But all I could feel was that acute burn of shame. I turned away from her, downing the cup of whatever it was, not wanting to be anywhere near her, or Rachel, or anyone for that matter... pushing through the backs and elbows, fighting for air along a hallway filled with heat and people, suffocating in the tang of sweat and shouting... and then suddenly finding myself sprawling out of a doorway into a kind of yard, a concrete space, gulping down the chill of the fresh night, my ears buzzing oddly, my eyes unable to focus as though I'd stumbled into a black sack of nothing.

A movement on my right and my head skewed round.

There was a shadow. It moved weirdly: lengthening and looming, before being joined by another. Two of them, like a pair of bad spirits.

'Hello?' I said tentatively, but my voice came back at me as though an echo from very far away. I glanced back at the doorway, but there was no doorway, no yard. I had the sensation of being lifted but I didn't know how. There was whispering close to my ear, and I managed to look up into the night sky, the stars becoming bright searing pinpricks of light, so bright I had to shield my eyes from them.

Everything was heightened yet dulled. I became acutely aware of my surroundings, but in flick-book flashes that made no sense. I was outside and then I was inside, but not the party, a quieter claustrophobic space with the smell of oil – something over my face... A hand? A cloth? A sharp sear of pain inside me, coupled with an instant panic of not being able to breathe. A weight constricting my ribcage, an iron grip of lead weight choking me as I tried to draw breath into my lungs... no air, no oxygen, the pressure building up and up, fighting for a single sip... and then suddenly gone. Dragging my lungs to inflate, and heaving... lying on my side and retching with a hand on my arm that I tried to fight off...

'Hannah?'

The smell of grass and earth filling my nostrils as I heaved again, the pooling liquid hot, and then cold against my cheek, as tiny cooling drops of summer rain pattered suddenly and then stopped.

'Hannah?... God, Hannah?' A girl's voice.

But my eyes wouldn't open, as though they'd been glued tight shut.

'Can you help me, someone? Can you help me here?'

And the hand on my arm becoming tighter, gripping me, sliding across my back and around my wait to hoist me up.

'Let's get her inside, there's a downstairs loo... All these people. Can I get through, please? Sorry, could you move? My friend's not very well...' Alison's voice. And then she was gone and Matt was there with me, and I was in my own bed and he was bringing me water and unravelling yards of toilet tissue, his face full of worry.

I just about managed to focus, my hand reaching for him as I attempted to struggle to sit up, but my arms giving way, unable to support my weight. I felt as weak as a kitten.

My memories after that are vague. Snapshots of moments: of me opening my eyes and being alone; a hard shard of daylight etched into the dim ceiling; an then that moment of waking with a gasp of pain, my legs rigid with the agony of it, trying to move, my skin not feeling like my skin, as I peeled myself from the sheet, and glanced down at what was there beneath me as my head failed to compute what had happened.

I don't think I left my room over the next few days. I remember Rachel knocking on my door a few times, and I remember Matt's concerned face in the gap, standing there with a tray of food that I couldn't touch and tea I couldn't drink. I remember waiting until I was sure they'd all gone out before I ventured into the bathroom for the first time, running myself a bath that was so searing hot, my skin reddened and prickled with pins and needles at the merest touch of the water. I lay in it anyway, watching the swirls change from aqua to a yellowy brown. I couldn't look at my body. I was an alien.

I knew something bad had happened, but I blocked it from my mind.

I couldn't formulate words, not even in my own head.

I couldn't think, couldn't speak, couldn't see anyone.

I wrote an email to my university supervisor telling her that I had 'personal problems at home' that I needed to sort out. She told me to take as long as I wanted. And that's precisely what I did. I moved through the following days and weeks not feeling as though time was passing; each day was a replica of the previous one. Outwardly, I was functioning normally. I laughed off the notion that I'd got so hammered at the party that Alison had to haul me home. I feigned surprise at Rachel having missed her train. I was courteous and friendly to Alison when I saw her, apologising and rolling my eyes at my behaviour. I started going out in the daytime as though I was attending lectures or working in the library, when I wasn't. I even made out that I'd 'met up with some new people and started socialising a bit', when actually I was staying in my room with the door locked.

I convinced Matt, Rachel and Alison that I was fine – busy, but fine. On the occasions when I bumped into Rachel in the kitchen, I was jokey and blasé. She was always smiley and kind, asking how I was doing? I told her all about my new-found friends and where we'd been and what we'd seen and she, in turn, smiled even more and patted my arm and told me how pleased she was that I seemed to be 'getting things together.'

I gave no clues to contradict – not to her, or to Matt, and definitely not to Alison.

When I think back, most of that time barely registers at all. I outwardly functioned in a way that suited everyone. Inwardly, though, was quite another matter.

I was holding it together, or so I thought, not allowing myself to think too deeply or feel too much, quiet there behind my locked bedroom door so that they had no idea I was there.

And that was how I overheard them.

Rachel and Alison.

They came in through the front door about mid-morning one day, giggling and twittering about something I couldn't hear properly. My heart stopped. I held my breath as, whispering, they stopped on the other side of my door, pausing for a moment. Their whispers got more insistent and then there was a tiny rapping and the shifting of feet.

'Hannah?' It was Rachel. 'Hannah? Are you there?'

I stayed quiet.

'I don't think she is,' I heard Alison say. 'I think I heard her go out earlier.'

'Well, we're going to have to tell her at some point,' Rachel said.

Some soft patter of alarm clutched at my heart.

'You don't have to do this, you know, Rachel', Alison chimed in. 'It's very kind of you to suggest it, but I'm happy to live by myself. You don't have to come with me. It won't change our friendship – we'll still see just as much of each other. I just need to have more space.' She breathed out in a long sigh. 'It's sweet of you, but—'

'You can't live alone,' Rachel put in. 'That's no fun. No, it'll be good for Hannah and Matt to stand on their own two feet, won't it?'

No, no, no, no.

'I mean I've supported her as much as I can; she has to make an effort too, doesn't she?'

The patter around my heart turned into a thud.

'I just don't know how well she'll take the notion of us two sharing a flat next year and not including her.'

'She'll be fine here with Matt.' Rachel laughed. 'They'll find another couple of oddbods to move in and create a proper little family.'

They were both laughing as they wandered off into the kitchen leaving me, breath held, standing by the door, head cocked and unable to move, terrified that they'd hear me. Their voices came back again, Alison calling out to Rachel.

'It's really sunny out there and there's not a lot of shade in that garden. Do we need hats?'

'Yeah, good idea. Matt's got mine in his car. He'll be there already probably. He's got crates of booze and he's dropping it round to them,' Rachel called back, 'so he'll meet us there...'

There was the sound of feet and rustling and words I couldn't make out, and then the front door opened and slammed shut and their voices rang out in the quiet street as they walked away from the house and then silence descended.

The pent-up sob scoured the back of my throat. I couldn't, I wouldn't, let it out.

Alison had played Rachel perfectly.

I saw the ploy, the way she'd hooked her carefully with tears and tales of how awful I'd been, and then let her swim gently away before quietly reeling her in. Oh, I saw it all.

Rachel was leaving me.

That's all I could think.

Rachel was leaving me.

Despite everything that had happened, everything that she'd said about me, my anger was only masking a deep, deep hurt that clawed at my insides until I felt as though my guts had been hauled out and exposed for all to see.

Alison had duped her. Rachel had allowed herself to be duped.

But she wasn't the bad one – no, she wasn't bad, just trusting and easily led.

No matter how furious I was, all I remembered were the moments of pure unadulterated happiness I'd felt since I'd met her.

That was the real Rachel.

The cups of tea in bed together, the giggling, the showing me how to do makeup, the experimenting with hairstyles, the clothes, the shopping, the cooking together, the squawking and messing about... all that.

The tears came then, silently choking out of me in great heaving swathes of pain from somewhere deep inside of me. I got up, viciously grabbing at the duvet and violently chucking it onto the floor, casting around the room and viciously sweeping all the books and cups off my bedside table. A whirl around, and then all the bottles and jars and pots tumbled from the dresser in one go. I stamped and smashed and trampled as I went, flinging the wardrobe door wide, dragging and tearing at clothes, my rage and hurt and humiliation singing in my ears as I pulled everything out in one great bundle.

And then there it was in my hands.

The dress that Rachel had left for me the night of the party, the mustard skirt, thin and flimsy in my fingers.

I should have burned it.

One dig and pull and I could have the thing in two. But I couldn't do anything. I could only stare down at its stained folds, the me before that night and the me after, the images sliding, one over the other, swapping and changing in front of my eyes.

How happy I'd been when she's left it for me. How beautiful I'd felt putting it on. How cared-for and loved and looked-after.

And now she was leaving me.

I'd probably never see her again.

The panic rose up in me, a desperate thing, and with it a pain like the grip of a vice. A spring of sweat slicked my hairline and I winced, biting my lip.

If only I could stop her.

If only I could make her care about me, and me alone – no Alison, no Matt, no one, just me and her, like how it used to be.

She was all I'd ever wanted.

And I always got what I wanted.

SEVENTEEN

'She doesn't want to see you.' Emily stands at her front door, her arms folded staunchly. Her eyes are clear and direct boring straight into mine.

'It's you I want to talk to.' I hold my ground, trying not to shiver as the light around me changes to grey.

'Thanks so much for setting me up with your friend Geraldine, Emily. Thank you for betraying my confidence. You lied to me, brutally and blatantly. You lied to me to protect Leach. A stinking rapist.'

She lets out a tiny snort of derision. 'Me? Well, thank God I did, Hannah. Thank God I didn't jeopardise a man's freedom for your delusions. While I have absolute empathy for the chaos and abuse you've experienced in your life, you can't hold innocent parties to account with no evidence against them at all.'

'Innocent parties?' The words take my breath away.

'You're convincing though, Hannah, I'll give you that.' She gives me that patronising earnest smile again. 'I was almost taken in by what you told me last night in the kitchen.'

I feel a queasy tingle of anxiety.

'Yes. Almost. But I had another call last night. A very interesting one, actually.'

My throat constricts involuntarily.

'I've been trying to put it all together, your turning up on Rachel's doorstep after all these years, this story about Leach—'

'It's not a story,' I interject. 'It's the truth.'

She purses her lips into a tiny smile. 'I think it's fair to say your relationship with the truth is pretty shaky though, isn't it?'

'I want to speak to Rachel,' I demand.

'Seventeen years,' she continues. 'Where have you been for seventeen years?

'There were no jobs, were there, Hannah? There was no conference. You were never a caseworker or a social worker or a teacher or even a volunteer. You had a caseworker. You had a social worker. You were sectioned.'

A sudden gust of rain stings the side of my face.

'There's no shame in it, Hannah. Just own it.' The purse of Emily's lips draws tighter and she gives me that oh-so-superior nod again. 'If you were prepared to be straight with Rachel now, I'm sure she'd listen.'

'What lies have you told her?'

'She deserved to know.'

'I struggled for a while, that's all. You didn't have to say all that.' I find I am almost crying. 'You didn't have to be that cruel.'

'But I did, Hannah. Truthfulness and honesty in a friendship are very important. It's the basis of trust, isn't it?' She gives me a condescending look. 'But I'll leave you to tell her about Matt.' She tips her head on one side. 'It's only fair that comes directly from you.'

I feel the noose of control slip quietly around my neck, but I'm not giving in that easily.

'Me and Matt? Don't make me laugh.' I stare her down, holding my ground. 'Nothing's happened. Rachel won't believe it has, no matter how you try and spin it.' My face burns red.

'Nonsense?' She feigns puzzlement. 'But I *saw* you, Hannah. I saw the two of you together.'

'Saw us? When? What are you talking about?'

'In the park.'

The wind gathers in a swirl behind me, bringing a patter of rain. I gather myself. 'I was getting some air. We were talking, that's all. You followed us?'

'Rachel said she had a headache and I told her to go and lie down, and I'd already noticed the vibe between you and Matt. I took the opportunity to see what you two were up to. I'm very glad I did.' She looks down at me for a moment, and then leans forward to draw me in.

'You see, I know who, and what you are, Hannah. I *know* you.' Her mask of professionalism slips a little.

'You know nothing, Emily.'

'Oh, I think I've worked you out.' She's trying not to smirk in triumph. 'You're bad news, Hannah. You're no good for Rachel, no good at all. You take advantage of her good nature.'

Something inside me tightens.

'I want to see her,' I repeat stonily.

'Well, she doesn't want to see you. And there's no point in keeping on turning up here. We're going away. She needs a break from all this, somewhere a long way away: from you, from Matt – the awfulness that you've dragged her into.'

'And James. What about him?'

I see a hesitance flicker behind her eyes.

'What about him?'

'I don't think Rachel will just walk away from James. He's what she wants.'

The flicker hardens into a defiant stare. 'There is no James, Hannah. She ended it. You don't know what you're talking about.'

'Are you sure about that, Emily?' I see the hesitance become something more. 'Because I know James has been on Rachel's mind a lot. He's been on her phone a lot too...

All the gifts and phone calls and messages? Of course she's told you all about that, hasn't she?' I feel the momentum gathering into my hands. 'She's told me she can't stop thinking about him.'

I say it loud enough just in case Rachel might be listening.

'And then of course, you say there's no evidence against Leach. Did you know he'd written to me, confessing? Oh yes, he has. And with his confession comes yet another problem. But I'm assuming Rachel hasn't told you about her involvement in that either?'

There's a split-second query on her face.

'What are you talking about? Rachel and Hugo Leach?'

'It's either a "yes" or "no", Emily. Simple question. Do you know how Rachel helped me after I was raped?' My voice rings out loud and clear. I let the word hang in the air; it feels good to articulate it: real and true and honest.

'How she *helped* you? What the hell are you talking about?'

'*Ask* her.' I gesture into the space behind her. 'Ask her in front of both of us, here and now. Let's have the truth out in the open.'

That sanctimonious smirk wavers and I take a step towards her.

'Well? Can I come in?'

Her shoulders collapse a little and I take my chance to push past her into the hallway.

'She's in the kitchen.'

I hurry to find her. The space feels strange. The odd, stormy light reflects dully, lingering on the dirty wine glasses still on the side, plates and cups stacked, but no Rachel. I look back at Emily.

'She must be upstairs. One minute.'

She disappears and I listen to the sound of her feet on the stairs and the movement overhead.

I have no idea what I'll say when I see her. I have no clue how to explain what happened to me all those years ago: what happened after I walked away from that patch of waste ground; how she was the one good memory I held on to; the promise we made, the one I knew she'd keep.

'She's not there.' Emily appears breathless in the doorway. 'I don't know where she is. I've tried phoning her, but she's not picking up.'

My eyes go to the back door. It's sitting ajar. Emily follows my gaze in shock. 'But where would she have gone?' She suddenly panics. 'Her things are still upstairs. Why would she leave like this?'

'Maybe she heard me speaking the truth, Emily. Have you thought of that? And maybe...' I let the pause hang in the air. '...maybe she's gone to James after all.'

There are seconds where her face only registers a kind of blind terror.

'No. No. No. She wouldn't.' Her face drops. 'You don't understand, Hannah. She wouldn't do that to me.'

I watch as her fevered anxiety gears up. 'She can't do this... She wouldn't do this.' She searches frantically around for her car keys. 'She can't have gone far. I have to find her.'

The sheer scale of her panic ramps into a frenzy as something begins to dawn on me.

'Rachel's a grown woman, Emily.'

'She can't do this to me. She can't.'

She finds the keys and heads for the door with me following close on her heels.

'What's all this about?' I press. I'm two steps behind her. 'Why are you so desperate? Why did you pretend you'd help me and then throw me under the bus?'

She doesn't answer as she heads for her car.

'Why did you need to go snooping into my private life? Why? What is—' I peter off as she swings the driver's door wide and then it hits me.

'Oh my god. You have real feelings. You're in love with her.'

She falters as though I've punched her.

'You're in *love* with her,' I say again, my fingertips curling around the door frame and holding on tight so that she can't get away.

'Just tell me, Emily. Let me understand what all this has been about.'

Her face slowly rises to meet mine.

'I don't have to tell you anything,' she spits.

'No, you're right, you don't.' And within seconds I'm around at the passenger side and yanking the door open. 'But you're not going anywhere without me either.'

'Get out of my car.' Her teeth are gritted tight.

'No.'

'Get out of my car, Hannah! Get out of my space. Get out of my life. Things were fine before you turned up.'

I bite my bottom lip as I haul the door shut with a slam. 'Shame.'

'If you don't—'

'If I don't, what? What are you going to do, Emily? You've already decided to destroy my relationships, you've destroyed my chance to confront the man who ruined my life. What else are you planning on doing?' I skew round in my seat to face her directly.

'You've put all this together very cleverly. You've presented it to Rachel tied up in a neat bow – but you don't know the actual truth. I have *not* been having an affair with Matt, because I wouldn't do that to my closest friend. I came to her house to tell her what kind of a man she was married to – I owed her that – but then I discovered things, and I wanted answers to things, and I wanted my oldest friend to help me. But now, thanks to you, she thinks I betrayed her from the beginning.' I wave angrily. 'So if you want to find her, I'm betting she's gone to confront Matt. She'll be on foot, so I suggest you stop fighting with me and go after her.'

We drive with Emily's furious silence filling the space between us as we both desperately search the streets left and right for a sight of her. Emily stabs again and again at the Bluetooth console, shouting Rachel's name in desperation as the ringing tone echoes into the car's interior. But Rachel doesn't reply.

There's another rumbling boom of soft thunder as we pull up outside Rachel and Matt's house. I am out of the car immediately, with Emily close on my heels, but we both stop abruptly at the sight of the front door. The wintery light slides for a second and then comes back.

It's open. There's a flurry of rainy snow partway into the hall, blown in by the wind. My heart skitters.

'Rachel?' I call out nervously. But there's no reply.

I prod the door wider.

'Matt?' I shout tentatively. 'Rachel? Matt? Are you here?'

A feeling comes – a definite wrongness in a sharp band of pain around my chest. There's a scatter of torn paper on the hall floor, the edges lifting a little in the draught. An odd patterning of light flickers on the wall, and I turn my head. The ornate mirror is smashed into a spider's web of cracks; my face reflects back, weird and disjointed.

'Rachel!' The anxiety gathers faster now. 'Rachel?'

I look back at Emily.

'I'm ringing the police.' Her hand goes to her pocket.

'What was that?' I instinctively touch her sleeve.

There's a strange sound coming from somewhere deep in the house. It sounds like an animal that's been wounded. I wheel around.

'There it is again.'

Treading carefully over the broken glass, we pause at the bottom of the stairs.

'Up here!'

But Emily hangs back. 'Hannah! Don't go up there.' Her voice is a terrified whisper, but I ignore her. Treading quickly, I get to the top. The door to my room is open. Even from here I can see the wreckage. The mattress has been hauled from the bed, the wardrobe is lying across it.

I almost don't see the crumpled figure amongst the strewn clothes.

'Matt!'

He's on his knees, head down, one hand lifted to a gash on his forehead.

'Oh my god.' I rush forward, but he holds me off, his arm floundering wildly. 'It's me, Matt. It's Hannah. What's happened? Where's Rachel?'

'I don't know... I don't know.' He moans. 'She rang me... We were having an argument. She was saying all kinds of stuff.' He glances at me. 'She was screaming at me about me having an affair with you.' He looks around, dazed. 'When suddenly there was a terrific crash like someone was smashing in the front door. I came out of my office, and there was this... this...' A shaking hand comes up to his face. '...figure. A man, coming towards me so fast – then the force of him slammed into me. I hit the wall – I hit my head maybe... I don't know – suddenly everything went black.' He winces.

Emily appears behind me, kneeling amongst the debris, trying to see the wound.

'I'm definitely calling an ambulance and the police right now.' Her fingers tremble as she tries to unlock her phone. 'We need something for your head.' She looks around as the tiny voice of the operator answers. 'Can you grab a towel or something Hannah? Something – anything... Yes, hello, we need police and an ambulance.'

Leach. A sudden wash of dread comes over me. Who else would it be? I reach out and grab Emily's hand.

'What if he's got her?'

Emily freezes mid word. I am aware of the tinny whine of the person on the other end of the line.

'What?'

'Leach. What if he's got Rachel?'

Matt's dazed eyes skim from me to her. 'What are you talking about Hannah? What is this?'

'We'll have to tell the police what we did: Rachel... Me...'

All I can hear is the operator down the line. Emily is staring at me.

'We *did* something. My coming back here. My going to see Leach... He knows where I've been staying. It's all connected.'

I pull out a wad of tissue from my pocket and begin to dab at the wound near Matt's temple. The twittering insect whine from the phone shuts off abruptly as Emily pockets her phone.

'I'll ring them back in a second.'

Matt and I can only stare at her.

'You're still protecting him, aren't you?' I hiss. 'I cannot, cannot—'

But Matt puts a hand on my arm. 'You said Rachel... You and Rachel did what?' Matt sits unsteadily back on his heels.

'After Leach drugged and raped me' – I'm breathless and shaking as I look from one to the other – 'I became pregnant. I couldn't hide it. I decided to run away but started to miscarry. I hid on a building site. I rang Rachel and asked her to help me. We didn't report it and I didn't go to a doctor. We buried the... the remains.'

'You buried a baby?' Emily's mouth hangs open. Her eyes dart from me to Matt.

'*We* did. I made Rachel help me. We'll have to tell the police that's what we did. That's why I went to see Leach.'

All I can hear is Matt's breathing.

'I threatened him.'

'You threatened him?' She's incredulous.

'By telling him I have his DNA. I showed him photographs of the building site beyond the cemetery where they're planning the new housing development. I wanted him to confess.'

I'm panting; everything feels high up in my lungs. 'He had no idea what I had on him. He must've thought, whatever it was, I would've brought it here for safekeeping.'

'Was it that night...?' Matt's voice is soft and I look at him. 'The night of that party when you were so out of it?' I look at him. He's barely hearing what I'm saying. 'That's the night he attacked you?'

I don't speak.

'Oh my god, Hannah. Is that why you backed away from everyone? Is that why you disappeared so suddenly?'

'Where's Rachel, Matt?' Emily's voice cuts across him, scared and insistent. 'Where is she?'

His eyes are wide and staring. 'I – I don't know. I told you, she was screaming down the phone at me. That's the last thing I remember, she—' He halts abruptly, his eyes widening.

'What?' Emily insists. 'What?'

'The last thing I remember... the last thing...' Matt is already struggling to his feet. 'She was shouting about those messages on her phone. About someone wanting to meet her. Hannah? You remember – she told you about it too. I didn't believe her, but—'

My eyes follow him upwards in horror.

'I think I might know,' says Emily quietly.

Matt and I look at her.

She licks her lips. 'I had a message too, asking me to meet. Mine was a veiled threat. I should've said something – I should have told someone,' she says dully.

'What? What are you talking about?' I'm nearly screaming with frustration.

'From Hugo Leach.'

I glare at her. 'How the hell can it be Leach?'

'Because he got hold of my phone when I was at a meeting in the prison.'

'He did what?'

She swallows. 'I took it onto the wing by accident. I'm supposed to report a breach in security like that, but he's so high profile, and there'd be an investigation.' Her hands come up to her eyes to shut out the horror. 'I thought I'd lose my job. I'd lose everything I've worked for.'

She shakes her head. 'It only happened once, but of course he only needed one chance,' she mumbles. 'He said he wanted to meet me when he got released. He said we could be very helpful to each other. He said it would be nice to meet all my friends.' She takes a breath, staring at us. 'I deleted and blocked his number, but he must've seen all my contacts.'

My spine feels as though it's made of ice, but Matt is already floundering towards the window.

'Matt... Matt. Stop. Where are you going?'

He's already heading for the door with Emily close behind him.

'Matt!' I'm scrabbling after him. 'You're in no fit state.'

But he's down the stairs, grabbing for his coat, pushing Emily back and yanking the front door open.

'Matt!' I shout as Emily tries desperately to follow. 'Matt... You can't. No!'

But he's only slams it behind him, leaving Emily and I fumbling at the lock. By the time we have it open, he's got to his car.

'Stop!' I yell, slithering in the slushy snow and grabbing the handle. I desperately try to hang on, but my fingertips barely skim the paintwork as he screeches away. I stand in the road watching in panic as he slews into an oncoming car. A horn blares violently before he veers away again, gunning the engine.

'I'm ringing the police and then I'm ringing Rachel to warn her,' Emily breathes, pulling out her phone.

She starts to pace, agitated as she rings with no one answering. The light is fading fast. The temperature is dropping by degrees. All I can do is stand and watch pathetically, praying and praying that somehow Emily has this all wrong.

Emily's face suddenly drops with relief. 'Rachel. God... Thank God. Where are you?' She looks past me as my heart hammers wildly in my chest.

Oh, thank you God, my heart says. *Rachel is on the other end of that phone. She's safe.* It takes all my control not to snatch it out of Emily's hands.

'Where is she?' I hiss, but Emily only holds up a hand to quieten me and begins to walk away.

'Yes, but, Rachel, listen. Listen... That text might not be from a woman. No, listen Rachel. I'm being deathly serious. It could be Hugo Leach... No, Rachel, look... You're not listening... You can't know that,' Emily insists, pushing the wet hair from her face in frustration. 'I'm at your house... Yes. Someone has broken in and Matt was attacked... No, he's fine. He's coming to find you... Has he rung you? Well, you need to contact him then. Promise me you won't meet anyone. Where are you?... Oh, okay. Right. Right... Look, Rachel. Promise m— Rachel? Rachel?'

Emily heads for her car.

'What's happened? Where are you going?' I'm frantic as I go after her. 'Emily! Answer me. Where's Rachel? Is she with Leach?' I go to grab her arm.

'Emily? Tell me!'

But she wheels me away, elbowing me sharply.

'Get off! Get off me. I don't know, okay? She says she's

meeting someone she knows and it's all fine. Just leave me alone. Leave us both alone.'

She goes to get in, but I grab the keys from her hand, dropping breathlessly behind the wheel and staring up at her.

'What the hell do you think you're doing?' she shrieks.

'I've already told you, you're not going anywhere without me. If you know where Rachel is and she could be in danger, then I'm coming with you.'

'I'll give you one chance,' Emily snarls.

'Or what?' I look up at her blankly. 'I'm in your car and I have your car keys and your house keys. I can drive away now – or you can get in and we can go and find Rachel. Your choice, Emily.'

She stands mute and furious for a moment, and then runs round to the passenger side.

'She's at a café down by the river.' She stares resolutely ahead. 'Just drive if you're going to.'

My legs are jelly as I start the car, anxiety washing through my stomach. I drive, scared to brake, scared to steer, begging the road to let me get there faster.

The streetlamps reflect a weird orange in the banked-up drifts of snow. The street signs have disappeared. Nothing is familiar anymore. I lean in closer to the windshield, desperate for anything to show me where I am, and then suddenly I see it – the turning

where I know the tow path begins, and I'm throwing the door open, practically abandoning the car and pulling out my phone to find Matt's number.

'Where are you?' I say frantically to his voicemail message. 'Emily knows where Rachel is. We're heading for a café by the river. Ring me.'

Emily is walking away from me and I hurry after her,

following her down to where the bright lights from a two-tier boat café at the river side burn fiercely into the foggy mist. The boat's heavy mooring chains are illuminated by hazy blue and pink lights. On the bank, a few figures huddle around outdoor tables, watching children shriek along the towpath throwing snowballs at each other. None of them are Rachel. The creeping sensation up my spine tingles with a tightening charge.

'Can you see her? Is she there?'

But Emily is staunchly silent, crunching down the snow-laden gravel path towards the bright lights.

'She must have said something,' I pant beside her. 'She said it was all fine. It can't be Leach then, can it? How could she know this person, Emily? How could she kn—?'

'Wow! Enough already.' Emily rounds on me in a flash of temper. 'It turns out the person is an old friend.' She snaps angrily. 'Will that snippet shut you up? It's some woman called Alison.'

EIGHTEEN

'Alison?' I halt abruptly, grabbing her sleeve. 'That's not possible.'

'And why's that?' Emily tries to unwind my fingers, but I'm holding on for dear life.

'Because... because she...' My head won't compute. I pull out my phone and search for Rachel's number. 'Why would she be here? Why would she be here now?'

'You know her?'

Rachel's phone rings out, over and over. I feel a rising sense of panic. 'This doesn't feel right, Emily. Alison is someone that we used to share the house with. Matt mentioned her recently... Rachel didn't keep in touch with her as far as I know. She would have mentioned it, I'm sure she would.'

'Oh, Rachel tells you everything, doesn't she?' Emily pulls herself free.

'She would've *said*,' I insist.

'Oh, for God's sake, Hannah.' Emily shakes me off. 'You just don't get it, do you?' She begins to walk away from me.

'Get what?' I'm forced to jog after her. The icy snowflakes drive in hard gusts, stinging my face.

'Rachel can't stand you. She never could.' Her words are whipped over her shoulder and a dull rumble of thunder booms far away.

'That's a lie! A dirty stinking lie. Rachel wouldn't say that.' A sob catches in my throat.

But Emily shakes me away angrily. 'She always knew there was something weird about you – something off. She said she pitied you, that's all.'

I catch her up, panting at her side. 'No. She wouldn't. You weren't there. It wasn't like that. I had problems, sure. Like we all do when we're young. Rachel was the one who helped me—'

'Helped you?' she snorts. 'Was forced to deal with you, you mean.'

'She's just a bit needy and insecure, that's all. I honestly feel sorry for her.'

Rachel's own words drift back to me.

'Rachel was on my side. She had my back when it counted.'

The light on the pathway dims and brightens as the storm clouds shift.

'You manipulated her, you mean. You lied about things you'd said. Is that what friends do, Hannah?'

'I didn't lie, Emily. I'm not the person you're making me out to be.'

I hear Rachel's voice, all concerned: *'Mmm-mmm.'* She *sighed again. 'You know the other girl who shares the house – Alison, yeah? Well, Hannah created a whole load of drama with her, telling her stuff – about how she felt that I'd excluded her, chosen to spend time with other people, and generally been a shit friend – and then, when I tried to speak to her, absolutely made out she hadn't said it. Practically called Alison a liar. It's all very odd. It's a way of getting me to choose her, I suppose. A kind of massive insecurity... Making out she didn't say stuff... It's a way of getting me to choose her over other people.'*

'What was it you said, Hannah? *"You always get what you*

want." That's right, isn't it?' I hear the words coming at me in the strange light. The sound of the river behind her icily clucks and chuckles.

'But I saw through all that, Hannah. Right from the start. I've seen how you manoeuvre her and take advantage. You can't help yourself. Rachel has a good heart. She needs protecting from people like you.' She marches away from me, hunched and head down, to where the shadows bloom darker on the path.

'And you're here to rescue her are you, Emily?' I shout after her. 'Fight us off until you've got Rachel all to yourself? Is that the grand plan? You're in for one big shock, you know that? I know Rachel better than anyone. You're nothing but a passing fad,' I spit. 'An amusement, that's all. You can't compete with me, Emily. No matter what happens, Rachel and I are bound together with what we did. We're bound for life.' I'm breathless with it.

She turns slowly. 'Jeez, can you actually hear yourself, Hannah?' she sneers. 'How old are you? Seriously. You need to grow up.' She shakes her head, chuckling horribly.

'Bound together?' she mimics. 'What a silly delusional bitch you are.' And with that she walks away from me towards the boat café, all brightly lit as the thunder echoes again.

I am alone, here, on the towpath. A cloak of snowy shadow settles around me. I can only stand there, trapped in my own bubble of dumb shock.

Something comes to me.

'Was that you?' I shout after her, but she ignores me.

'Was that you?' I say again louder, more forcefully, striding after her. 'Was that you who left the snowman and the rose petals?'

That stops her.

'What?' She wrinkles her nose incredulously. 'What the hell are you going on about now?'

'You left a snowman outside with a heart on it. They had

them at the prison, you could easily have got hold of one. Then there was the bath and the rose petals. It was you, wasn't it?' I go right up to her. Her eye sockets are dead like pits of shade. There's a sound.

She begins to giggle.

Her face distorts in the weird half-light, her nose and mouth like some Punch and Judy character. The river water laps, dark, black and oily. A sudden flash of lightning illuminates the path beneath my feet, and then it goes dark. I shift, feeling the crunch of it, the slew of grit beneath the soles of my shoes.

'You tried to intimidate me,' I say quietly. 'You came into the house. You knew I was terrified of Leach. Rachel would have told you.'

'Oh, wow! Dear me.' She laughs, like a hiss of air. 'You've really lost it big time, haven't you?'

I look at the lights from the café reflecting out onto the white towpath. There's no one about. A narrow wooden gangplank bridges the towpath to the boat's door.

'I'm going in here to meet Rachel, Hannah. I might also meet her friend Alison. I suggest you go away now – back to wherever it is you came from. I suggest you get some professional help too. Clearly you aren't ready to deal with the stresses of life outside.' She smiles that appallingly condescending smile of hers, pausing to reach for the rope handrail, but also successfully barring my way.

'I mean, nobody wants you here, do they?' Emily bites her lip, but I see the flinch of a smile. 'There's nothing and no one here for you. You really should do yourself a favour.'

But I'm not listening to her. I'm staring at the bright whiteness of the boat café window: Rachel is alone and sitting facing the door. She's looking up expectantly, with her coffee cup paused in both hands. She must be aware of the shadows moving but can't see us in the darkness. She can't see me. But I can see her – and who is sitting two tables behind her.

It's not Alison.

It's Leach.

'Oh my god—' The words spill from my mouth as Emily turns to look, her hand reaching out to grab the rope rail.

There's a moment, a kind of slow-motion flounder, where she tries, but somehow fails to get a hold. She steps awkwardly sideways from the gangplank, her ankle twisting, her shoulder buckling.

The thunder cracks and roars.

There are seconds, *just seconds – one... two...* – where I see the shock registering on her pale face, her hand reaching out for mine, but I hold still. Very still.

One minute she's there, and the next, there's a splash of black water.

I look down into the oily turbulence, where the anchor for the boat is secured. I think she might call out again and I look behind me. There's no one. The thunder roils again, and I count the seconds.

Three... Four...

There's a flash of electricity, lighting up the sky before it all goes dark.

Five... Six...

My eyes adjust to the darkness, looking for signs of movement, but there's only the sensation of the air around me tightening in a little shiver. Dark water laps up the hull of the boat: a greedy suck and draw. I look down at the gangplank where Emily once was. She was there and now she's gone.

I am alone.

My eyes search the café window. Leach is pushing his chair back. I see Rachel turn her head slightly towards the sound. I know what he's going to do and I'm not going to let him.

My hand reaches for the café door and I push it open. Rachel, him, me – no one else.

Leach looks up. His jaw drops in mock alarm. 'Hannah.'

Rachel turns in her seat. Leach hasn't taken his eyes from me.

'What?' she says.

I glance round. The café owner is out the back. I see her moving around the tiny kitchen with her back to me. There's a half-made sandwich on the countertop.

I don't say anything. I saunter, almost casually towards Rachel.

'Who...' she says. '... Leach?' She goes to stand up but I body block his path to her.

'Keep away from her.' I hold up a hand at his smiling face. The table behind me hasn't been cleared. *Steak*, my brain says. *The customers had steak* – and my other hand slides the serrated knife quietly into my sleeve.

My phone buzzes. Leach's eyes flit to my jacket. I know it must be Matt.

'Calm down, ladies.' Leach smiles his ruined smile. 'I'm only here for a chat. Like I told you, Rachel, there are things you should know.'

I see the sudden jolt as her spine stiffens. 'You're...' Rachel starts in horror. 'You're the one that messaged me?'

'The very same.'

'But how—?'

There's the sound of scuffing feet as the café owner appears. 'Sorry, love. I didn't hear you come in.'

'Oh, don't worry, we're just leaving.' Leach gets up quickly – so quickly I don't have a chance to react. He takes Rachel by the arm.

'But your—' the woman starts, but he's already hustling Rachel towards the door. I see the mute shock on Rachel's bowed face. Her terror forces my fingers to curl towards the blade at my wrist, and I feel the reassuring sharpness of its tip.

Leach shoves Rachel brusquely down the gangplank. The snow begins to fall, thick and fast, billowing down.

'I said a deal is a deal.' He looks back at me, teeth slightly bared. 'You have something of mine, and I want it. Now I have something of yours.' He gives Rachel a little shake, pushing her into the shadows of the towpath. The dark water splashes and eddies amongst the reeds of the riverbank. He blinks through the teeming flurries, his eyes darting around. Did he see Emily here? The memory of her feels almost like something half-remembered as a sense of complete calms come over me. I press the knife closer.

'Thing is, you women are just so *easy* in so many ways.' His eyes meet mine and I feel my guts twist. 'You believe what you want to believe.' He tuts, shaking his head. 'You believe what's in front of you.'

'How did you get Rachel's number, Leach? How did you track me down?' I demand.

'Mmm-mm, I wonder,' he muses. 'Now, how could I have got information? Let me think now…'

'Where's Emily?' Rachel blurts suddenly, but he twists Rachel's arm behind her back so hard she cries out. My right hand grips my sleeve.

'The problem with phones and people, is that their whole lives are in there for the taking. Emily thinks she's so clever, talking about me and showing me off. I'm the little feather in her cap, doncha know?' He winks. 'Where is she, by the way? I thought she'd be here by now.'

'She's gone to get help.' I throw at him. 'She's contacted the police.'

'Really?' He cocks a hand to his ear. 'Can't hear any sirens and flashing lights, can you? And anyway, by the time they turn up, we'll be well away from here. Where is our transport parked?'

I say nothing, but Rachel's back instantly arches with pain.

'At the street that joins the towpath,' I splutter. 'Just don't hurt her.'

He shoves Rachel roughly in front of him, wrapping his arm around her as though trying to keep her warm. We bundle awkwardly along the path. People pass us and I desperately try to catch their eyes, but they're muffled in hats and scarves, so focussed on getting home they barely notice we're there.

A sense of unreality washes over me as we cut up through the gap to the side street. The windows of the houses either side are warm with light. There must be people behind them, people who would help us if only they knew what was happening – but all the time I know, deep down, that there's nothing and no one between us and what this man is about to do.

'Here.' I head towards my car.

'You're driving, and Rachel goes in front of me.' Leach points towards the passenger seat. 'We don't want any accidents. I'll be right behind her, just remember that.'

I grimly get in, keeping my arm pressed across my stomach, feeling the reassuring dig of the handle. *I can do this*, my head says. *I can wait until he's distracted. One swift skew round in the seat and I can plunge—*

He slides in behind Rachel. There's a rustling and I see her head jerk back. He's slipped a wire noose around her neck.

'Just in case of any funny ideas.' The thin metal shines dully in the dim light. 'You know where we're going, I take it? You said some waste ground, didn't you. You must know where it is.'

'It's getting dark,' I stutter, panicking. 'We won't be able to find anything in the dark.'

'Drive,' he commands.

I fumble as I attempt to start the engine. From the corner of my eye I see Rachel is crying in absolute terror. My hands are shaking so much I can barely grip the wheel.

'I said drive.'

The tyres spin a little in the slush as we jerk forward. I can barely use my feet. A bubble of fear escapes from between Rachel's lips.

'Shut up, you stupid bitch,' he snaps.

My rage doubles, trebles. There's a white-hot burning inside my chest that might explode at any minute.

The snow-laden streets trail past, the illuminated shopfronts shining out onto the streets. Everything looks ordinary. Buses roar away from bus stops; the fumes hang grimly in the cold air. The passengers inside stare blankly out at us.

There's a stone in my gut.

Only I have the power to stop this thing happening. Fear is a driver all by itself. *Own it*, my head says. *It's yours. Own it*. Rachel's terror comes at me in waves. I glance across at her, watching her eyes widen like a helpless animal. I combine hers and mine and I harness it; locking it inside me, feeling the surge buzzing with adrenaline and turning it into rage. I am no longer ordinary. I am no longer a victim. I have real power.

Rachel hiccoughs a sob as we head to the other side of town. The chain-link fence tells us we're there.

'Pull up,' Leach says.

'It's too dark and covered with snow,' I say again. 'We can't find anything in this.'

'Just shut up and get out.'

Rachel doesn't look as though she can move, but he jerks her noose, and she yelps, fumbling for the door handle, almost falling to a crawl on the side of the road.

I stand, watching, as he stoops to haul her up again, pushing her forward in front of him, his hand between her shoulder blades, his fist gripping the wire tightly.

There's a gap of broken links between the chain fence and the gate and he propels her towards it. She ducks her head, her hair catching on the wire. My fingers trail over the curly strands, plucking them free, winding them tight.

'You don't know where we're going,' I pant, sliding and slipping over frozen bricks. Massive snow-topped timbers stand upright spiked with cast iron rods. Split pottery pipes yawn in shards from craters in the white-turned earth.

'You don't know where it is.'

Leach wheels round abruptly. I don't even see the fist before it slams into the side of my head. There's a burst of stars. My palms hit the solid ground just before my face does, a smash of pain into my jaw and the burning sting of ice as it slices my skin. I'm winded for a second, can't move, before he hauls me up, shoving me forward so hard my knees buckle again.

'Will you SHUT UP!' he yells close to my ear. 'Jesus.'

I splutter and cough, trying not to cry out with the pain as I manage to lift my head a little. In front of me is a newly dug pit in the frozen ground. A digger looms out of the snow-filled shadows. The horror of it grips me tight as a movement flickers just out of the corner of my eye. I know Leach doesn't see it.

There's the slight shush of feet.

My eyes bat, hope fluttering through my heart.

Matt.

The sound of boots creaks across the snow. I blink upward.

Trouser legs. *Matt... It's Matt.*

The feet step back.

All I can hear is Rachel crying. Leach is saying something, but all I want is Matt.

What is he doing? Why is he standing there?

Leach's voice lifts and falls. I look up.

Matt is planted stock-still, hands shoved into his pockets, staring down at me. 'Where's Emily?' he asks dully.

I'm so stunned I can't answer. I look at Leach. He's standing close by with the same expression etched into his face. His head twists right and left as he peers into the darkness.

He glances at Matt. 'Who cares? We don't have a lot of time. Let's just do this.'

Do this?

Rachel whimpers and her eyes roll upward.

'*Matt!* Please. What is this? What's happening?' she moans. 'You can't—' But she stops abruptly, wheezing and gasping, gargling as she struggles to breathe as Leach drags her to the edge of the pit as I desperately feel for that knife.

'I've told people that you're leaving me, Rachel.' Matt almost sounds pained. 'I've told loads of people I think you're having an affair. I've cried and sobbed about how you're going to leave me. They won't question when you disappear for a while. I've even had chats with your work colleagues about the stress you're under... Plus, you've been confiding in various people, haven't you? About leaving me. Now, that *was* silly, wasn't it?'

'Emily's contacted the police. She's gone to get help. It won't be long before—'

But Matt only stands there, shaking his head slowly and tutting.

'Who would've thought you'd have it in you, eh, Hannah?' he says sadly. 'There I am, all parked up and getting out of the car to help my friend here with Rachel, and who do I see? Hmm? You and Emily.'

My heart goes cold.

'Having a little altercation. Oh...' He holds a hand up to cup his ear. 'I'm surprised you didn't hear them before. The sound of sirens.... Only, they're not coming here. Who do you think might've called them to help poor old Emily?'

My head is a mass of things that don't make sense. Nothing makes any sense.

'But we did make a deal though, didn't we, Hannah?' Leach's voice sends a chill through me in the dying light. 'And a deal *is* a deal,' he sniggers. 'You wanted to know what happened that night, and so I thought I'd bring us all together again. A foursome. Just like the old days.'

There's a pounding of blood that hisses in my ears. A heart-beat jumps, pulsing beneath my dry tongue.

'I gave you most of the story, didn't I? So now you need the end of it. It's quite funny really.' He chuckles. 'When you look back.'

I twist my head to get a glimpse of Rachel. She can't move. Her eyes are wide and staring, the wire around her neck cuts deeper into the flesh.

'It was never intended to be you, you see.' Leach giggles. 'It was supposed to be that other chick, that other one you lived with. That's the irony.'

'Alison,' Matt says, gleefully joining. 'Now, she was the *really* ugly one. She's the sort who would've been grateful to have a bit of attention. It was all set up so nicely, wasn't it?' They smile at each other. 'Only Chris here' – Matt thumbs across to him – '*he* goes and louses the whole thing up.'

My head doesn't compute.

'Chris?' The name leaves my lips. I blink up, painfully.

'You don't recognise him then? No, I didn't think you did... God, it's all the old friends together, isn't it? Hang on... Let me do the formal intro, although I believe you've been informally introduced.' He sniggers, clearing his throat. 'Hugo Christopher Leach.' He bows a little. 'Also known as "Chris" to his very good friends.'

My brain stumbles as I cast my mind back: the boy that helped Matt move in... The pain in my eyes burns like fire and I close them.

'Me lousing the whole thing up,' Leach protests, laughing. 'That was all on you. Totally your cock-up. It was going so well. I'd poured the silly bitch the Cosby cocktail, and what does she go and do? Wanders off and gives it to *this* one. I couldn't believe it!' He gives me a look. 'What a night.'

'Do you remember what you said though?' Matt is still laughing.

'No, what did I say?'

'You said, "*Any hole's a goal*".'

They both burst out laughing.

'Did I?'

'Yeah... Proper wingman.' Matt hoots gleefully. 'Both of us taking it in turns, one after the other.'

'I had to go back and finish the ugly one though, didn't I?'

'But I was the one who gave you her new address, remember?' Matt waggles an admonishing finger. 'Without me, you'd never have known.'

'Wow!' Leach giggles. 'What bloody *legends* we were that summer.'

The cold stone shifts and settles into its proper place.

Fear. Gone. Anger. Gone. Cowering and crying, gone, all gone.

'You.'

My voice is deep and steady.

'You. it was you. You raped me. You raped me and then looked after me. You made me trust you.'

The darkness inside me that I've carried for seventeen years rises like a black veil, lifting me with it. I am unfurling slowly, blooming like a time-lapse flower, up and up until my face meets Matt's face, my eyes meeting his eyes.

They stare down at me with a kind of blank surprise. I see he wonders what I'm doing.

Past tense.

He actually should be wondering *what I've just done.*

I watch his bottom jaw dropping a little as I step back and away from him. He frowns, making a grab for me, going to step forward but then immediately stumbling as he realises too late, what's just happened. There's a spatter of something wet as it hits the snow. The inside of his trouser leg blooms dark and he staggers back, sitting hard like a toddler that's just fallen. He grabs at his crotch.

'Jesus!' he gasps.

I look at Leach, who has tightened the noose around Rachel's neck and is backing away. Rachel's hands have come up to her throat. She claws, her eyes bulging as the wire begins to bite.

'Come near me and she'll be sliced right through,' he warns, his feet blundering and staggering over the debris.

But the hard stone in my gut feels nothing. I am empty: I have no emotion, no thought, just a dead, dogged, relentless motion that my feet are forced to take without my asking them to.

'I *said*, keep away!' he yells.

There's a spring of blood in a wide smile under Rachel's chin that immediately soaks down the front of her coat.

Only I don't keep away. My feet move faster, I close in on her, watching her eyelids flutter and her hands begin to drop as Leach tightens his grip.

'Get back. I'll do this. I really will,' he screams, right at the very moment that I raise the knife over my head as though I'm about to plunge.

He does exactly as I expected: lurches backwards, attempting to yank Rachel with him.

But I've already seen what was behind him.

He steps back, his eyes lighting up in shock. I watch with an almost fascinated horror as his arms come up, opening wide like a Christ-figure, as he lets go, Rachel falling to her knees, gasping.

I stare at him, his outstretched arms, his mouth open as though about to say something profound, only there's a black iron spike jutting out just below his jawline. He gasps. A solid wooden post looms white in the darkness above his head; it's topped with snow, crowning him as its nail drives deep, his tongue writhing the dark hole of his mouth.

I scramble to Rachel's side, loosening the garotte and flinging it away, my fingers sticky with blood, murmuring over and over that she'll be okay now, she'll be okay.

Her eyes flicker open in shock, looking at me, and then at

the crucified form, silhouetted black against the whiteness. He's gurgling now, mouth open, a gap in his face hissing pleas for us to help, as I pull Rachel to her feet.

'Come on!' I urge. 'We have to get out of here.'

She's like a lamb, all mute and compliant as she leans on me, letting me guide her in whatever direction; she's totally mine.

I gather her to me, like a child, half-carrying, half dragging her back towards the fence. I look over to the main road where blue-and-red flashing lights speed towards the river.

She starts a little, coming to. 'They're coming to get us?' Her face is a confusion of pain and fear.

'We just need to get out of here, Rachel.'

'But—'

I'm almost lugging her along the pavement, our feet skidding in the slush.

'I need help,' Rachel rasps. 'I need to go to the hospital.'

'Yes, yes, we'll go to the hospital,' I reassure her. 'The police will find us there.'

I manage to get her as far as the car, leaning her against its side as I glance up. The blue eye of a CCTV camera stares unblinking down at the site gates as my fingers close around the reassuring metal.

'Come on, Rachel, not long now. Let's get you somewhere safe.'

Bundling her into the passenger side, I drop down behind the wheel. Her hands cup her neck as she stares in front, stupefied and vacant as I pull away, driving towards the flashing lights.

I imagine those passers-by all gathered, whispering, on the riverbank. The police, their incident tape unravelling, cordoning the path, putting up their forensic tents and ushering the crowds away. I see the woman in the café answering their questions and giving a description. Would she know a knife was missing?

'Matt...' Rachel whispers into the quiet. 'It was Matt?' Her face turns to me. 'Alison too. Poor Alison. I can't get my head around it. I never knew... I never knew.... Oh my god.' She turns away again, staring out.

Alison?

I glance at her.

After all I went through. *What about me?*

'What about what happened to me, Rachel?'

My voice shakes a little in the quiet interior. I glance across at her, but she's staring mutely out of the side window, her breath fogging the glass.

She's not hearing me.

I know how to make her hear me. I know how to make her listen.

'Rachel?' I say.

She doesn't respond.

'Do you want to know what really happened?'

I look across. She doesn't even blink.

'I heard you, Rachel. You and Alison in the hallway that afternoon. Talking about how you were going to move out and leave me.'

Not a flinch. She doesn't register.

'And I couldn't let that happen, Rachel, I just couldn't.'

I heard their chatter as they walked away from the house, the pain inside me sweeping from my gut, banging into the top of my head and making me gasp.

Life without Rachel.

My life going back to being just me, alone again, dragging myself through my grey days devoid of her light and her laughter. I didn't think I could bear it, not now I'd had a glimpse of sunshine. I couldn't bring down the shutters and block out my only chance of happiness.

'Shall I tell you, Rachel?'

She doesn't look at me.

There's a voice. It sounds like mine. I don't know if I'm speaking out loud, or if it's all in my head.

I looked around my room, at the clothes I'd borrowed from her, at all the things that I felt had made my life complete: the ring of dried daisies from our time at the riverbank I had pinned to the wall; the silly cartoon postcard that always made me laugh, her bits of jewellery lying around – but without her physical presence, none of it meant anything anymore.

I was numb. Dead on the inside. I stood there, looking down on myself, a dishevelled, greasy girl, standing alone in a rented room in a student house with nothing and no one – cut adrift and out at sea with no chance of survival. I watched myself as though from somewhere near the ceiling, as the girl in the room swept an arm out like a dancer, dragging the clothes from the bed and then the things from the dresser, flinging the wardrobe door wide and tearing at everything she found there. Until she stopped suddenly, a tatter of silk in her hands as a grinding pain loomed up in her, building and building like a pressure cooker desperate for release. She knew the signs... But then a sudden recognition of what was in her hands; and just as suddenly she swooped to the little broken box on the floor and picked up the thing she knew she needed right now: the razorblade... And she wrapped it up in the shredded silk and she headed out of the door.

She meant to do it.

She really meant to do it.

She found herself walking, the roll and push of the pavement under her feet, the houses and hedges skimming past, knowing they would never find her where she was going, not for days maybe. She'd hide herself away to make sure. She'd seen the place, the very place where the workmen had stopped working weeks ago, and she trod across the broken ground, her ankles turning over in a wince of pain with the agony in her belly building along with the agony in her heart, almost as vicious and intense, but knowing that soon... soon it would be over, as she found an 'L'-shaped bit of wall, tucked away, hidden from view.

Hunkering down in the dust, she listened to the pigeons crooning on the overhead wires as she slid the tiny sliver of a blade from out of the fabric folds and pulling off her shorts, she stretched out her leg. The whiteness of her inner thigh, so smooth, but silvered here and there with tiny lines of old cuts between the fine blue veins. Her eyes were drawn to the press of the blade edge as it depressed the skin, tightening it more and more, her breath held with the tension... Just a bit harder, just a bit... And then feeling everything give in a gush of blood and the relief, the absolute relief. Cutting deeper then, again and again, tipping her head back against the jagged brickwork, feeling the reassuring press of it, her eyes closed against the sunlight that sent brilliant flashes of red and blue to the inside of her lids. Soon it would go dark. Soon she wouldn't have to see, or feel, or hear anything ever again...

Her eyes flickered open. One last look at the sunshine. One last sensation of warmth on her skin... and in those seconds, the sun shifted and there was a halo of bright blonde hair there in front of her. A smiling face looking down at her. A mouth moving as it came closer... so much closer...

'*Hannah*,' it said, the smile dropping into shock. '*What are you doing? You can't leave me, Hannah. You can't do that.*'

And the voice was so real, and so present, and so there, the girl came to as though from a trance, fumbling for her phone, her fingers slipping and sticky with blood, as she dialled the number; the number and the person that she knew would be her lifeline, and you came, Rachel. You came.

· · ·

'I never said there was a baby, Rachel. I didn't lie. I never said there was.'

The car's interior is completely silent. The wheels whine, slipping beneath us like fluid. I look across at Rachel next to me. She's staring at me as though she's never seen me before. She looks odd, like a mannequin in a brightly-lit shop window – when suddenly a bank of searing headlights bear up in a blaze of hot white and a lorry thunders past.

I look back at the road again. I hear my own voice whispering into the quiet.

'I needed a mother back then, Rachel.' I look across at her expressionless face.

'I needed a mother to put her arms around me and say that whatever happened, she'd be there to hold me. I needed a father to carry me upstairs to my old bedroom and sit on the side of the bed and stroke my face and tell me whatever else was happening out there, with him I was safe from all the bad things. But I had nothing like that. I'd never had anything like that. There was no one there for me.'

My fingers tighten on the wheel as the main road opens out into black. The bushes and trees on either side lean in, silvered with snow. For moments there are no other cars as we reach the mouth of the underpass.

I wince, squinting and blinded, my palms hard against the wheel as the glare ribbons past in a stream of white light. Suddenly we plunge into deep black, the road curling away in front into nothingness.

'Say something, Rach,' I plead. 'Say anything.'

But she doesn't answer.

Nothing, my brain says. *I could drive straight through this and into nothing. I could do that.*

'The police,' she says suddenly, and I jump.

'What?'

'This isn't the way to the police.'

'No.'

I feel the surge of her instant panic.

'Where's Emily, Hannah?'

'We came together to the café to find you.'

'So where is she now?'

'We'll tell the police everything we know,' I answer firmly. 'Everything. All of it. From the beginning.'

'You're saying you were sad and lonely, Hannah. You're saying you were neglected and so you made things up,' she says carefully. But I see she's reaching for her phone; it sits loosely in her palm on her lap.

I count the silence. It comes in drips – *One, Two, Three, Four*. All I am aware of is the sound of her swallowing over and over, the dry grate of air as it sucks into her lungs, all papery and thin.

'You assumed there was a baby,' I continue. 'I just didn't put you straight. I only told you that because I thought you wouldn't come.'

'Hannah.'

'What? You wouldn't've. You know you wouldn't. You said —' I take a breath. 'I was too needy.'

'Hannah, I didn't. I wouldn't.'

'Don't lie!' I shriek. 'Don't you dare lie! Not now.'

I see her fingers fiddling with her phone as my foot presses down on the accelerator.

'Put that away, Rachel.' My hand comes out to snatch it from her but misses. 'Not after everything I've done for you.'

I'm aware of her stare – stunned disbelief. Wary. The fear building behind her eyes.

'But all of this...?'

'I was raped, but I never said... I never, never said anything about a baby,' I begin to gabble. 'You thought there was, that's all. I just let you think it.'

'Okay.'

'Don't say "okay" like that.' My temper explodes and she winces. 'That's how they talk to you in the hospitals. Don't you get it? It was because of you I wanted to die. It was true, what I said, I couldn't stand to be here anymore. I didn't want to think, or breathe, or feel anything ever again. I wanted it all to stop. I wanted to go back to feeling the way you always made me feel, Rachel. I felt *happy*. Do you get they? *Happy*. I'd never had that. I'd never been as happy as I was when it was just the two of us.'

'Yes, I knew how you felt when we were together. It was great, wasn't it? In the beginning…'

I wanted to just disappear. Rachel made it disappear.

'I was so happy. *We* were. *Both* of us.' She beams. 'I was happiest when it was just us and no one else.'

I can't quite believe she's saying this now. There's a leap of joy that makes my heart sing. That bird of joy that I've been searching for all these years.

And then I see what she's done. The screen of her phone is lit into white as she's dialled the police.

She sees my gaze as I see hers – right into her. All masks gone. All pretence over. All the theatre of it, the love, the friend-ship, the possibility of happiness.

Gone.

Over.

'Why did you have to do that, Rachel?'

My calf muscle tenses as the engine begins to ramp up into a shrill warning note.

'Hannah, stop! No! Stop!'

I look into the rear-view mirror. I see that summer dawn, the dusty pavements, the weight of my sandals in the hook of my fingers, the feel of the warm concrete beneath the soles of my bare feet, that gauzy sky-blue day spangled with stars just waiting to be born, and the smell of baking. That sudden press of her skin as she grabs my hand.

Hold on to that moment, the voice in her head says. *Hold on to what being alive really felt like, if only for the minutest fleeting second; you know what really living and really loving actually felt like.*

'Hannah!'

And then she does it again – the heat of her hand on mine, the touch of her skin. But this time her fingers close around my hand on the wheel. I fight her. The headlights swing wildly as I shoot a look up.

There's the outline of a hill up ahead.

A corner.

The tunnel of darkness seeping from black to a pulsing sparkle of red-and-blue stars and the outline of police cars parked horizontally across the road. A white searchlight illuminates the trees, ratcheting up into the sky and my heart ratchets with it.

They know. Matt told them about what I did to Emily.

They'll believe it. Rachel will convince them.

My future rolls out in front of me; it's sitting up ahead: the gather of grainy-white cars in the darkness, the black uniforms, the tinny, chattering radios, the smell of vinyl of the police car's interior, the whitened, skull-like profile of the driver who'll drive me to—

Back to the place I can't ever go again – with the groups and their nodding heads and the shiny understanding eyes of therapists, and the bars on the windows and the stark single bed of a stark single room, and no way out this time. They'll never let me out again.

My fingers tighten around the wheel as Rachel's shrieking cries reach a terrible pitch. I glance at my hands: they look like someone else's. The shadowed, frightened eyes in the mirror aren't mine at all. My shoulders flex, dragging the steering sharply as the tyres object beneath us in a screaming skid of hot rubber as they slew sideways looking for purchase. The other lane yawns widely into the stink of hot rubber and a plume of smoke and grit.

The engine stalls.

Rachel stops screaming.

And for one infinitesimal second, there's only my heartbeat in the silence.

And then a roar.

The blackness unfolds, revealing a monster lorry – blue-and-red lights twinkling like a fairground ride, bearing down in a giddy tumult of light and noise.

My face in the mirror is a mask.

'I love you,' I hear someone whispering before the gunshot blast of shattering glass and a torquing twist as I'm ripped in a shock of agony, my nerve endings shrieking and echoing into the night sky.

And then there's nothing but black.

NINETEEN

What wakes me is the lack of noise.

The chattering voices and strike of metal on metal all stop. There's a webbing of hazy light and movement.

'She's back again,' someone says.

I don't know what they mean. *Back?* I don't know where I've been.

'Hannah.'

They're calling me from far away. I shift my head.

There's a blurred balloon hanging above me. It bobs and weaves; I can't get a fix on it.

'Can you look at me, Hannah?'

The balloon becomes a face. A woman. Glasses. Green rimmed. Brown short hair. She shines a bright light, so white it hurts.

'Hello,' the face says. It's smiling.

'Hello,' I say.

The room comes into focus. A soft shush of doors swinging wide brings with it a scent of disinfectant, polish. I know that smell. I've been here before.

'Just sit. Give her a while. See how she goes,' Green-

Rimmed says over her shoulder. I peer, but there's only a shape in the corner of the room. Whoever it is, is sitting with their back to the light.

'I'll leave you to see if she'll chat. Would you like some tea?'

Whoever it is in the corner says 'yes', and I have this sudden lurch.

'Rachel?'

There's the screech of chair legs against the floor and the figure gets up. My eyes narrow.

'It's not, it's— Hang on, I'll pull the curtain,' they say and then come around, dragging a chair up to the side of the bed. They blur in and out and then suddenly I see them.

'Alison?' Her name leaves my lips on my outward breath. 'Alison?'

Her face, older, but the same; hair shorter, cheeks thinner. She inches her chair closer so that she can touch my hand.

'Oh my god, Hannah. I couldn't believe it when I saw the news. It was like... it was like...' She shakes her head, biting her trembling lip.

I can only nod, the tears leaking from the corners of my eyes. Words don't count; they're not enough.

My fingers scrabble across the sheet towards her. 'Where's Rachel?' I manage. 'Where is she?'

The door opens and a woman bustles noisily in with a tea trolley.

'Milk and sugar?' The woman ignores me, hissing boiling water from an urn into a metal teapot, clanking the lid shut and rattling two cups onto the table at the bottom of the bed.

'Oh – just milk, thanks.'

Something bad has happened, I know it. The ordinariness of all this shakes me with a fear I can barely contain. The woman trundles away again, the door closing. We both stare at it for a moment.

'Is Rachel—? Is she—?' I whisper, unable to say the last word, the violent thudding of shaking my chest.

'She's in ITU.' Alison's eyes search my face. I know there's something else; I can feel it.

'What?' I whisper.

The door opens again and Green-Rimmed comes back.

'Oh, you're looking brighter.' She smiles. 'You've done her good.' The nurse picks up the teapot from the end of the bed and pours me a cup. 'You might need yours in a beaker.' She eyes me. 'I'm sure your friend will help you if you ask her nicely.' She winks, handing Alison the cup. 'Oh, by the way, the police want to come in at some point. Maybe you'd like to arrange to be here then too?'

Alison nods, taking the cup. 'She's worrying about Rachel.'

I see the look that passes between the two of them. They've spoken about this already: I can tell.

'Then maybe you could take her to see her?' The nurse looks at her pointedly. 'Whenever she feels up to it?'

She leaves us alone in the quiet room. I'm aware that Alison isn't looking at me as she studiously drinks her tea.

'Tell me,' I croak. 'Tell me what I don't know. Tell me, have they found Matt?'

She shrugs a little as she puts down her cup. 'Matt was still alive when they got to him. He's admitted his part in aiding and abetting Leach. They'll bring charges of kidnapping too as Rachel was taken against her will. They have the footage from the towpath. I think they'll want to know at what point did Leach take the knife from the café. The café owner says he must've taken it from one of the tables.'

I find my head is swinging from side to side slowly as my brain begins to piece it together.

'And then the footage from the building site – Leach forcing Rachel through the fence. That's pretty clear. They just need to know what happened after that.'

My head swims. *Aiding and abetting. Kidnapping. Rape. My word against his.*

Alison closes her eyes. 'I've been such a coward, Hannah. Such a coward. I've lived with this thing for too long, just like you. Now all I want is to make it stop.'

She opens them. 'You and I, both of us.' Her fingers saw against each other in her lap. 'I had a feeling something bad had happened to you. I had no idea what was going to happen to me too. I ran away; I think you did too.' She looks up at me shyly. 'It ruined my life. I'm guessing it ruined yours too... And then when Leach was convicted... Oh, I don't know.' Her hands come to her face. 'It plagued me, like I guess it plagued you. And I made up my mind. I went to the prison to see Leach."

I swallow and nod.

'Only this was years ago.' She shakes her head. 'When he was in Ravensmoor prison in the middle of nowhere. I was standing in the Visits line when I saw him.'

'Who?'

'Matt.'

I look at her.

'And I couldn't work out why Matt would be visiting a prison, unless...' She shakes her head. 'The coincidence was too much. So, I waited and I wondered what to do and I started digging and investigating all of Leach's victims.'

'So did I.'

'And I worked out Leach was either extremely clever and very, very lucky.'

'Or?'

'He wasn't committing his offences alone.'

I watch her face.

'So I found Matt on Twitter and I confronted him about that night, only—' She stops 'Only I wasn't expecting what happened next. He denied it, of course, but then weird shit started happening to me. He found out where I lived, God knows how. All kinds of freaky stuff went on: I knew someone had been in my house, moving my things, touching my underwear, laying it out on the bed. There were notes and messages left for me, the kind of things that were so small and insignificant and unprovable, I couldn't go to the police with them, but it was menacing. God, it was menacing.'

I can barely dare to ask: 'What kind of notes?' But I already know. 'Did one of them say, *You're Mine?*'

'Yes. How did you—?' And then she falters. 'Oh, wow! Oh jeez.' She shakes her head determinedly. 'But I wouldn't let it go. I wouldn't just let it drop. I messaged Rachel, but I wouldn't tell her who I was. I kept begging her to meet me, telling her there were things she needed to know, but she would never agree to meet me. In the end I decided to come looking for her. I never dreamed I'd find all this.'

I close my eyes, thinking back to that night at Emily's when Matt grabbed Rachel's phone. He would've seen, he would've guessed. It gave him an ideal opportunity for Leach to lure her in, knowing that she would be the bait for both me and Emily. They would've got all three of us in one foul sweep.

'If only we'd known about each other.' Alison touches my hand. 'If only we'd trusted each other with our secret.'

But I remember that conversation in the hallway; the taking Rachel away from me. I remember it word for word.

'Look, let me take you to see Rachel, how about that?' Alison says carefully, as though I'm a small child. 'Would that be good?'

'Has she mentioned me? Has she said anything about what happened?' I plead. 'I just need to know.'

But she only changes the subject and starts chatting on about 'If I'm feeling up to it' and 'Making sure I'm warm enough' and telling me 'It's not far'. I know there's something else though.

She's talking too much and too fast as she calls the nurse,

and they get me into a wheelchair. They're both too solicitous with the blankets and the tubes and the tucking in and the patting of my arm and the clucking and the fussing. I know something else is coming, I can feel it.

We follow the green and red markers on the floor taking us to ITU. Alison hasn't stopped burbling on and on. We pause at the doors, and she swings the chair around and crouches down beside me. I want to scream.

Here is the thing: whatever it is, it's coming now.

'I've been in discussion with the nurses over the last few days, Hannah. It was thought – *we* thought – that it would be better that you saw Rachel for yourself, rather than being told about her and then imagining things. This way, you can process it all in your own good time.'

Process?

I'm now scared to think at all. The only thing I can do is nod as she manoeuvres me round and forward, the footrests of the chair clattering against the doors as they let us in to the ITU.

It's much quieter in here. A kind of reverential hush. There are rooms with glass windows, vertical blinds turned so you can't see the horror within. A nurse walks past us quickly, the plastic of her apron flapping as she rustles by.

We turn into a dimmed bay. Rachel is lying flat on the pillows, tubes and bags and lines everywhere hooked up to pulsing monitors. Her eyes are closed. Her hair is scraped back. Her face is cut and bruised above a thick white tube taped to her mouth.

I look up questioningly.

'It's too early to tell...' Alison begins to explain.

'What?'

'The scans. Of the brain. It's too early to tell.'

'What?'

'If she'll ever wake up.'

I stare and stare at Rachel's face. It doesn't really look like Rachel – and yet more like Rachel than I've ever seen her before.

She seems younger somehow; all the lines and worry are gone. She looks more as she did when we were eighteen.

'Can you give us a minute? Please?'

Alison hesitates, then nods. 'Sure. Of course.'

She pulls the door almost closed behind her and I manage to ease myself closer to the side of the bed. I take Rachel's hand in mine.

Click, goes the machine, and it takes a mechanical breath.

'Rachel.' I give her hand a tiny shake.

The bed shivers and her head moves a little.

'Rachel, can you hear me? It's me, Hannah.'

Click.

I stare. 'Rachel? Can you hear me? Blink if you can hear me, Rach.'

Do I imagine it, or did her eyelashes just flinch, just a tiny, tiny bit?

'You're in hospital, Rach. You're not very well at the moment, but I know you're going to get better.'

There it is again: that minute tremor.

'I promise you're going to get well, Rachel, because I'm going to make it happen. We haven't come this far, or been through this much, to give up now. Are you listening?'

Click.

I look at the machine. I'm sure that click was different just then.

'And I'm never leaving your side. I'll be here every day to look after you. You and me, Rachel, no one else this time.'

Click again. Her breathing changes imperceptibly and I know she knows I'm here.

'Rachel?'

Click. Click.

I sit back in my chair as a quiet certainty settles. From now on there's no Matt, no Leach, no Emily; no past, no present, there is only future.

'There's only us from now on,' I whisper, leaning in to kiss her cheek, when a sound behind me makes me look round.

'You're so right, Hannah.' Alison is standing in the doorway. I am aware of the soft smile on her face. Her eyes linger over the prone body lying on the bed. 'You, and me, and Rachel. It'll be like the old days, Hannah: the three of us, just like it used to be.'

I can only stare blankly at the beaming smile.

'You'll never be alone again.'

A LETTER FROM THE AUTHOR

Thank you so much for reading *The Broken Marriage*. It was exciting to write and explore Hannah's journey. If you want to join other readers in hearing about my new releases and bonus content, you can sign up here.

www.stormpublishing.co/elena-wilkes

If you enjoyed this book and are able to take a moment to leave a review it would be so appreciated. Every review means so much to an author, and I'd really love to hear your thoughts. Thank you so much!

The Broken Marriage is about the complexity and intensity of female friendships; the ups and the downs – particularly the downs that I find so fascinating.

Women, I think, share something very special with their female friends. Someone once said, 'Women bond over detail'; I think that's so true. They share bits of themselves in all kinds of ways: the things that make them laugh, and the things that make them cry. The stressful and sad things, the endless minutiae of their lives, passed back and forth in endless hours of café lunches and copious bottles of wine. Friends become like co-conspirators: opening up and being vulnerable with each other, showing our best (and sometimes our worst) selves, knowing that our best friends always have time for us and ultimately have our back, no matter what.

But what happens when something goes wrong with that relationship?

When the shared lunches start getting shorter and those intimate moments feel like they're being invaded by newer faces – all shiny and more interesting, ready to whisk your best friend away.

It's the worst thing in the world, especially for Hannah: that desperate moment when she feels she's been replaced.

She's devastated, heartbroken, and frantic.

But Hannah doesn't give up without a fight.

There's one thing about Hannah that no one's realised.

Hannah doesn't lose.

Thanks again for being part of this amazing journey with me and I hope you'll stay in touch.

ELENA WILKES

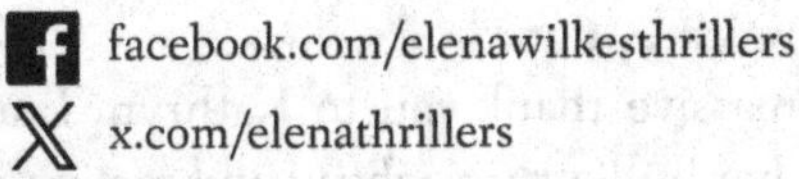

ACKNOWLEDGMENTS

There's a calculation I've often wondered about: just how many friends, bottles of cava and packets of crisps does it take to write a single book?

For me, the answer to the first part of the question is three. Amy Beashel, Ko Porteous and Tess James-Mackey. The answer to the second part of the question is... well, probably best not to put a number on it.

Therein lies the reality of writing: it's a lonely occupation, but we don't do it alone. There's a kind of 'ripple chart' of supportive people that bring a book to fruition and *The Broken Marriage* was no exception.

Firstly, a massive thank-you to Kathryn Taussig at Storm publishing for her brilliant, insightful and meticulous editorial – someone who 'gets' what I'm trying to achieve, when I clearly don't. A huge thank-you too, to Hannah Bond and her plot suggestions, who pointed out all the 'soggy' bits and showed me how to get the plot moving in a way I couldn't see – And to Natasha Hodgson for her eagle-sharp editorial eye and getting right to the nitty-gritty. Huge hugs for that.

Thank you too to all those writer friends who are there for the coffees and the lunches and the writerly advice: Carys Jones, Ginette Sears, Jenny Blackhurst, Lou Mins, Tat Effby, Annie Garthwaite. And then there's my lovely friends and neighbours in my potty Shropshire village, who are generous enough to buy my books and ask, 'So how's the new one going then?': Joan Owen and Rebecca Owen-Keats, Sarah and Mick,

Vincent and Isobel, Jill and Dave, Robin and Jenny, and the newbie-to-the-nutty-neighbourhood, Imogen – all lovely people who are amazingly encouraging.

And finally to my husband, Ian, who endures being married to a writer and all that entails – thank you for everything.

www.ingramcontent.com/pod-product-compliance
Lightning Source LLC
Chambersburg PA
CBHW011132190726
48289CB00012B/3010